ANOTHER VICTIM

Charlie lifted the blanket away from the top of the stretcher, disclosing what lay beneath. "Oh, Gawd!" Annie exclaimed, throwing her hands in front of her face and breaking into noisy tears. "It's awful."

"Do you know her?" Matt said urgently.

"Oh, Gawd, oh, Gawd, I wish I never looked. Oh, Gawd!"

"Do you know her?"

"I never seen her before in my life. Oh, Miss Cassidy. Miss Cassidy?"

Brooke stepped back, feeling the color drain from her face. Sounds reached her dimly, as if from a very great distance. It *was* awful. Her knees too rubbery to support her, she sank down onto a rock at the edge of the cliff, as far from the stretcher as she could get. It wasn't a maid who had been killed. It wasn't a maid at all. Dear God, this was worse than she could ever have imagined.

"Brooke?" Matt stood before her, and she looked up. "What is it?"

"I know her."

"What?" He crouched down.

"I know her. Dear God." She closed her eyes, trying to shut out what she had just seen, knowing she would remember it forever. "It's Rosalind Sinclair."

DEATH ON THE CLIFF WALK

MARY KRUGER

ZEBRA BOOKS
KENSINGTON PUBLISHING CORP.

ZEBRA BOOKS are published by

Kensington Publishing Corp.
850 Third Avenue
New York, NY 10022

First Kensington Hardcover Printing: December, 1994
First Zebra Paperback Printing: December, 1995

Printed in the United States of America

To the Silver City critiquers: Nancy Bulk, Kathy Shannon, Sharon Winn, and Rona Zable. Thanks for being good friends and good writers. I couldn't have done it without you.

And to my mother, Madelyn Sweeney Kruger, who has always believed in me. I really couldn't do it without you.

Prologue

Newport, Rhode Island, 1895

She snatched the starched white cap from her head, letting her hair tumble down her back, and laughed to the night sky. She had done it! All the hours of planning, all the months of risk, had finally paid off. There'd be some scandal at first, but that only added to the deliciousness of it. She had won, and she was going to run her life as she saw fit. Not what her mother wanted, or her father, but what she wanted, freedom to be herself, and, of course, enough money to ensure that freedom. Soon she would be Mrs.—well, she'd best keep that a secret for a while, even from the crickets chirping in the rambling roses growing wild to her left, or the booming surf to her right. Who knew who else might be about on Newport's famed Cliff Walk on such a glorious summer night? Doubtless there were maids and men-servants, returning, like her, from their secret trysts. After all, that was what the Cliff Walk was for, wasn't it? For servants, and sometimes their employers, to go from one cottage to another. It could be a tricky stretch of walking, with several dark, delightfully frightening tunnels, and, far below, the sea pounding on jagged rocks left by some long-ago glacier. But she wasn't afraid. She'd traveled this way many times before.

A tiny sound behind her made her turn, and for the first time unease crept into her triumph. No one was there. Oh, perhaps a gull, landing with its meal of crab or something else, but no person. Only shadows. Nothing was going to happen to her, not on this night of nights, and again she threw back her head and laughed. Anyone seeing her would, at first glance, take her for a maid in her black dress and crisp white apron, but *he* knew better. He knew she could ruin him if she wanted to. But she didn't want to, and tonight he had agreed, surprisingly easily, to all her demands. Her parents would be horrified, but what choice would they have? She had, at long last, won.

Clouds ghosted across the moon, momentarily dimming her view, and behind her there was another sound, as of a rock falling, falling, to the restless waves below. Again she whirled, shock surging through her. "Who's there?" Again, there was no one. Was there? Didn't that shadow look like someone—oh, nonsense! But her skin tingled and her back tightened as she hurried on, no longer exulting, wishing she had brought a lantern to light her way. It was late, high time for her to be home. There she could rejoice, there she could celebrate—

It was unmistakable this time, a footfall, measured and deliberate. Following her. She made a noise, a small cry, and broke into a run, hampered by her petticoats and the heavy serge skirt, no longer trying to avoid any stray rocks in her path. She was careful only to stay far from the cliff edge and the sheer drop to the sea. Home, and safety, and—yes, more footsteps, running, pursuing her. Too late she remembered the events of the past month, too late she recalled the gruesome fate met by other young maids walking alone on the Cliff Walk, late at night. *But I'm not a maid,* she thought, and whirled to face her pursuer.

The breath went out of her in a great woosh! of relief. "Oh!" She put her hand to her heart. "You gave me such a start! Do you know, for a moment there I thought you were—what are you doing? No, don't—"

One black-gloved hand shoved at her mouth, suffocating her, pushing her back against the cliff wall. Stones scattered everywhere as she struggled, her feet shuffling and kicking, and nearby, some nocturnal creature, disturbed by the noise, rustled in the bushes. Another gloved hand caught her throat, and there was an odd sound, a gurgle that might only have been the

tide rushing out of some hidden cave far below. A whisper of sound, starched cotton crinkling, a thump of something falling, and then silence.

And, far below, the surf crashed on the rocks.

1

Detective Matthew Devlin felt tired. In the bright morning sun, he looked down at the crumpled form lying on the dirt path and resisted the urge to rub his hand over his face. Another one. The fourth maid strangled in less than a month, and no one cared. Except him.

His face a still mask, he crouched beside the body, not touching it, studying it for clues. Rigor mortis had set in, indicating that she had been dead for some time, while the bruises on her throat gave him a clear idea of how she had died. Behind him the police artist carefully sketched the scene so that they would have a record of it later. Other police were at work as well, one talking to the sobbing girl who had had the misfortune to find the body, while the retired patrolman who guarded the nearby estate kept the reporters and the curious at bay past the hastily erected rope barricades. All respected both the detective's silent scrutiny, and his anger. Matt Devlin's Irish temper was legendary among the Newport police.

Poor little girl, he thought, studying the victim's hand impassively. Matt was good at hiding his feelings; he had to be. Studying a crime scene was part of his job. The rage and sorrow he felt, however, was real: overwhelming sorrow for the victim, overwhelming rage at whoever had caused her death. She'd fought her attacker, judging by the state of her fingernails, broken and torn, with the blue tinge caused by asphyxiation. Those that weren't, though, were perfect ovals, with a shine that could have come only from long hours of patient attention. Matt grunted in surprise, the first emotion he'd shown all day. A maid with long nails? He touched the small, cold hand. Slender, shapely, soft, and white. Not a working hand. Not at all the hand of a maid.

The thought chilled him and he glanced away, absently watching the uniformed patrolmen at their tasks. He wouldn't be one of them again, wearing heavy blue wool buttoned to the throat in this heat, he thought irrelevantly, before forcibly reminding himself of what he had to do. Rubbing a finger across his mustache, he studied the body again. It sprawled in the indignity of death, the head, propped up by the cliff wall, lolling forward, the skirts of the uniform rucked up to reveal heavy black wool stockings and high-laced shoes. Lying nearby was the one piece of evidence that conclusively linked this murder to the others, the one clue. A single red rose. One had been found carefully placed by each of the bodies. What it meant was anybody's guess, although Matt had a sinking feeling he knew. For it was not a rambling rose, plucked from one of the bushes that grew in abundance along the Cliff Walk. It was, instead, full-blown and perfect, deep bloodred. A hothouse rose, beyond the means of most people. A rich person's rose. An important clue, and yet the image of the girl's fingernails, mute testimony to her futile struggle for life, jarred him more. He had a feeling that the case had just taken a drastic change.

Abruptly, he rose. Though all the bodies had been found on the Cliff Walk, none had been at the same place. Here the Walk dipped several feet below the level of the property it passed, but the small rise didn't block his view. Across a broad, velvety swath of lawn, he could see the cottage. Cottage. *Ha*. Newport had been a summer resort for many years, but it was only recently that the wealthy had discovered the town and had descended upon it in droves. Vanderbilts, Astors, Lorillards—all these and more found it stylish to spend the summer here. All along Bellevue Avenue and Ocean Avenue, at Ochre Point and Brenton Point, fabulous houses were being built, each outrivaling the other with their lavish use of marble, gilt, and antiques. Not Matt's idea of a cottage.

Using the eraser of his pencil, he turned the page of his notebook, and then looked up at the house. Belle Mer, this "cottage" was called, and its construction had been the talk of Newport for the past two years, the largest house the town had yet seen. Massive and solid, an interpretation of an Italian palazzo, with collonades and loggias looking out over the sea, it looked out of place on this rocky stretch of the New England coast. It was common knowledge that Belle Mer had over seventy rooms, its own generator for electricity, and more staff than a person could count. Because the murder had taken place nearby, everyone inside, staff and owners alike, would have to be interviewed. Not that they'd tell him much. So far the wealthy people who had employed the murdered girls hadn't been cooperative. Apparently it was beneath their dignity to talk to a common policeman.

The girl who had found the body looked up, her eyes red with weeping, when he crouched before her. Like the murder victim, she, too, wore the black dress and crisp white apron of a maid. "I'm Detective Devlin," he said. "I understand you found the body, Miss—?"

"Machado," the girl said, her voice lightly accented with the rhythms of her native Portugal. "Teresa Machado."

Matt nodded; her name and address would already have been noted by one of his team. "You're local?"

"Yes, sir. Middletown. I wish I was there now."

Matt let a smile appear briefly on his face. With witnesses it didn't hurt to let up a little, especially if they were female. It tended to make them open up more, tell what they knew more easily. Matt was well aware of the effect his Black Irish looks had on people, and was not averse to using them. "I don't blame you. I won't keep you long, Miss Machado, and then you can go."

"Thank you, sir." The girl let out a shaky breath. "The mistress'll probably sack me after this. I was supposed to be back a long time ago."

"You work at—?"

"Seacliff. I told this to that man already."

Matt nodded. "Yes, I know, and I'll read his report. But

humor me, Miss Machado." He smiled, and was glad to see her smile back, if uncertainly. "You were on an errand?"

"Yes. I'm a parlor maid. Mrs. Madison, she's the housekeeper, sent me to The Beeches for something, and of course I took the Walk. We always do."

"Of course." Matt nodded encouragingly. The Cliff Walk had been used by the citizens of Newport long before the wealthy had made it their playground; it would be used long after they were gone. "You didn't hear anything? Any screams?"

"Yes," she said, surprising him; the girl had been dead long before Teresa Machado had come along. "But it was only a gull. I seen the gulls before I saw her. Thought it was a bundle of rags, at first." Her voice trailed off, and she buried her head in her hands. Matt leaned back, waiting. "It was only when I got closer that I seen . . ."

"Easy." He laid a hand on her arm. Her eyes squeezed shut and he thought his sympathy would be her undoing, but then she seemed to shake herself.

"It was awful. The gulls, they was all around her. I chased 'em away, and then I ran up there"—she indicated Belle Mer with a jerk of her thumb—"to get help. But I knew she was dead, the way her eyes popped out." She looked up at him, her throat working. "Is it the same man? Is he going to go on killing maids until no one's left? Why don't you stop him?"

"We will." Matt rose, his face grim, wishing he felt as confident as he sounded. Four weeks, four dead girls. A month since New York's wealthy had arrived for the summer. He didn't like the conclusion that was forming in his mind. The chief would like it even less. "One more thing, Miss Machado, and then you can go. Do you know her?"

"The dead girl? Never seen her before in my life. If she's a maid, she's one of them New York ones."

"If?" he said, sharply. "You think she isn't?"

The girl gaped at him. "Don't know, sir. Don't know what made me say that. The way she's dressed, of course she's a maid."

Matt nodded, signaling to the patrolman on guard that

Teresa Machado could leave. So, something about the dead girl had aroused her suspicions as well. He didn't like this situation at all. "Let me know when Dr. Chandler gets here. I'm going up there," he said, jerking his head toward Belle Mer. "Charlie, come with me."

"Yes, Cap." Charlie Sweeney, red-haired and freckle-faced, deceptively young-looking, fell into step beside Matt as they walked the narrow path past the barricade. Where the Cliff Walk intersected with the street, filled now with police carriages and the horse-drawn police ambulance, was an impressive set of wrought iron and brass gates, leading to Belle Mer. "Need a chaperon?"

Matt gave him a look. "I need you to take notes," he said, as if this weren't a routine they'd perfected over the past few weeks. "And don't call me Cap. I'm not the captain yet."

"Yes, Cap. I mean, sir. And you want someone with a face that won't scare people off."

"Sometimes people deserve to be scared." Matt's tone was mild as they crossed the lawn, heading toward the house.

"Well, don't scare these people, Cap. Remember what happened last time, when you interviewed the last one's boss. Mrs. Belmont, remember?"

Matt frowned. "Only trying to do my job."

"Uh-huh. And the Belmonts complained to the chief, and he chewed you out, and you chewed me out. Rather not get one of your lectures again, Cap." They walked along in silence for a moment. "How long do you think the chief will keep you on this case if you keep getting these people mad?"

"I don't care what they do," Matt said, sharply. "Even if they have money, they have to talk to us."

"Well, it's your funeral, Cap."

Silence fell again. "What did Mr."—Matt looked down at his notes—"do to earn his money?"

"Olmstead. Nothing. He—"

"Olmstead?"

"Yeah." Charlie looked up at him. "What about it?"

"Nothing. Go on. How did he make his money?"

"He didn't. It's an old Knickerbocker family. The fortune

comes from land first, and then the China trade. Henry Olmstead spends most of his time in the Reading Room. He likes his whiskey. I hear—Jeez!"

"What?"

"Look at that, will you." Charlie pointed toward the house. On the terrace a man catapulted off a slanting board, turned a somersault in midair, and landed on his feet, his arms upraised. Another man turned a cartwheel, while still another vaulted off the board and onto the shoulders of the first man. Then all three stopped and stood together, pointing toward the board and arguing. Past them, on the lawn, small brightly colored tents had been set up in two orderly rows, with equally colorful flags strung between them, and workmen were busy erecting lightpoles and signs. The atmosphere was unmistakably, and incongruously, that of a carnival.

Matt and Charlie exchanged looks. "I thought I'd seen everything," Charlie said. "This should be interesting."

"Or insane." Matt eyed the tents with eyebrows lowered as they passed by. "God save me from the rich."

"You're a Newport cop, Cap. Means you're going to have to come up against them from time to time."

"Yes, but I don't have to like it." They had reached the house now. Going down a few steps, below ground level, he knocked on the door. "Might be we'll find some answers here."

"You don't think someone here did it? One of the staff?"

"I doubt it. I think we have something a lot more serious on our hands, Charlie."

Charlie made a noise of surprise, but was stopped from answering when the door was opened by a short, stout woman. "Yes, what is it now—oh, it's you. Cops."

Matt nodded as he stepped inside, taking off his bowler hat. Before him was a short hallway, and beyond that an enormous kitchen. He stopped, surveying the room. Never knew what might be important in a murder case, especially if the girl had come from here. Five huge iron stoves took up most of one wall, with flues leading upward, while in the center of the room stood a long table with a marble top. Above, copper pots hung from racks suspended from the tin ceiling. The people who had been at work, a maid arranging flowers at the soapstone sink, a man in shirtsleeves and striped vest polishing silver, a woman rolling out pastry on the marble tabletop, had stopped what they were doing and were staring. "We'd like to see the owners of the house. And you are—?"

"Aggie Smith, the housekeeper. That'll be Mr. and Mrs. Olmstead. Mr. Olmstead's out, and her ladyship never gets up this time of morning." Her eyes were avid with curiosity. "Should I wake her and tell her what you want?"

"I'll take them, Mrs. Smith." The man who had been polishing silver came toward them, shrugging into a frock coat. "I am Hutton, the butler. Is this about the body?"

Matt nodded. "Yes."

"Then you'll want to speak with Miss Cassidy. She is in the Italian Hall. If you'll follow me, please."

"Do you suppose there's a French hall, or an English one?" Sweeney whispered, and Matt gestured him to silence with his hand. "Miss Cassidy is the niece," he added under his breath.

"I know," Matt said. He was smiling, an ironic smile. "I think we're in for our first piece of luck."

"How so, Cap?" Charlie asked as they followed Hutton from the kitchen up a narrow flight of iron stairs, into the main part of the house. Here the floor was of highly polished parquet, and on it a huge porcelain urn was placed almost casually against the wall. To the side and above him rose the bulk of a broad, freestanding marble staircase, with, of all things, a working fountain tucked in the sloping space underneath. "I think— Jeez, will you look at that?" Just ahead was an enormous room, set off from the corridor by a row of columns. The ceiling soared high above, a good two stories. Running around the walls halfway up were galleries, hung with garlands of flowers and, of all things, clown masks. Charlie's mouth fell open. "Fifteen generations of my ancestors in Ireland could live in that room. And that vase. Do you suppose it's real gold?"

"We're here to work, not gawk," Matt snapped. "Pay attention."

"Sorry, Cap," Charlie said, sounding not at all contrite.

"Miss Cassidy," Hutton said, and, across the room, a girl in a blue dress with enormous sleeves, perched precariously on a stepladder high above the marble floor, turned to look at them. Her face went white, and the mask she held, suspended by velvet ribbons, slipped from her fingers to shatter on the marble floor. "Miss Cassidy!"

"Miss, are you all right?" the maid who was holding the ladder chimed in.

"Matt." She stayed where she was, and for a moment there was taut silence. "You're here about the murder."

"Miss Cassidy." Matt acknowledged her with an expressionless face, though Charlie glanced at him curiously. He was acutely aware of where he was, and who he was. Five years ago, in what seemed like another lifetime, he had looked on this girl almost as a sister. Now she was one of the cottagers, and more than her position lay between them. Five years, and an act of betrayal. "We'd like to talk to you."

Gathering her voluminous skirts, Brooke scurried down from the ladder. All morning she had been expecting this, since the news of the body found on the Cliff Walk had spread through the house, stunning everybody. Another murder. Dear heavens. Would it never end? "Of course. I imagine you'll want to speak to everyone in the house."

Matt inclined his head. "We do."

Brooke nodded. How she was holding on to her composure, she wasn't certain. "Hutton, will you see to it?"

"Do you know these—gentlemen—miss?" Hutton said.

"Yes." Oh, yes. How strange to see Matt after all this time, and here, of all places. He was from another time and another place, when their fathers had been partners on the Newport police force. She hadn't been one of the cottagers then, but a townie, living an ordinary life in Newport's Fifth Ward. Returning here every summer since was strange. Once it had been home; now she was an outsider, and her old friends were uncomfortable with her. Including, apparently, Matt. Of course she'd known he had become a cop. It was a natural choice of occupation for a policeman's son. "Hutton, please gather the staff together and explain what is happening."

"What of Mr. and Mrs. Olmstead, miss?"

"I'll talk with them."

"Very well, miss." His back ramrod straight, the butler turned and stalked out of the room.

Brooke blew out her breath, lifting a strand of hair off her forehead. "I'm sorry about the confusion around here. There's a party tonight, and—but you don't want to hear about that." She turned to the man standing next to Matt, looking about with unabashed curiosity. "And you are—"

"Sergeant Sweeney, miss." He smiled at her. "This is some place."

"It's not much, but we call it home," she murmured, the corners of her mouth tilting. "Please, gentlemen, sit down." She indicated the chairs grouped on the Persian rug in the center of the room.

"Miss?" a voice said behind her, and she turned to see Annie, the maid who had been helping her decorate before the arrival of the police. "Should I clean up the mask?"

"The mask?" Brooke looked down at the shards of porcelain littering the floor. "Oh, dear. Aunt Winifred will have kittens. Yes, clean it up, Annie, and then you can get on with your other tasks. I am sorry," she said again, turning to Matt. "We're all at sixes and sevens today. Please, sit. Would you like something to drink?"

Matt looked at the gilt and satin chair she indicated and then sat, rather gingerly, as if afraid it wouldn't hold him. Charlie showed no such fear, sitting solidly and flipping open his notebook. "No, thank you. We're on duty."

Brooke sat across from them, her feeling of unreality deepening. In the old days, the good days, her father had sometimes discussed his cases with her. Now she was the one being questioned. "Of course."

"Now." Matt frowned at his notebook. "Miss Cassidy—"

"Matt." The distance between them hurt. "We've known each other too long to be so formal."

"As you wish. Miss—Brooke. Have you noticed anyone missing from the staff?"

"Oh, Gawd!" Annie exclaimed, the dustpan falling with a clatter.

Brooke jumped, her hand going to her throat. "You think she's—one of ours?"

"We haven't identified the body yet."

"Oh. Is it the same as the others?"

"Looks that way."

"Oh, dear. Do you have any idea who did it?"

Matt grunted, a sound that could mean anything. "Where were you last night?"

"I was at Wakehurst, with my aunt, for a musicale, and Uncle Henry was at a meeting of the Casino board, I believe."

"We'll want to talk with them later. What time did you get home?"

"Rather early. Around eleven."

Matt looked up from his notebook. "That's early?"

Brooke lifted her chin at the note of criticism in his voice. "Actually, yes. I found it too warm for sleeping, though, so I went onto the second-floor loggia for a time."

"Mm-hm." He noted that down. "It overlooks the Cliff Walk, doesn't it?"

"Yes."

At that he looked up, his eyes so piercing that she was glad she wasn't guilty of anything. He would surely discover it if she were. "Did you hear anything?"

"Not out of the ordinary, no. But then, so many people use the Cliff Walk."

"Mm-hm." Matt looked down at his notebook, formulating his next question. "Have you—what the—!" He stopped, staring outside, as a man in leotards flew into the air, executed a perfect somersault, and then descended from view. "What is going on?"

"Who? Oh." In spite of the seriousness of the situation, Brooke smiled. "My aunt's party." She waved her hand in dismissal. "It's a circus."

Matt looked at her from under his brows. "Apparently."

"No, I mean it literally. I'm sorry, I should explain. You see, my aunt wants tonight to be special. After all, it's our housewarming. Up until last week we had an indoor garden party planned, with turf, trees in tubs, and a stream. All quite standard."

Matt and Charlie exchanged quick looks. "Quite."

"But Aunt Winifred thought it sounded boring. Where she ever got the idea of a circus!" Brooke reached up to brush a strand of hair away from her face, and his gaze fastened on her hand. It was as white, and as soft-looking, as the victim's. Matt's uneasiness grew. "I can't tell you what I've gone through, getting the tents for the midway and finding entertainment at such short notice. But you don't want to hear about that."

"Only if it pertains to the case." He paused. "Why are you doing the work, and not your aunt?"

Brooke stiffened. "I act as her social secretary."

"Oh." He thought of a number of things he could say to that, and dismissed them all. Now was not the time to bring up the past. "Now, as we were saying. You heard nothing suspicious last night?"

"No, nothing."

Matt turned to Annie, who had long ago given up any pretense of cleaning, and was listening avidly. "What about you?"

"Me, sir?"

"Yes, you."

Annie shrank back against the wall. "N-nothing, sir."

Brooke turned to look at her. "Annie, do you know anything about this?"

Annie's hands twisted together. "Oh, miss, I didn't do anything wrong, I swear."

"No one is saying you did. Were you out last night?"

"No. Yes."

"Well? Which is it?" Matt said, crisply.

Brooke gave him a look. "My aunt has a rule about servants going out without permission. Especially if they're not alone." She made her voice gentle. "You won't lose your job, Annie. Who were you with?"

Annie stared at the floor. "Sam, miss."

"Sam?" Matt said.

"Sam Thompson. He's a footman at Bealieu. We're keeping company," she added, defiantly.

"On the Walk, Annie?"

"Yes, sir."

"Did you see anything?"

"No, sir, nor heard nothing, neither. We went down to the Forty Steps." She glanced quickly over at Brooke. "There was a sort of party there."

Matt nodded. He was well aware that servants from the cottages often met at the Forty Steps, the steep stone staircase that led from the Cliff Walk down to treacherous rocks and pounding surf. As a patrolman, he'd been called to disturbances there more than once. "When was this?"

"Around midnight."

"Hm." Matt leaned back, rubbing his chin. "We don't know the time of death yet, but . . ."

"The murder had to happen after that," Brooke said. "The body was found between the Forty Steps and our gate."

"Hm?" Matt gave her a look. "Yes, looks that way. Who else might have seen something last night?"

"I don't know, Matt. I haven't heard of anything. But then, our staff wants to keep their jobs."

"Anything they tell me will be kept private unless it's necessary to the investigation." He frowned. "Would your aunt really fire people for going out?"

"No. She'd make me do it."

"Nice lady. Well." He stood up. "I'll want to talk to the staff."

"Of course. You won't keep them too long, will you?"

"If there's someone who knows something, we'll have to."

"But everyone's so busy, with the party—" She stopped herself. Living as a cottager, sometimes she got so caught up in the social world that she forgot what really mattered. "Forgive me. Of course this is more important. Aunt Winifred won't be pleased about this," she added under her breath.

"Detective." A patrolman appeared at the glass door leading from the loggia. "The medical examiner's here."

"I'll be right there." Matt flipped his notebook shut. "Anything else you can think of to tell me?"

"No." Brooke shook her head. "But I'll get in touch with you if I do."

"Sir?" Annie said, her voice hesitant, and Matt turned. "Who was it?"

"We don't know. Is anyone missing from the staff here?"

Brooke and Annie exchanged a look. "Not that I know of, but I'd have to check with Mrs. Smith to be certain. Dear heavens." Brooke walked with them to the glass doors leading out to the loggia overlooking the lawn, Annie following behind. "I hope not."

"How well do you know the staff in the other houses, Annie?" Charlie said, speaking for the first time since the interview had started.

"Pretty good, sir." She swallowed, hard. "You mean—you think it might be someone I know."

"Would you mind taking a look to see?" Matt asked gently.

She swallowed again. "No. I suppose not."

"Matt," Brooke protested. "Is this necessary?"

"We need to find out who it is," Matt said.

"Then I'm coming with you."

Annie turned a grateful look on her. "Thank you, miss."

"It's not necessary, Brooke."

"Annie is a friend." Brooke's chin was set at a determined angle. "Of course I'll come with her."

"A friend?"

Brooke held her ground. "Yes. A friend."

"Fine." Matt turned away. "It won't take long."

"Well, then, let's go." Brooke turned away, her back very straight and her head held high, Annie behind her. Wondering just when control of the interview had slipped away from him, Matt followed.

"I'm proud of you, Cap," Charlie muttered as they crossed the lawn again, behind the two women. "You didn't lose your temper this time. Maybe you'll keep your job, after all."

"I told you. We've had a lucky break."

"What?"

"Miss Cassidy."

"How do you know her, Cap? She's a lady from the ground up."

"So?"

"So I thought you didn't have nothing to do with the cottagers."

"She's Michael Cassidy's daughter."

Charlie stopped dead. "Big Mike Cassidy?"

Brooke looked around at them. "Did I hear my name?"

"You're Big Mike Cassidy's daughter?"

Brooke's smile was strained. "Yes."

"Jeez!" Charlie looked back at the house. "How did you end up here?"

"My aunt and uncle took me in after my parents died." She slowed as they walked through the huge gates onto the Cliff Walk. "Is that—her?"

Matt looked past her. Beyond the rope barricades, a stretcher held a blanket-wrapped bundle. Nearby the medical examiner wrote something in a notebook, his old-fashioned Prince Albert coat buttoned to his throat. The crowd of bystanders had increased, while the reporters scribbled down their stories. "Yes. Wait here for a moment. Dr. Chandler." The man looked up as Matt came forward, and slid his glasses up to his forehead. "Sorry to make you wait. Anything to tell me?"

"Death was by strangulation, but you know that." The medical examiner's voice boomed out as he lifted a corner of the blanket and looked down at the stretcher. "Hard to say time of death for certain, but I'd put it around midnight. I'll know more after the autopsy." He looked down again, and then lowered the blanket. "Any idea who she is?"

Matt looked back at Annie and Brooke, and then stepped closer, his voice pitched low enough so that the onlookers couldn't hear. The look on Dr. Chandler's face turned from professional interest to surprise at whatever Matt was saying, and he glanced over at the two girls. "They're talking about us, miss," Annie said. "Do they think one of us did it?"

"Don't be foolish," Brooke said, sharply, though she longed to know what they were saying. "Of course they don't."

"I'm sorry I agreed to this, miss. Do you think, if I go back to the house—"

"I'm here, Annie. Nothing's going to happen to you."

"I've never seen a dead person before. Not one that's not laid out proper, that is."

"It will be all right, Annie." Brooke shifted from foot to foot. The attention of the crowd seemed to be divided between her and the body, with the reporters calling out questions that she ignored. She, too, wished she were back in the safety of Belle Mer.

"Well, could be that way." Dr. Chandler's voice boomed out again. Putting his glasses in his jacket pocket, he held out his hand to Matt and then ducked under the rope, held high by the patrolman on guard. "I'll let you know as soon as the autopsy's done. Ladies." He nodded to Brooke and Annie as he passed them, and walked to his buggy, waiting in the street.

It was their turn now. Brooke could see it in Matt's face. "Annie. If you'll just come this way," he said.

Annie turned to her, her face pleading. "Oh, miss—"

"I'm right here with you, Annie."

"You don't have to come, Brooke." Matt blocked her way. "It's not a pretty sight."

"She needs me." Brooke brushed past him and caught up with Annie, now standing by the stretcher. "I'm here, Annie."

"Oh, miss—"

"Whenever you're ready," Charlie said, quietly. He stood by the stretcher as well, and Annie looked from him to Brooke. Then her head rose, and she nodded.

Charlie lifted the blanket away from the top of the stretcher, disclosing what lay beneath. "Oh, Gawd!" Annie exclaimed, throwing her hands in front of her face and breaking into noisy tears. "It's awful."

"Do you know her?" Matt said urgently.

"Oh, Gawd, oh, Gawd, I wish I never looked. Oh, Gawd!"

"Do you know her?"

"I never seen her before in my life. Oh, Miss Cassidy. Miss Cassidy?"

Brooke stepped back, feeling the color drain from her face.

Sounds reached her dimly, as if from a very great distance. It *was* awful. Her knees too rubbery to support her, she sank down onto a rock at the edge of the cliff, as far from the stretcher as she could get. It wasn't a maid who had been killed. It wasn't a maid at all. Dear God, this was worse than she could ever have imagined.

"Brooke?" Matt stood before her, and she looked up. "What is it?"

"I know her."

"What?" He crouched down.

"I know her. Dear God." She closed her eyes, trying to shut out what she had just seen, knowing she would remember it forever. "It's Rosalind Sinclair."

2

The Flying Bellissima Brothers had performed their acrobatics, to the delight and approval of all the guests. Moths and other insects flew at the fairy lights that illuminated the circus tents, where guests in evening gowns from Worth or well-tailored dinner jackets from Brooks Brothers flitted, gawking at the fortune-teller, the juggler, the games of chance, munching on peanuts, sipping pink lemonade, and having a grand time. Inside the house, the orchestra, set up on the second-floor gallery of the Italian Hall, was tuning up, while in the dining room the staff was laying out a supper to tempt even the most jaded appetite. All in vain. On this warm summer night, the guests at Belle Mer's housewarming party could not be persuaded inside, away from the novelty of a circus, or the more lurid attraction of a genuine murder scene.

Brooke stood on the loggia, several steps up from the lawn, looking out over the scene, a part of the party in her evening gown of azure faille and silver lace, and yet very much removed from it all. It was how she had felt far too often in the past five years, but it was more pronounced now. Try though she might, she couldn't join in the festive merrymaking below her. What she had seen and done earlier that day stayed very much on her mind.

"Brooke, how could you?" Aunt Winifred had wailed, her blue eyes huge and reproachful. "To identify a dead body is just not done."

"I'm sorry, Aunt," Brooke murmured mechanically, sipping

at tea that had gone cold. Several hours had passed since she had seen Rosalind's body on the Cliff Walk, and still she felt shaky, though she was now safe in her aunt's oval-shaped bedroom. Winifred, wearing a frilly white bed jacket, sat ensconced in her magnificent gilt and white bed, an enameled *chinoiserie* bed tray set across her lap. Her dogs, rare Chihuahuas from Mexico, lolled on the pink satin quilt. For some reason, Winifred had named them after English poets, but to Brooke they resembled nothing so much as bad-tempered rats. She was never quite comfortable in this room—so much her aunt's, with its beruffled vanity table and satin-upholstered chairs in too many shades of pink—but today it was a haven. In times of crisis she needed family.

"Really, I don't know what you were thinking of. Grace!" Winifred's voice rose sharply. "This tea is cold. A fresh pot, if you please. Really," she said again as Grace, her maid, removed the offending teapot, "and on today of all days, when we're having our very first party here."

"I assure you, that was on my mind."

"Do not be snide, Brooke. It doesn't become you. Now. We must think how to salvage this situation."

Brooke's cup clinked as she set it down on the saucer, hard. "Surely we're not still going to have the party!"

"Why shouldn't we? What happens on the Cliff Walk doesn't affect us. We are constantly being reminded, are we not, that it is public property? Why, we cannot even fence off our own section." She made a face. "Distasteful thing. I imagine the *hoi polloi* is out there even now."

"Yes, people are there. Aunt, we should cancel, if only out of common decency—"

"Indeed, we will not! No one can reasonably expect it of us at such short notice. And after all the work I've done. I find it terribly rude of that policeman—what was his name?"

"Detective Devlin."

"Devlin. Yes. Irish, of course. He was very rude. Telling me to cancel the party. As if he had the right!" She sat up straighter, her face flushing. "A common policeman, telling me what to do!"

"Aunt, your heart," Brooke said, alarmed by Winifred's color. Winifred subsided, falling back against the pillows, and Brooke breathed easier. Of all today's trials, she suspected her aunt found being summoned downstairs by a policeman, and before she had had a proper breakfast, the worst. "Please don't distress yourself so. Uncle Henry has promised you we'll have the party."

"Yes." Winifred's voice was smug. "I am very glad he's friendly with Senator Burdick. He should be able to control the police. That Detective Devon—"

"Devlin."

"Whichever. He needs to know his place. Much too aggressive a young man."

"Matt was only doing his job, Aunt."

"Matt?" Winifred eyed her. "Are you already on a first-name basis with that—person?"

"I've known Matt for years, Aunt. He and I were friends."

"A common policeman?" Winifred's voice rose several octaves.

"My father was a common policeman."

"Please don't remind me. Oh, my heart." She patted at her chest. "I'm having palpitations. Grace! My medicine, please. At once!"

"Oh, for heaven's sake," Brooke muttered, though she rose and bent over the bed. Winifred's color was normal, and her breathing, regular. "Please calm down."

"Calm down!" Winifred glared at her over the familiar brown bottle of Mrs. Pinkham's elixir, which Grace held out to her. "When I learn that my niece is consorting with a cop?"

"It's hardly that."

"It had better not be. Oh, give me that." Winifred grabbed the bottle and took a healthy swig, grimacing at the taste. "You are close to making a decent match with Eliot Payson, and I want nothing to ruin that. You must promise me you will not see Devlin again, Brooke."

Guilt sizzled through Brooke at the mention of Eliot. She'd hardly thought of him today, and yet they were close to an engagement. Aunt Winifred was right. That was important. "I won't, but—"

"Promise me, Brooke."

"I promise, Aunt." Not a difficult promise to keep, since Matt had shown little interest in her. "But he's bound to be back to talk with us."

"Let him. But I will not have you going the way of your mother." Winifred grasped Brooke's hand tightly. "It's bad enough I lost my only sister. I will not lose you, too."

Brooke turned her hand in her aunt's grip, squeezing back. "You're not going to lose me, Aunt."

"I should hope not. I have much better plans in mind for you, Brooke."

"Yes, I know." Brooke released her hand, unreasonably disappointed. Aunt Winifred was far more concerned about Brooke's social standing than anything else. She should have known. Brooke's past life in Newport was best forgotten. And yet, never in that life had she had to face something like this. . . .

"You look as if you could use this," a voice said at Brooke's elbow, jarring her from her thoughts. Before her the party went on, seeming unreal after all that had happened. Yet for now all she could do was be a good hostess. She looked up to see Miles Vandenberg, holding a cut crystal flute of champagne out to her.

Brooke managed to smile as she took the glass. "Thank you, Mr. Vandenberg. Though I think lemonade would probably be more sensible," she said, carefully setting the champagne down on the broad granite balustrade.

He leaned his forearms on the balustrade, a youngish man of medium height, dark-haired and dark-eyed and attired in a tuxedo jacket, a rose tucked into his lapel. The new style of dinner jacket was scorned by some, but Brooke liked it. For all his isolation from the fashionable world, Miles managed to stay *au courant*. "Are you always so sensible, Miss Cassidy?"

"With my aunt, someone has to be." She took a sip of the champagne. "Ah, that is good. Thank you, Mr. Vandenberg."

"Please, call me Miles. I think we've known each other long

enough to dispense with formalities. You are looking charming tonight, my dear."

Brooke gazed off toward the Cliff Walk before answering. "Thank you, Mr.—Miles."

Miles turned toward her, frowning. "You sound distracted. Am I boring you?"

"What? Oh no, of course not." Brooke smiled briefly. "I was thinking of the tragedy this morning. I'm afraid I haven't been able to get it out of my mind all day."

"The tragedy? Oh, Rosalind." Miles drained his glass. "Adds some excitement to the evening, doesn't it?"

"That's a terrible thing to say."

"Is it? Take a look out there, my dear." He gestured toward the lawn. "It's all anyone is talking about. Can you deny that it's made your party a success?"

Brooke looked out. "It's horrid," she said, slowly.

"Yes, but true. Why else do you think some people are here? For the sensation, of course. Freddie Jamison, for example. He never comes to affairs like this."

"He's lucky he wasn't arrested, jumping over the police barrier the way he did."

"Indeed. But it was smart of the police officer not to do so, considering that Freddie's father is active in local politics. It was, after all, just high spirits."

"Of the liquid kind."

Miles shrugged. "What of it?"

Brooke sent him a troubled glance. Ordinarily she liked Miles Vandenberg. He was handsome, easy to talk to, and, like her, a bit of an outsider. His wife's health made her an invalid and kept her immured in their mansion, the Point, which meant the Vandenbergs lived in Newport the year 'round. It didn't seem to bother Miles; he was that most valuable of commodities, an agreeable male available to dance court on the ladies of Newport. At a moment's notice he could be counted on to make up the proper number at dinner, or to escort a society matron whose husband might be gamboling on his yacht or still at work on Wall Street, to a concert at the Casino or a picnic at Bailey's Beach. He was always perfectly groomed and attired, perfectly charming. Without thinking about it much, Brooke had always liked him. Tonight, however, his attitude and that of the guests' bothered her. A girl had died, and people seemed to care only about the sensation it caused.

"It's terrible," she said, abruptly.

"What is?"

Brooke looked up at him in surprise. "Why, the murders, of course."

"Let's be honest, my dear. No one really liked Rosalind. No one's sorry she's gone."

Brooke gasped. "That's awful!"

"But true. Or do you plan to tell me that you liked her?"

"I—felt sorry for her."

"There, you see my point? No one mourns her. Except perhaps her parents."

"It's terrible," Brooke repeated, and shivered, because it was true. Rosalind hadn't been well liked; her sharp tongue had seen to that. Still, her death should mean more than just scandal. "She was a person. So were the other poor girls."

"No one cares much about them either. After all, they were only maids."

Brooke gripped the edge of the balustrade. It might very well be true that the Four Hundred cared little about the deaths, but for Brooke, who counted more friends among the servants than among society, they meant something. "They didn't deserve what happened to them," she said, through gritted teeth.

"Oh, undoubtedly not. I met one of them, you know."

Brooke looked up. "Did you? Where?"

"Oh, it was purely by chance. She was keeping company with one of my servants, I forget his name. In any event she was at the Point one day. Pretty girl. What a shame," he added, absently.

"That's right. A footman, wasn't it? I'd imagine he's a suspect."

"I imagine so. I wonder if I should keep him on?" He stared out over the lawn for a moment, and then turned to her, smiling. "This is a boring conversation, Brooke. Could we go on to something else?"

"Did you tell the police?"

"About what? Seeing the girl at my cottage? No, why should I?"

"It might help them."

"I can't imagine how." Miles lifted his glass, frowning at it when he realized it was empty. "No, I don't plan to tell them, Brooke. I don't plan to talk to them about anything."

"How are they supposed to solve the crimes, if no one will help?"

Miles set his glass down and turned to her. "This has you worried," he said, slowly. "I wonder why."

"Brooke," a voice called behind them, and, distracted, Brooke turned.

"Oh. Eliot."

"Why are you hiding up here, darling? Evening, Vandenberg," Eliot Payson added, leaning forward to kiss Brooke on the cheek.

Miles nodded. "Payson."

"People are wondering where you are," Eliot went on, standing by Brooke's side.

Brooke glanced up at him. His light brown hair was ruffled, and there was a scent of brandy on his breath. If he'd indulged too much, however, it showed neither in his appearance nor his voice. It never did. She had a brief image of how she must look, flanked by two well-dressed, attractive men, and wondered what people would think if they knew how she really felt at the moment. "Are you enjoying the evening?"

"I'd enjoy it more if you were with me." He bared his teeth in a smile at Miles. "Mustn't monopolize her, Vandenberg."

Miles returned the forced courtesy with a nod. "I wouldn't dream of it, old man. She's all yours."

"Oh, honestly!" Brooke broke away from Eliot's grasp, annoyed with both men. "Was there something you wanted, Eliot? Because I have to go inside to make sure everything's ready."

"Er, no." Eliot's gaze was so blank it angered her further. "Just wanted to see you, that's all. Oh, and your aunt thought maybe we could start getting everyone inside."

"A good idea. Please go and tell them," she snapped, and, turning on her heel, stalked across the loggia to the glass doors that led inside, leaving the two men to stare at her in bewilderment.

Once inside, Brooke blew out her breath, lifting a strand of hair away from her face. Drat, her hair was coming loose again, she thought absently, shoving the strand back into place. Her momentary fit of temper was already passing, as it usually did. It wasn't fair of her to be angry at Eliot for something that wasn't his fault. He was what he was, and usually she accepted that. She couldn't change him, or any of the guests, mortified though she might be by their behavior. Surely someone truly mourned Rosalind; surely many thought the deaths of four young women, whether maids or not, tragic. She had overreacted to one man's opinion. Her unease remained, however, as she walked into the dining room to check on preparations there. Something was very wrong in her world.

Annie was just laying out silver cutlery in precise rows on the huge mahogany sideboard, under Hutton's watchful eye, when Brooke walked into the dining room. "Oh, miss! Are the guests coming in so soon?" she exclaimed.

"Ahem." Hutton cleared his throat. "That's no way to speak to Miss Cassidy, McKenna."

"It's all right, Hutton." She sent them both a quick, strained smile. She liked Annie, and tonight she felt even closer to her, because of what they had both gone through that morning. "Yes, we're trying to get them inside now. The circus is too successful, it seems."

"Then I'll make sure everything else is ready, miss," Hutton said, and left the room.

"Phew!" Annie let a heavy silver fork clatter to the table. "Didn't think I'd do anything right with old fish-eyes there watching me."

"Annie," Brooke reproved.

Annie grinned without apology. "Sorry, miss. I don't mind Mr. Hutton, but it's been that kind of a day." Her smile faded. "You all right, miss?"

"Yes, why shouldn't I be?"

"I can't stop thinking about—well, you know."

"Yes, I do know, Annie." The last of Brooke's annoyance fled. Now why couldn't Eliot, or her aunt, for that matter, be concerned about her reactions to what she had seen, rather than treating it as a nuisance? "It will fade."

"I do hope so, miss." Annie frowned as she polished the handle of a spoon on her apron, and then set it down. "Miss?"

Brooke, about to return to the Italian Hall, turned. "What?"

"I—oh, nothing."

Brooke walked back into the room. Annie's face was troubled, and her brow was creased. "What is it, Annie?"

"Oh, it's nothing, miss. You'll think I'm foolish."

"Maybe I will." Brooke smiled. "But tell me anyway. I can see something's bothering you."

Annie shot her a brief glance, and then returned her attention to the silverware. "It's just that—well, I thought I heard someone."

Brooke frowned. "Someone? I don't understand."

"No, miss. But there was a voice tonight I heard before."

Brooke waited. "So?" she prompted.

"I think I heard it on the Cliff Walk."

"The Cliff Walk! When?"

Annie set down the silver and looked straight at her. "The night of one of the murders, miss."

Brooke drew in her breath. "Annie! Were you out there on other nights besides last night?"

"Yes, miss." Annie wouldn't meet her gaze. "The night the third girl was killed."

"Dear heavens. Why didn't you tell me?"

"Thought you'd scold me, miss."

"You'd have deserved it," she said, sternly. "But what do you mean, you heard a voice? I don't understand."

"Neither do I." The furrows on Annie's brow deepened. "I didn't think much of it at the time, you understand, and I've been trying to get it clear in my head since. But what I remember is, I was just coming back in. Just got through the gates, as a matter of fact, but I didn't want to go inside yet. So I stayed out by the edge of the lawn. It was a lovely night. Warm, and a lot of stars."

"I remember."

"I'd just got there when I heard someone go by on the path. Now I didn't think anything of that, because there were a lot of people on the cliffs, but he was talking to himself. And what he said was, 'That's number three.' "

A chill ran down Brooke's spine. "You're sure that's what he said?"

"Yes, miss, far as I can remember. But I was distracted, see."

Brooke looked at her from under her brows. "Were you alone, Annie?"

"No, miss." Annie wouldn't return Brooke's gaze. "Sam was with me."

"Hm. I see. Did he hear the voice?"

"He says not. But he was distracted, too."

In spite of the seriousness of the situation, Brooke had to fight the urge to smile. "Oh. Are you sure you weren't imagining things, Annie?"

"No, miss. I've gone over it and over it, and I'm sure that's what he said. 'That's number three.' I'd know that voice if I heard it again. Knew it tonight, didn't I?"

That chill went down Brooke's spine again. "Tonight?" she said, sharply. "Where?"

"Here, miss." Annie looked up at Brooke, and then quickly away. "It's one of the guests, miss."

3

"It can't be!" Brooke exclaimed.

"All I know is what I heard, miss, and I heard that voice again tonight," Annie said.

"But it doesn't mean anything."

"No? Someone walks along the Cliff Walk saying something about the third one on the night the third girl is murdered? Fair gives me the creeps, it does."

It gave Brooke the creeps, too. But to think that one of their guests, someone she knew, could be the murderer, was ridiculous. "The murderer is a maniac," she said, repeating what everyone had been saying over the past few weeks. "Heaven knows why he's choosing to kill maids, but—"

"Miss Sinclair wasn't a maid, miss."

Annie's words stopped Brooke cold. No, Rosalind hadn't been a maid. Why, then, had she been dressed as one? And could the killer possibly have known she would be on the Cliff Walk? The thought made that shiver run down her spine again. "Where did she get the maid's uniform, Annie?"

"Don't know, miss." Annie's eyes wouldn't meet Brooke's. "I'm done here, miss. Can I go back to the kitchen now?"

"I—yes. No, wait." There was one logical place where Rosalind could have gotten the uniform. Her own home. "Did she get it from one of the maids at Claremont?"

Annie's eyes flickered. "Dunno, miss. Can I go now?"

Brooke gazed at her a moment. Annie's eyes were guileless, but something about the way she held herself, her arms crossed, told a different story. Clearly Annie knew something. Just as clearly, she wasn't going to say what it was. "You'll have to tell the police what you heard."

"Me? Not on your life! I mean, beggin' your pardon, miss, no."

"Why not?"

"You think they'll believe me? Me, a maid, accusing someone wealthy?"

"I think Detective Devlin would."

"No, miss. I don't think anyone would. Anyway, it's better not to get mixed up with cops."

"Annie—"

"I gotta go, miss," Annie said, and practically ran from the dining room, leaving Brooke to stare after her in frustration. Two people she had talked to tonight knew something that might help the investigation, and neither would talk to the police. In a strange way, she understood their reluctance, Annie's conviction that she wouldn't be believed, and Miles, with the self-assurance of the wealthy, believing the investigation was beneath him. He wasn't the only cottager who felt that way; from what she had heard tonight in conversation, she doubted that any had cooperated fully with the police. Earlier that wouldn't have mattered, but now, hearing what Annie knew . . .

Shuddering, Brooke turned away and walked, almost in a trance, into the Italian Hall, her arms crossed and her hands chafing her skin, as if for warmth. People were beginning to drift into the Hall, their voices echoing against the high ceiling, but she hardly noticed. If Annie were right, the murderer could be a cottager. It was hard to believe, almost impossible, and yet—. And yet her father hadn't tried to protect her from human nature, and she had grown up knowing that the wealthy were as capable of wrongdoing as anyone else. She'd certainly seen evidence of that herself, though never anything this serious. It would be futile to press Annie to tell her story. That meant that Brooke, the only other person with the information, would have to do so.

She stopped dead. "Brooke?" a voice said, and she looked up to see Eliot. "Are you all right?"

"What? Yes." Of course she had to go to the police. It was what her father would have expected her to do. In fact, had he lived, and had she been a boy, she'd probably be on the force herself by now, making him proud of her at last.

"Brooke," Eliot said again.

"What?" She blinked, and he came into focus. "Yes, Eliot, what is it?"

"I asked if you're all right. You're pale."

"Am I?" She put a hand to her cheek. "It's rather chilly, isn't it?"

"I don't think so. Well, never mind, so long as you're all right. Once everyone's inside, your aunt wants us to start the dancing."

"Yes, of course." She placed her hand on his arm, letting him lead her deeper into the Hall. Tonight she had to go through with this farce of a ball. Tomorrow, however, was another story. She would go to Matt with what she knew, and she didn't care what her aunt, or anyone else, would say. She rather thought her father would have been proud of her.

The Newport police station was located on an unpaved street near the waterfront, down Market Square from City Hall and the custom house, facing the old Trinity Church. Though it wasn't far from Bellevue Avenue and its mansions, this area of town was another world. True, nearby was the harbor where the trials for the prestigious America's Cup race were held, and the wharves for the great steamers of the Fall River Line, with their wealthy passengers from New York. There were also, however, the piers of the fishing fleet; the landing for the ferry from Jamestown, on Conanicut, the island across the bay; and, farther down, the Torpedo Station and the docks belonging to the Navy. Newport's lifeline had always been the sea. It always would be.

In the winter the town was generally quiet, except for the occasional barroom brawl on Thames Street. None of your high-class folk there; this was the Newport of the townies, the men who went fishing in all kinds of weather, the tradesmen who charged exorbitant prices in the summer and then saw their business fall off come autumn. This Newport had survived invasion by the British during the Revolution, and lustily fought the rival city of Providence for the honor of being capital of Rhode Island. This city had its own concerns. In the winter, Newport slept, both dreading and anticipating the return of the summer residents.

In the summer, though, in the summer things were very different. The narrow, dusty streets leading down to the harbor and the wide paved avenues near the mansions were filled with traffic of all descriptions: drays, barouches, victorias, even the rare electric motor car, driven with magnificent disdain by liveried coachmen. No one knew when the tension that was always present between the summer folk and the townies would break out. By and large each group kept apart, but there was the occasional clash between wealthy young men out on the town, and local residents. There were also times when the wilder, or more eccentric, of the summer residents would do something outrageous, such as the time one man rode his horse onto the piazza of the Reading Room, that staid and exclusive bastion of Newport gentlemen escaping from their females. Accidents were common, and so was theft. During those hectic two months in the summer, the Newport police were often hard-pressed to keep up with their duties. Too often those duties included mollifying the summer residents, who had the wealth, and the power, to demand special treatment. No one on the force liked it; no one was pleased that the two worlds had collided again.

In his small, cluttered office in the station house, Matt leaned back in his creaking wooden chair, rubbing a finger across his mustache. It was Sunday morning, a time of rest for most people, but in the station house it mostly meant that those who had been arrested the night before for disorderliness or other minor infractions were being released. "All right, Tom," Matt said, his voice genial. "Let's go over it again."

Tom Pierce, the man sitting across the desk from Matt, hunched his shoulders and turned his cap around in his hands again. "Don't know nothin'," he muttered.

"I don't believe that. You know where you were the night before last, don't you?"

"Told you. I was in my room."

"Mm-hm." Pierce not only had been keeping company with Maureen Quick, the first girl murdered, but also was employed at Claremont as a gardener, placing him high on the list of suspects. He could have done it, too, Matt thought, sizing him up. He was a big man, almost hulking, with broad shoulders and strong hands that could easily choke the life out of a small woman. Matt could well believe that he was the culprit, except for two things: the almost delicate way his long fingers held his cap, and the look of misery in his eyes whenever Maureen was mentioned. "Did anyone see you there?"

"I was alone. Told you that before, too."

"But no one saw you go in your room, Tom." Matt's voice was soft. "We asked. No one. Not only that, someone knocked on your door at twelve-thirty, and there was no answer." He paused. "Want to tell us where you really were?"

"In my room."

"You're lying." Matt's voice hardened, causing Pierce to shift uneasily in his chair. "Do you know where I think you were? I think you were on the Cliff Walk."

"No."

"I can understand what happened with Maureen. You had an argument. Maybe she told you she wanted to see someone else and you lost your temper. It wouldn't be the first time a man has strangled a woman for that reason."

Pierce looked wildly about the room at the accusation, as if seeking escape. "I would never have hurt Maureen! Ask anyone. Ask her friends."

"Oh, we did." Matt bared his teeth in a smile. "They say you got jealous when you saw her flirting with someone else and you hit her."

"She deserved it," Pierce said, sullenly.

"Did she, now? Did she deserve choking, Tom?" Matt leaned forward. "What was it like, putting your hands around her neck, squeezing, squeezing—"

"I didn't!" Pierce jumped to his feet. "I swear I didn't."

"—and then finding you'd gone too far," Matt went on. "Must have been a shock, eh? Maybe unhinged you a little bit. So whenever you go on the Cliff Walk and see a maid—"

"No. No." Pierce shook his head violently from side to side.

"—you remember Maureen and what you did. Isn't that how it happened, Tom, night before last?"

"No!" Pierce shouted. "I swear to you I wasn't there!"

"Then where were you?" Charlie put in, quietly. He had been in the room throughout the interrogation, but only now did he speak, prompted by a quick look from Matt.

"I was in my room. I swear."

"Come on, Tom. We know different," Matt said, rising as well. He wasn't as tall as Pierce, but somehow the other man appeared diminished next to Matt's air of authority. "If you were in your room, why didn't you answer when someone knocked?"

"Because I was crying!" Pierce shouted, and dropped into the chair, his hands over his face. "I was crying."

"Crying. Huh. Tough man like you. Do you expect us to believe that?" Matt's tone was scornful, but over Pierce's bent head he sent Charlie a look that mingled surprise with resignation. The admission had the ring of truth to it.

"I was." Pierce looked up, his gaze defiant and sheepish at the same time. "Losing Maureen—well, it was about the worst thing that's ever happened to me. Think I wanted anyone to see me? Oh, I heard him—Lawton, it was, the head gardener. Don't know why he needed me so late, but he called me a lazy son of a bitch and then went away. I tell you"—Tom raised his head and looked at Matt—"if he called me that at any other time, I'd have gone for him. But not then." Tom's face was not without dignity. "I was missing Maureen."

Matt kept his face impassive, in spite of his frustration. Pierce was at last telling them the truth. Not just because Lawton had indeed called him such a name and had proudly said so when Matt interviewed him; but because of what Pierce had claimed to be doing. A man like him wouldn't easily admit to any weakness. "Take him away," he said, feeling tired. They weren't going to accomplish anything more today.

Pierce's hands bunched into fists. "I'm not letting you arrest me."

"We're not arresting you yet." Matt stared steadily at Pierce. "But don't go anywhere. We'll want to talk to you again. Now, get him out of here, sergeant."

"Yes, sir. Come on." Charlie took Pierce's arm, and the two men left the room.

Left alone, Matt leaned back for a moment and then rose, crossing the room to study the charts hanging on the wall. Carefully constructed, they listed the movements and whereabouts of every suspect in the case, no matter how unlikely. Matt took a pencil, scribbled something next to Pierce's name, and then turned away. He didn't think Pierce was the killer. He wasn't sure he ever had.

Next to the charts, he had tacked up sketches and photographs, taken by the press, of the four victims. Hands tucked into his pockets, Matt studied them, paying particular attention to the most recent ones. Rosalind Sinclair, as first she had been found; the marks around her neck that indicated strangulation; a larger view showing the entire scene of the crime. Not that Matt was likely to forget any of it, ever, but looking at the sketches might jog his memory, or inspire a line of investigation. This time, however, not even the photographs, which he usually found useful, showed anything he hadn't yet followed up.

A noise at the door made him turn. "See anything?" William Tripp asked, pulling on his pipe and studying the sketches.

"Some things," Matt said, shortly. In contrast to Tripp's natty appearance in tweed jacket, with his hair pomaded, Matt was in shirtsleeves and suspenders and already looked rumpled. But then, Matt had never known Tripp to do anything that required hard work.

"I see there was another rose found by the body." Tripp indicated a sketch with the stem of his pipe. "I assume the bushes nearby were checked to see if any were missing."

Matt snorted. Of course everything near the crime scene had been thoroughly studied. "Even if one was, it wouldn't mean anything. The Cliff Walk's a public way."

"It would tell us if the murderer came prepared, or picked

something handy." Hands behind his back, Tripp rocked up on his toes and then back down. "It could mean the difference between premeditation, or a crime committed on the spur of the moment. A good detective looks for these things."

"I'm aware of that."

"Are you? I wouldn't have let Pierce go. He's our man."

"Where's the evidence?"

"You have to look for it. Mark my words, Devlin, he did it. He had motive, the ability, and no alibi."

"Is there something you want?" Matt said, cutting across his words. "I'm busy."

"Thought I'd offer my help."

"Oh?" Matt sat behind the desk. "The chief tell you to?"

"After yesterday, I should think you'd want the benefit of my expertise. Considering how everyone reacted when they found out who the victim was." He shook his head. "Bad form, letting one of the summer people see the body. You know we try to shield them from things like that."

"Did Chief Read tell you to help?" Matt repeated.

"No, but he will." Tripp perched on the edge of Matt's desk, one leg swinging back and forth. "After all, I did solve that series of burglaries last year."

Matt snorted again. That had been his case, until Tripp had taken over. Both knew quite well who had really solved it, even if Tripp had taken the credit. Matt's gaze was steady, and, after a moment, Tripp looked away. "I'm busy," Matt repeated.

"Think about it, Devlin. We both know how you are with the summer people. Ordering the Olmsteads to cancel their party, and those questions you asked Mr. Sinclair about his daughter. You made the girl sound like a common streetwalker. Not well done, Devlin." Tripp shook his head as he lighted another match, touching it to his pipe. "I heard the chief's not too pleased with the way you're handling things."

"This is my case," Matt said through gritted teeth. "You're not going to take it away from me."

"I wouldn't think of such a thing. Have you forgotten, though, that we are supposed to work together? You're not a one-man police force, Devlin."

"I never claimed to be." Matt pulled some papers toward him. "I'm busy," he said, yet again.

Tripp rose at last. "Just remember, if you want my help, I'm available."

"More reports, Cap," Sweeney said, breezing in and slapping a sheaf of papers down onto Matt's scarred desk, already littered with papers. "Morning, Detective Tripp. This is some case. You're going to make your name with it, Cap."

"Huh," Tripp said, and stalked out.

Charlie stared after him. "What did I say?"

"Nothing." Matt grinned for the first time that day. "You reminded him that he's not the one getting publicity out of this."

"Oh." Charlie grinned back, pulling over a chair and straddling it. "He trying to take over again?"

"As usual." Matt pulled the reports toward him. "What have we got?"

"Not much. Reports from three of the mansions. Nobody saw nothin', or so they say."

"I'm not surprised." Since yesterday afternoon, teams of patrolmen had been going to all the mansions to interview people, with Charlie supervising.

"What do you think about Pierce, Cap?"

Matt scanned the first report. "I think he was telling the truth."

"Yeah. So do I. Doesn't mean he's innocent, though."

"I realize that. Still, I don't think—these reports are only about the servants," he said, sharply, raising his head and glaring at Charlie. "I thought I said the summer people were to be interviewed as well."

"We've got problems there, Cap. None of them want to talk to an ordinary patrolman. Some demanded to see the chief."

"That's all we need. All right, maybe they'll talk to me." He tossed the report back with the others. "I'll look at that later. What do you think, Charlie?"

"About the cottagers? I think they're pulling in, Cap. It was different when it was all maids getting killed. Now that it's one of their own, they're scared. Getting anything out of them is going to be hard." Charlie paused. "You're not going to like this, but I think Tripp's right about one thing. You don't handle the cottagers too well. Even I wouldn't have asked Mr. Sinclair anything when he came to identify the body."

Matt looked at him and then, reluctantly, nodded. "All right, so maybe that wasn't the time for that. But they have to cooperate, like everyone else."

"Yeah, but Cap, they have money, and they're ruthless. If they don't like how you handle things, they'll get the chief to take you off the case."

"And replace me with who? Tripp? Ha. He wouldn't have a job if he wasn't related to an alderman."

"Same could be said for all of us, Cap. Anyway, he knows how to talk to the cottagers. You want to get anything out of them, you'll have to be careful."

"I will be." He pushed the papers away. "So all we know so far is that Miss Sinclair somehow managed to get herself killed, and no one saw it. No one knows why she was on the Cliff Walk, and no one knows why she was in a maid's uniform." He frowned. "Something funny about that."

"Something funny about all of it. When's the autopsy report coming in?"

"Chandler said he might have something for us today. At least we know how she died." He rose, crossing to the sketches and studying them. "It's about all the victims have in common, except for being maids. Or appearing to be a maid."

Charlie joined him. "Same man, though."

Matt grunted in agreement. It was likely that this latest murder had been committed by the same person. Even if the rose hadn't been left as a signature, the similarities between this case and the others were obvious. All the girls had been strangled, probably by a man, possibly left-handed, judging by the size of the bruises left on their throats. All had been left on the Cliff Walk; all had been maids, in the employ of the summer people, and all apparently had been alone when attacked. Other than that, they had little in common, not their appearance, not their nationalities, not even their activities before their untimely deaths. One had been returning from a secret tryst with a lover who worked at another mansion; another had visited friends;

the third had gone out only for a brief walk. "We don't know if he chose them because he knew them, or if it was at random," Matt said. "They all struggled, but that doesn't mean he was a stranger."

"Not much physical evidence, either." Charlie pointed to an area on the sketch showing the overview of the crime scene. Faint lines indicated a scuffle, and what might be a man's footprint. A plaster cast of it had confirmed that guess; it belonged to a man wearing heavy work shoes that showed little sign of wear. It could have been any man's footprint, but its nearness to the body was suspicious. It did not, however, belong to Tom Pierce; his shoes were larger than those that had left the print. "It'd be a job interviewing men who are five seven, five nine."

"Anything strike you about those shoes, Charlie?"

"What?"

"They were new."

"So? He needed new shoes."

"Or he bought them for this purpose."

"So we interview left-handed men who recently bought new work shoes."

"He could have bought them in New York."

"You do like to make things tough, Cap." He pointed to another part of the sketch. "What about the roses?"

"What about them?" he said mildly, wondering if Charlie had noticed the same thing about the roses he had. Tripp obviously hadn't.

"I was thinking, we should check with florists—"

"Or anyone with a hothouse."

"But no one around here can afford hothouses except florists or the cottagers, and—" Charlie's head whipped around. "Jeez, Cap, are you thinking it's one of the summer people?"

"Those weren't wild roses, Charlie. Doesn't that make you wonder?"

"Jeez. That's going to cause a hell of an uproar. You could lose your job if you annoy the wrong people." Charlie let his breath out through his teeth. "You told the chief?"

"This morning." He smiled, without mirth. "He wasn't pleased."

"I'd say not. It's tough enough dealing with the summer people. How do you think they're going to react if they find out you suspect one of them of murder?"

Matt didn't answer right away. He had a good idea how they would react. It could cost him his job. But, still. Four girls killed. "I have a bad feeling about this. Four murders in four weeks, all unsolved. Our man must be feeling pretty well satisfied with himself. I think—I hope—he'll get careless."

"And kill again?"

"I hope not. No, I was thinking more on the lines of bragging, or knowing too much about the crimes. God help us if he does kill again."

"Detective." A patrolman stuck his head around the doorjamb. "There's a lady here to see you. A Miss Cassidy."

Charlie and Matt exchanged looks. "Now what the hell is she doing here?" Matt muttered. "Okay, bring her in."

Brooke took a deep breath as she entered the small, dingy office. Though she hadn't been in the police station since her parents' death, it was all familiar: tired-looking detectives and patrolmen in their blue wool uniforms; the clamor of voices raised in despair or anger; smells of moldering paper, bitter coffee, and human misery. Talking to Matt yesterday in the safety of Belle Mer was one thing; coming to see him at the police station was quite another.

Matt rose as she entered, shrugging into his jacket. "Miss Cassidy," he said, not smiling. "What can I do for you?"

"Good morning, Matt. Sergeant." She smiled at them both; only Charlie responded. "I thought we weren't going to stand on ceremony."

There was a long pause. "Is there something you need, Brooke?" Matt asked, finally.

"Well." She sat down, her back very straight, her hands playing with the clasp of her handbag. She had decided to come here after attending services at Trinity Church, and had dressed accordingly. Wanting to look businesslike and serious, she had chosen her beige linen walking suit with the brown velvet collar and a matching small toque hat. Yet, in this world of men, she felt out of place. "I heard something last night I think you should know. In fact, I heard several things."

"At your party?" he said, brows lowered.

Brooke raised her chin. "Yes. Something that could be important."

"Something important." Matt leaned back in his chair, bracing his head on his hands. "And just when did you hear it? During the dancing, the supper, or the circus?"

"The circus, actually," she said, refusing to be goaded by his casual attitude, or his sarcasm. "One of the maids heard something on the Cliff Walk."

"So?"

She gripped her small leather purse tighter. She would not lose her temper. She would not. "It was the night of one of the murders, the third one. She was on the lawn and she heard someone going by say, 'That's number three.'"

"Jeez," Charlie said. "Did she see who it was?"

"No, but—"

"It doesn't necessarily mean anything," Matt interrupted. "It could mean three waves, or three people, or—"

"Or three murders," Brooke retorted, finally losing patience. "I don't know why you're so angry at me—"

"I'm not angry."

"—or why you're behaving this way, but I think this could mean something. Whatever you feel about me, you shouldn't let it interfere with your investigation."

He sat forward, the legs of his chair banging down. "Don't lecture me," he said, in the soft voice that more than one miscreant had learned meant danger. She met his glare with her chin up, determined not to be the first to look away. "I'll do my job my way."

"Really. Without letting your personal feelings get in the way?"

"My personal feelings?" His smile was ironic. "Right now I have no feelings, one way or the other."

Brooke rose jerkily, pulling on her gloves. "I don't know why I bothered. If this is the way you interview people, it's no wonder you're not getting anywhere."

"Jeez, Cap," Charlie said. "This is what I warned you about."

Matt gave him the same look he'd earlier given Brooke. "I'll handle this, sergeant."

"Yeah?" Charlie appeared undaunted. "If Miss Cassidy has something to tell us, I think we should listen."

"Never mind, sergeant." Brooke smiled at him. "He's just like his father, a bullheaded Mick."

Matt stood as quickly as she had, and Charlie let out a burst of laughter. "You've got that right, miss. I—"

"Sergeant," Matt said in that same, quiet voice, and Charlie subsided. For a moment there was tense silence in the room, and then Matt ran a hand through his hair. "All right. Sit down. You might as well tell us whatever it is."

"How kind of you." Brooke sank gracefully into the chair, her chin still raised. She knew what was wrong, even if he wouldn't admit it. Matt hadn't forgiven her for her decision five years ago, after the death of her parents, when she had chosen to live with her aunt and uncle rather than with his family. "I'd think whatever Annie heard is worth investigating. Especially since she heard the voice last night at Belle Mer. One of our guests."

Matt's head snapped up at that, affording her great satisfaction. "One of your—who?"

"She doesn't know. She thinks she'd recognize the voice again, though."

"Jeez," Charlie said, looking at Matt.

"Will she talk to us?" Matt asked.

"She doesn't want to, but yes, I'll see to it that she does."

"This is the same Annie we talked to the other day?"

"Yes."

"Good." Matt noted that down. "You said there was something else?" he went on, coolly professional now.

"Yes. One of the guests said he had seen one of the murdered girls at his house. Kathleen Shannon, I believe it was. She was keeping company with one of his footmen."

"That'd be Vandenberg, at the Point," Charlie said.

"I know." Matt toyed with a pencil. "Did he say anything

else? When this was, or if she was quarreling with her boyfriend?"

"No. In fact, I doubt it means anything. The point is, he said he wouldn't talk to the police about it, or anything else."

"So?"

"Annie said she wouldn't talk to the police, either. But they both talked to me."

Matt let the pencil drop. "So?" he said again.

"If they won't talk to you, you'll need someone who can get information." She took a deep breath. "I could do it."

Both men stared at her in astonishment. "I beg your pardon?" Matt said.

"I know the staff in most of the houses." She gripped her purse more firmly, as startled by what she had said as they were. It certainly wasn't what she had planned, but Matt's indifference had awakened something in her. It reminded her too much of the times when she had made suggestions to her father about his cases, and he had ignored her. "They'll trust me. They'll talk to me."

Matt rubbed his mustache. "Let me get this straight. You're offering to help."

"Yes."

Putting back his head, he let out a laugh. "What do you think of that, Charlie? A debutante detective."

Brooke straightened her spine, angry again. She was Big Mike Cassidy's daughter, not the social butterfly Matt thought her. "I can reach the people you can't. I can ask them the questions you can't. I can help, Matt."

Matt's laughter stopped as abruptly as it had started, and his gaze bored into her. "Thank you for the offer, Miss Cassidy, but it's out of the question."

"Why? I know what I'm doing. I listened to my father's stories enough times. I know how an investigation is done. I also know you need help. This way I can do something useful, instead of writing invitations and arranging teas."

"This is not a party, Miss Cassidy. Or have you forgotten there's a murderer on the loose? If you're bored, I suggest you find something else to do, rather than setting yourself up as one of his victims."

"You think I'm suggesting this out of boredom?"

"Aren't you?"

"No." She sat frozen. "So what I have to say is of no use at all."

"I didn't say that." He shuffled through some papers until he found the one he wanted. "What you could do is tell me what she was like, places she went."

"There are others who can tell you that, Matt." She leaned forward, trying one last time to reach him. "Her family, other friends, Paul Radley—you do know who he is?"

"Yes. Her fiancé."

"Yes. *They* can give you that kind of information. *I* can find out other things. What the servants know, for example. What the cottagers know, but won't tell you. They'll close ranks to protect Rosalind's reputation, but they'll talk to me. I'm one of them, you see. I'm also a cop's daughter. I can help, Matt."

Matt looked up at the ceiling before answering. "No," he said, at last looking at her. "It's out of the question."

"But—"

"You just said yourself you're a cop's daughter. Not a cop. Leave this to us, Miss Cassidy."

"You won't take any help from me?"

"You can be of no help to us."

"Oh." Brooke rose, her back very straight. "Excuse me, then. I'm sorry I wasted your time," she said, and turning, walked out the door.

Matt stood for a moment, hands braced on his desk, before sitting down again. Damn, Charlie and Tripp were right. He didn't know how to handle the cottagers. But how was he supposed to react when faced with such a ridiculous offer?

Charlie pulled out a cigarette, tapped it on Matt's desk, and then struck a match. "That was interesting," he said.

"Mm." Matt sorted through the reports on his desk. "Who interviewed the staff at Belle Mer?"

"Edwards and Sullivan, and no, no one told them anything about overhearing someone on the Cliff Walk. You knew that already. Seems to me Miss Cassidy just told us something important."

"Maybe." If nothing else, it was evidence toward his own suspicion as to who the murderer was. It was the fact that Brooke had learned it, rather than he himself, that annoyed him. "Hell, give me one of those." Matt reached for the packet and lit a cigarette himself. "What was I supposed to do, Charlie? Tell her she could help? Think what the chief would say to that, involving a woman. A cottager, at that."

"A cop's daughter, Cap."

"Doesn't make her any more knowledgeable than any other civilian. Besides, she'd be bored in a week."

"I don't think so." Charlie crushed out his cigarette. "Anyway, too late now."

"Hell." Matt rose and began pacing the office. "It's out of the question, Charlie. I'm not going to endanger her like that." He tossed the report to the desk. "I want you to go to Belle Mer and find out about this."

"Yes, Cap. Say, do you think—"

"Hope you appreciate this." A voice cut across his words as Dr. Chandler came in, a sheaf of papers in his hand. He had taken off his homburg, and his wispy white hair stood up in its usual peaks. "Take a look. Hot one out there," he added, putting the papers on Matt's desk and dropping into the chair Brooke had just vacated.

"The autopsy report already?" Matt said in surprise, picking up the papers.

"Preliminary. Considering the victim, I hurried it up."

"Um-hum." Matt scanned the top page. "Holy God," he said, and looked up at Dr. Chandler. "This true?"

"Beyond a doubt."

Charlie craned his head to see. "What?"

"This changes things." Matt lowered the report. "Rosalind Sinclair was pregnant."

4

Brooke stood in the entrance hall at Belle Mer, waiting for her aunt to come down so that they could pay their condolences to the Sinclairs. Winifred was late, as usual, leaving Brooke with too much time to think. Not pleasant company, her thoughts. The responsibility she felt toward the staff was heightened now by the menace to them, and she couldn't do a thing to help. Oh, she'd tried, going to the police station this morning to talk to Matt, but little good that had done her. The memory of the way he had dismissed her concerns still rankled. She could help, not just because she had access to people in a way he didn't, but because she saw them differently. She was caught between two worlds, the workaday Newport of her childhood, and the glittering life of high society. What that usually made her feel was uncomfortable. She no longer fit in with her old friends, and her middle class origins kept her from fully being a part of the 400. Yet now it seemed to give her a distinct advantage. She saw both groups clearly; she also knew how to talk to each. She could help, she knew she could, and she needed to. For, underlying all her other emotions was the one image that would not go away: Rosalind, lying stiff and still in death.

Hutton, the butler, opened the front door, and she turned, smiling at the man who toddled in. "Uncle Henry."

"Hello, darlin'." Henry Olmstead slipped his arm about her waist and placed a whiskey-scented kiss upon her cheek. "Fine day out. Why are you dressed all in black?"

"Aunt Winifred and I are paying a condolence call on the Sinclairs."

"Ah. Bad business, that." His brow furrowed and his fingers reached up to toy with the red rose in his lapel, his habit when he was preoccupied. "Brookie, you don't go out on the Cliff Walk alone the way you used to, do you?"

She laid her hand on his arm. "No, Uncle, I'm very careful, and I've made certain the staff is, too."

"Good. Good. Wouldn't want anything to happen to you. Though you'd have more sense than the Sinclair girl." He fingered the rose again. "Wonder who she was seeing?"

Brooke's startled eyes met his. "Seeing? But she was engaged, Uncle Henry."

"Yes, darlin', I know. Just wondering why she was on the Walk at that time." He shrugged. "No concern of ours, so long as the police do their job."

"Unless it interferes with our socializing."

Henry winced. "Now, I'm not proud of what I did, darlin'. But you know your aunt. There'd be no livin' with her if she couldn't have her precious party."

"I suppose it's just as well we did have it."

Henry looked at her with eyes unexpectedly keen. "Do you really think so, Brookie girl?"

"No. But you knew that yesterday."

"So I did, so I did." He glanced away, his hands thrust into his pockets, his shoulders sagging. "Detective Devlin seems to be a good man." He looked back at her. "The name sounds familiar."

"Yes. His father and mine were partners once."

"Ah." His eyes twinkled, and the defeated look of a moment before vanished. "Don't let your aunt hear of that. She'll have hysterics. And speaking of her." He glanced up the stairs, at the sound of Winifred's sharp voice giving orders to her maid. "Excuse me, Brookie. Think I'll just check on my roses."

"Of course, Uncle Henry." Brooke at last smiled as he ambled out in the direction of his conservatory. If she found Aunt Winifred trying, she could only imagine how gentle, scholarly Uncle Henry, more interested in his prize roses and his books than anything else, coped with her. It was no wonder if he tended to drink more than he should at the Reading Room most mornings.

"A most distasteful task," Winifred declaimed, sweeping down the stairs and into the hall. The staccato click of her heels on the marble floor was echoed by the clacking nails of her dogs following her. "You are ready, Brooke?"

"Yes, Aunt."

"Good. I detest being kept waiting. No, no, my babies, you cannot come," she crooned to the dogs, turning as she drew on her gloves. "Mommy will be back soon. Brooke?" Her voice returned to normal. "Let us go."

The drive at Claremont was packed with carriages when the Olmsteads arrived in their victoria. It was a somber occasion, and yet in spite of that, the chatter that filled the mansion had a hectic, almost festive, air. Perhaps, Brooke reflected, standing in the receiving line with her aunt, almost as if this were any other social event, things would be different if Rosalind had been at all liked.

It shouldn't have been that way. Rosalind had been pretty, and could be charming when she wanted to be. But her sharp tongue had made her more enemies than friends, and won her fear rather than liking. When she had first come to live with her aunt and uncle, Brooke herself had felt the sting of Rosalind's wit, and had actively disliked her for a very long time. Once she had met Mrs. Sinclair, however, she had understood Rosalind far better. Mrs. Sinclair seemed to see her daughter as the means to social advancement, and not as a person. Brooke had felt a little sorry for Rosalind, and for that reason alone, Rosalind's dislike of her had been enormous.

"Dear Winifred." Mrs. Sinclair sniffled as she pressed Winifred's hand and touched a lace-trimmed handkerchief to eyes that were red and swollen, but, at the moment, dry and hardlooking. Nothing so common for her as to show emotion, Brooke thought. "So kind of you to come. Although, after last night, I would hope you would."

"I am so sorry for your loss, Linda," Winifred said, ignoring the reference to her party. "Such a tragedy. You remember my niece, Brooke Cassidy?"

Mrs. Sinclair looked up, and her eyes hardened even more. "Cassidy? Oh, yes. You found Rosalind, I understand?"

Brooke held on to her composure. At the best of times, Mrs. Sinclair was a trying woman, loud and aggressive and haughty. She was also, Brooke reminded herself, going through a terrible time. "Yes, ma'am. I'm so sorry for your loss."

"Thank you," Mrs. Sinclair said mechanically. "You are engaged to Eliot Payson, are you not?"

"We're seeing each other, ma'am," Brooke said politely.

"My Rosalind turned him down, you know, when he proposed to her. She could have had anyone she chose."

"Of course," Brooke murmured, and something Henry had said popped into her mind. Who had Rosalind been seeing when she went out in disguise? "How tragic that she was on the Cliff Walk at such an unfortunate time."

Something flashed in Mrs. Sinclair's eyes, something that Brooke couldn't quite identify. "It was not her fault," she said, "and for you to suggest otherwise shows how ill bred you are—"

"Linda." Winifred pressed Mrs. Sinclair's hand. "It's all right. We understand."

Mrs. Sinclair's eyes filled up, and she averted her head. "I'm sorry. I didn't mean that. But it's just so difficult."

"I know it is," Winifred murmured. "I lost a child myself. We all feel for you, Linda."

She dabbed at her eyes with the handkerchief. "Thank you. I—thank you."

"You should go rest."

"No." Mrs. Sinclair drew herself up, her bosom jutting forward impressively. "Rosalind would have wanted me to carry on."

Winifred nodded, as if in approval. "But be certain to take care of yourself. And do not hesitate to call on me if I can help at all."

"Thank you," she said again, her lips tucked back in an effort to smile.

"We'll leave you now. Come, Brooke."

"Yes, Aunt." Brooke touched Mrs. Sinclair's hand. "I'm terribly sorry, Mrs. Sinclair."

"I know you are, my dear." Mrs. Sinclair raised her head, recovering some of her poise. "Mrs. Mills," she said, looking past Brooke and Winifred to the lady behind them. "How kind of you to come."

Winifred and Brooke exchanged looks as they moved away from the sofa to a broad table, where tea was being served by a maid. "How did you know what she was feeling?" Brooke asked as they turned away, balancing shell-thin porcelain plates.

"Experience, child. Grief takes different people different ways. Though I must admit I was annoyed when she attacked you. As if she's so well bred herself." Her lips thinned. "New money, and not so much of it at that! Why, I hear they only have two million."

"Aunt, please," Brooke murmured. "She's going through a very difficult time."

Winifred glanced back at Mrs. Sinclair, and her face softened. "Yes, she is. It's a terrible thing to lose a child. I do feel for her. Thank heavens we have you."

"Why, thank you, Aunt."

"Yes. I always wanted a daughter to present to society."

"Oh. Yes. Of course. Society is so important."

"I have told you not to be snide," Winifred said, but she smiled. "Sometimes, you remind me so of your mother. Oh, look, there is Mrs. Goelet. I must have a word with her."

"Of course." Brooke followed behind her aunt, absurdly touched by her aunt's words, but thoughtful as well. If the Sinclairs knew why Rosalind had been on the Cliff Walk, they weren't saying. Brooke suspected, however, that they didn't know; it had been consternation and annoyance she had seen in Mrs. Sinclair's eyes. Rosalind's death was apparently as much of an embarrassment to her family as a bereavement, and that in itself was tragic.

"My dear Brooke," Mrs. Stanford gushed as Brooke wandered away from the tea table. "Such a terrible ordeal as you have had. You seem to be bearing up very well."

"Good morning, Mrs. Stanford. Emily." Brooke nodded to the woman and her daughter. Neither was a particular favorite of hers. Mrs. Stanford, a tall woman with a large nose and a penetrating voice, considered Brooke a poor relation and ordinarily paid her only the scantest of courtesies. Emily could talk of little else but men and fashion and gossip. Her black walking suit trimmed with white twill at the lapels and cuffs was stylish, yet Emily had a woebegone look. Brooke looked at her a bit more closely. If Rosalind had had a real friend, it was Emily, who must be feeling the loss. Remembering what her aunt had just said about grief, Brooke tamped down the annoyance Mrs. Stanford usually awoke in her. "Yes, of course I'm fine. Why wouldn't I be?"

"Well, dear." Mrs. Stanford's voice lowered. "I understand you saw—Rosalind."

Ah, so that was it. Brooke had already run this particular gauntlet, last evening and this morning; she suspected she would do so for a long time to come. "Yes, I did."

"Was it very awful?" Emily asked in a small voice.

"Of course it was, Emily! Don't talk nonsense," Mrs. Stanford reproved her. "What an awful thing for you to see, Brooke, dear. Tell me." She leaned closer. "Was she really dressed as a maid?"

"Yes," Brooke said shortly, scanning the crowd beyond, as if looking for her aunt. And all the time the question that had bothered her since yesterday nagged at her. Why had Rosalind been dressed as a maid?

"I don't know why she'd do such a thing," Emily said, still in that lost voice. "And just when everything was going so well for her."

"She was a foolish girl," Mrs. Stanford proclaimed. "Of good family, of course, but foolish."

"She would have calmed down," Emily said, displaying the first spark of spirit she'd shown that morning. "She would have! She was so happy, with all her plans coming true. She told me about it."

"When was this?" Brooke asked.

"The day before—before—oh, dear." Emily pressed a handkerchief to her eyes. "Oh, dear, I'm sorry. But she was so happy, talking about her marriage and how soon it would be."

"I thought she and Paul had set a date for the winter."

"Indeed, they had." Mrs. Stanford was eyeing her daughter with a mixture of sympathy and disapproval. "Come, Emily, it doesn't do to show one's emotions like this."

"I'm sorry, Mama."

"I know." She patted Emily's hand absently. "Of course, I can't help thinking that she brought it on herself."

Brooke frowned. "What do you mean?"

"Well, it wouldn't have happened had she been dressed properly. Tell me." Mrs. Stanford leaned forward. "I heard she was—violated."

Brooke recoiled. "Oh, surely not!"

"She was asking for it, after all. Going out alone, dressed as a maid—well, it's just not done."

"Please excuse me." Brooke set her cup down on the tea table, harder than necessary. She had had enough. "I see that my aunt needs me," she said, forcing a smile to her lips, and stalked away.

How dare they? she thought, her hands trembling with anger. How dare Mrs. Stanford and everyone else imply that not only Rosalind, but the other three girls, had somehow brought their violent fate upon themselves? Safe in their smug little world, didn't they realize that this was more than a topic for gossip? Four girls had died, and no one seemed really to care. Someone had to do something about that. She had to do something about it.

"Miss?" a voice said, and she blinked up at the footman who had spoken to her. "Do you need anything?"

"What? Oh. No. I'm afraid I was woolgathering."

"The reception room is that way, miss." He pointed behind her. "This is the way to the kitchen."

Of a sudden, Brooke made up her mind. No matter what Matt had said, no matter what her aunt would think, she had to find out the truth. Here in this house was someone who could tell it to her. "Yes, I know," she said, and walked on, her head erect.

Mrs. Dooley, Claremont's housekeeper, looked up from her mug of tea as Brooke walked into the kitchen, and hastily got to her feet. "Miss Cassidy. What are you doin' here?"

"Sit down, Mrs. Dooley." Brooke smiled as she pulled out a chair at the long deal table. In theory she wasn't supposed to be familiar with any but the public rooms in Newport's mansions, nor was she supposed to know the servants. In practice, though, things were different. At various times she had arranged to "borrow" staff from one or another of the houses when they were having an affair, reciprocating with Belle Mer's staff when needed. She had come to know many, if not all, of the housekeepers and butlers and cooks of the cottages, knowledge that had stood her in good stead in the past. Beyond that, Mrs. Dooley was an old friend, a neighbor from Brooke's childhood. She hoped the acquaintance would help her now.

Evidently the staff was taking a break. Monsieur LeClerc, Claremont's French chef, was sitting with a porcelain cup in front of him, while farther down the table, in strict precedence, were several maids. Brooke pretended not to notice the way they glanced at her, or at each other. "What an awful thing to have happened."

"Oh, indeed, 'tis terrible. Did Mrs. Sinclair send you for something?"

"No. Yes, I would like tea." Brooke smiled at the maid who handed her a porcelain cup. "I know how everyone at Belle Mer feels about what's happening. I've just come to make certain everyone here is all right."

"Thank you, miss. We've not lost anyone, thank the Lord, but you know that. We've heard you're not letting your girls go out alone, neither."

"No, not since the first one. I didn't realize that Miss Sinclair was in the habit of using the Cliff Walk, too."

Mrs. Dooley exchanged an uneasy look with the others. "Miss Sinclair's doin's were no business of ours, miss."

"No, of course not. You couldn't be expected to keep an eye on her." She paused, and for the first time doubts about what she was doing crept in. The people at the table were eyeing her warily, making her aware again of the gulf between servants and employer. "I suspect, though, that you had a pretty good idea of what she was doing."

"Well, that's not for me to say. Now, girls. Finish up your tea and go along, before Mrs. S. wonders where you all are. And don't think she doesn't know," Mrs. Dooley said, turning back toward Brooke as the maids scuttled out of the kitchen. "Not much gets by that one."

"And yet, her own daughter—"

"Now, miss, what's this all about?" The vast kitchen was nearly empty, except for Monsieur LeClerc, stirring something in a stock pot, and a kitchen maid carefully washing china. "I've had more people here askin' questions, police and Mrs. S. and whatnot, and now you! I've told them all I know."

Brooke propped her elbows on the table and, regarding the other woman, decided to take a chance. "I've heard there's a maid's uniform missing."

Mrs. Dooley drew in her breath. "Where'd you hear that?"

"Rumor," she said, vaguely. "Is it true?"

The housekeeper looked away. "It's not for me to say. Now, miss, if you'll excuse me, I've got a lot to do—"

"Did it belong to Rosalind's maid?"

Mrs. Dooley looked at her, her face somber. "They sacked Molly, she who was Miss Sinclair's maid, last night."

"No!" Brooke said, though she didn't know why she was so surprised. "Did you tell the police that?"

" 'Tis sure I did. I also told them that Molly had nothing to do with it. She didn't know a thing about what Miss Sinclair was doing."

"Then it's not her uniform missing?"

"Hardly, miss. She's short and plump as a dumpling, that one, and you know what Miss Sinclair was like."

"Yes. Willowy."

"And a sly one, if I may say so. Got whatever she wanted, however she could." Mrs. Dooley glanced at the others, who were pretending not to listen, and leaned forward, her voice low. "I told her just last week she should be careful."

Brooke leaned forward, too. "About what?"

"About going out on the Walk alone."

"What did she say?"

"She just laughed, told me I was **being foo**lish, and that he wasn't going to hurt her."

" 'He'?" Brooke said, sharply. "Who did she mean?"

"I don't know, miss." Mrs. Dooley looked puzzled. "I thought she meant whoever's doing these awful things. She'd think she was all right, her not bein' a maid and all."

"But she was wearing a uniform."

Mrs. Dooley's lips clamped shut, and she rose. "Excuse me, miss. Got a powerful lot to do today."

"Mrs. Dooley, please." Brooke rose as well, resting her hand on the other woman's arm. "I'm not asking questions out of curiosity. I'm scared, too. Everything's changed since Rosalind was killed. You know that as well as I."

Mrs. Dooley looked at her for a long moment. "You mean the upstairs folks are goin' to want this solved right away."

"Yes. And that means that perhaps the wrong person will be arrested, someone who didn't do it. I know you want to protect your people, Mrs. Dooley, but if you know anything, you have to tell."

Mrs. Dooley looked down at the floor, and sighed. "I suppose you're right, miss. All right. One of our maid's uniforms went missing in New York in the spring."

Brooke let out her breath in a rush, feeling relief and triumph. She had been right. She hadn't known how anxious she was about that until now. "Whose was it?"

"Now, that I'm not tellin', miss." Mrs. Dooley's lips set in a straight line. "It was bad enough when we found it gone. I don't want anyone else to get the sack."

"Mrs. Dooley." Brooke stared at her in frustration. "All right! I won't ask you about it anymore. But tell whoever it is to come to me. Tonight," she rushed on, as Mrs. Dooley shook her head. "In the kitchen at Belle Mer. Tell Molly, too, for that matter. No one need know about it."

Mrs. Dooley looked at her for a long moment. "Why do you care, Miss Cassidy?"

Why did she care so? "Because I'm scared. Not just for myself, but for the girls at Belle Mer. Whoever's doing this has to be stopped."

"Leave it to the police, miss. That Detective Devlin, he seems able to take care of things."

Detective Devlin had some surprises coming, Brooke thought, rising. "You've been a great help, Mrs. Dooley. Thank you."

"Miss Cassidy." Mrs. Dooley's voice stopped her at the door. "I hope you know what you're doing."

"Of course I do," Brooke said, and turned away.

Her smile faded, though, as she walked toward the public part of the house, her reassurance to Mrs. Dooley sounding hollow even to her own ears, like Rosalind's confidence in her own safety. Perhaps Rosalind had simply meant, with her inbred arrogance, that her status would keep her safe. Perhaps. But in that moment of revelation, Brooke had had another, more chilling thought. Was Annie right about the voice she had heard on the Cliff Walk? Had Rosalind known her killer? And, if that were so, did Brooke know him, too?

Matt hunched over the reins of the buggy as he drove down Bellevue Avenue. It had been a difficult, frustrating day, and it wasn't anywhere near over. He'd spent the afternoon interviewing the cottagers, who would not speak to anyone of lesser rank, and yet had little to say to him when asked their whereabouts on Friday night. From their indignation, however, some facts had emerged. Most had been at dinners or balls or other entertainments, and could provide proof; a few of the men, such as Miles Vandenberg, admitted sheepishly that they'd been at Blanche's, the flossiest cathouse in the city, or with a mistress. Very little of what he learned was of much help.

While Matt talked with the cottagers, other policemen again interviewed the servants. They knew more about Rosalind now, though not enough. Everyone agreed that she had been pretty, intelligent, and witty. Only a few had said outright that she had also been disliked, because of her sharp tongue and the way she treated people. Just last winter, she had broken off a long-standing attachment to Eliot Payson to become engaged to Paul Radley. That doing so had meant taking Radley away from his former fiancée, Iris Gardner, seemed not to have bothered her. Rosalind had made enemies; that much was certain. The question now was whether any of those enemies had enough motive to kill her, or whether her death was the random act it appeared. Nor did anyone know why she had been on the Cliff Walk dressed as a maid. Until the Sinclairs turned over Rosalind's diary, her secret was still safe.

Matt abruptly pulled on the reins, and the buggy turned on one wheel into a drive fronting a substantial cottage. "Jeez, Cap." Charlie grabbed the edge of his seat. "Slow down."

"Sorry," Matt said, absently. The interview ahead promised to be as difficult as any, if potentially more rewarding. Matt was about to talk to Paul Radley, Rosalind's erstwhile fiancé.

"Not bad," Charlie commented as they climbed down from the buggy, surveying the massive, turreted building. It was one of the oldest cottages on Bellevue Avenue, having been built when Newport was a summer place for Southern families, before the Civil War. It enjoyed the name "Hôtel Soleil," though it was shaded by massive copper beeches and towering elms. "I'd take it."

Matt grunted, looping the reins of the buggy over the horse's head and climbing the stairs of the house. "And where does the Radley money come from?"

Charlie consulted his notebook. "A little of everything. Railroads, oil, different things. Radley Senior is on the board of a dozen companies. Junior is on Wall Street."

Matt grunted again, his face expressionless. He knew about Paul Radley's work, and the fact that he came to Newport only on weekends, on one of the luxurious steamships of the Fall River line. This week he had taken the *Priscilla* on Friday night, which meant he had been en route at the time of Rosalind's death and could not possibly have killed her. Alibi or no, if he turned out to be the father of Rosalind's baby, Matt was going to look at him a lot more closely.

The entrance hall was of dark oak wainscoting and willow-patterned wallpaper, a stained-glass window throwing jewel colors onto the wall. Overhead the ceiling was painted in a design of flower garlands. The butler led them up a few stairs and showed them into a small, square room off the hall, a library, judging by the bookshelves lining the paneled walls. Also apparently not well used; Matt pulled down a book at random and opened it, finding that its pages were uncut. He was just replacing it on the shelf when the door opened and a young man stalked in. "I'm Paul Radley," he said, abruptly. "You Devlin?"

Matt turned slowly, sizing up the other man. College boy, he thought. Harvard, by the sound of his accent. Tall and blond and arrogant, thinking he owned the earth. Matt's hackles rose, and it was only by great effort that he calmed himself. Nothing would be served if he let his own feelings get in the way of the investigation. "Detective Devlin," he said, keeping his voice neutral and holding out his hand. "Thank you for agreeing to talk to us."

"Did I have a choice?" Radley threw himself into a leather armchair, his fingers drumming impatiently on the arm. "Ask your questions, and be done. I haven't got all day."

"All right." Matt hitched up his trouser legs and sat across from Radley, slowly and deliberately. So Mr. Radley wanted to be rid of the police. Interesting, if not particularly revealing. No one wanted to talk to the police about this case. "Mr. Radley, how long were you—"

"Have you caught him yet?" Paul demanded.

"Who?"

"The madman who's doing this. Rosalind—my God, I would think even you townies could find who it is."

"We're working on it." Matt licked a finger and turned a page of his notebook slowly, aware of Charlie's questioning look. Ordinarily he conducted interviews quickly, giving a suspect little time to think. This time was different. Let Radley think he was controlling the interview. Matt had a question or two that would likely stun him into cooperation. "How long were you and Miss Sinclair engaged?"

"Since Christmas. Is that what you needed to ask me? Anyone could have told you that."

"Christmas." Matt noted that down. "Did she often disguise herself as a maid?"

Paul waved his hand in dismissal. "A prank," he said. "It had to be. Anyone who knows—knew—Rosalind knows she enjoyed pranks."

"Except that this prank killed her, Mr. Radley."

"I say—"

"Was it something she was in the habit of doing?"

"I say, what are you implying?"

"If Rosalind often dressed as a maid, who would know of it? If not you."

"Rosalind never did such a thing."

"You sound positive of that, Mr. Radley."

"Of course I am. She is—was—my fiancée." His throat worked as he swallowed. "No one knew her better than I."

"I see." Matt appeared to consult his notebook, though in reality his mind was racing ahead, contemplating the outcome of his next question. It was time to bring Radley back to earth. "Then tell me. Were you the father of her child?"

5

"I—what? Damn you!" Paul jumped to his feet, knocking his chair back and assuming the classic boxer's stance. "I should take you out for that."

"Sit down, Mr. Radley." Matt sat still, unimpressed, and this time there was steel in his voice. Looking slightly surprised, Radley sat. "Rosalind Sinclair was three months pregnant. I ask you again. Were you her baby's father?"

"I don't believe it." Paul glared at him for a moment longer and then sagged, putting his hands to his face. "God. I don't believe she'd do such a thing."

In spite of himself, Matt began to feel pity for the man. "Were you the child's father, sir?"

"No. I wouldn't so dishonor Rosalind. But—"

"But someone did. I'm sorry, Mr. Radley. I realize you're upset, but those are the facts."

"There was someone else." Paul sounded stunned. "She was seeing someone else."

"You're sure of that?"

"I—yes. She wouldn't let me—I was going to marry her, for God's sake!"

Matt's sympathy for him strengthened. It was a betrayal, and he well remembered what that felt like. "I'm sorry," he said, and meant it. "Sweeney." Matt kept his gaze on Radley. "See if the butler will bring Mr. Radley something to drink."

Charlie rose. "Yes, sir."

"God." Paul walked shakily over to the window. "First to learn she's gone, and now—this."

"Sit down, Mr. Radley," Matt said, not unkindly. "I need to ask you some questions, and the sooner, the better. But if you'd rather wait, I can return at some other time."

Charlie, coming in just then with a crystal tumbler filled with an amber fluid, looked at Matt with eyebrows raised in surprise. "Here you are, Mr. Radley."

"Thank you." Paul drained the contents of the glass in one long gulp, and then set it down on the table next to him with a thump. There was a little more color in his face now, and his eyes had lost the glazed look of shock. "Will these questions help find her murderer?"

"Yes."

"Then ask them. I want to catch the bastard—"

"Thank you. Do you have any idea who she was seeing?"

"No. She wasn't that kind of girl. At least, I didn't think she was." His eyes were unfocused as he sat, hunched forward. "I can think of men she flirted with—I can't think of any she didn't flirt with—but to do this!"

"Is it possible she could have been friendly with someone on the staff?"

"I doubt it." Paul sat up straighter, more in command of himself. "It's not done to have an affair with a servant. Rosalind had too much pride in herself for that."

Matt nodded; that was his opinion, too. "You do realize what you're saying, don't you? About who the killer might be."

"One of us, you mean," he said, flatly.

"One of the cottagers, yes." He paused. "You don't seem shocked by the idea."

"When you've seen some of the things so-called gentlemen do on Wall Street—God!" Paul passed a shaky hand over his forehead. "Underhanded tactics, and sometimes outright fraud—there are times I think some of them could commit murder."

"You're sure you can't think of who she might have been seeing."

"No. Unless . . ."

"Unless?" Matt prompted when Radley stopped.

"No, I don't think he'd do such a thing. But you might want to talk to Eliot Payson."

Matt noted the name, as if he had never heard it before. "Who is he?"

"They saw each other for a while last fall. He was more serious about her than she was about him. Though I doubt it was him. He's been seeing Miss Cassidy lately. Of Belle Mer, you know."

Matt's head snapped up in surprise. "Oh?" Who the hell was Eliot Payson? "We'll talk to him anyway."

"Good. My God, this is inconceivable."

"If you don't know who she was seeing, can you think of someone who could tell us more about Rosalind?"

"No." He looked up, his eyes clear. "I loved Rosalind, but I wasn't blind to her faults. She could be difficult. And she didn't have any friends. Just acquaintances."

"Why not?"

"I don't know. Partly because they were jealous. She is—was—very beautiful, you know. But also—well, she could be difficult. Sarcastic. She had a sharp tongue, and I don't think she realized it kept people away."

"I see. The gentlemen, too?"

"No. Not the gentlemen, though I can't think of anyone she favored recently. But there was someone." His hands clenched. "When I find out who it was, I'll—" He stopped, and the madness in his eyes eased.

"You'll what, Mr. Radley?" Matt waited for an answer. "Kill him?"

"Of course not." Radley leaned back in his chair. "My temper got the better of me. Can't blame a man for getting mad, can you?"

"No," Matt said after a moment. "Can you think of anything else we should know?"

"No." He looked up, and his eyes were bewildered. "I never really knew her, did I?"

"I'm sorry." Matt and Charlie rose, and Radley followed

them, that bewildered look still on his face. "If you think of anything, call me."

"I will. Catch the bastard, Mr. Devlin."

"We will. Oh, and Mr. Radley." Matt turned at the door. "I'd appreciate it if you don't tell anyone what we discussed."

"Do you think I want to look like a total fool?" Radley snapped, and slammed the door behind them.

"Well." Charlie pursed his lips in a silent whistle. "I'd say we just got our walking papers, Cap."

"Yes." Matt frowned as he climbed into the buggy.

"Think he's the father?"

"I don't know." In his mind there remained a question mark next to Radley's name. He had a temper, that Matt had seen for himself, and a powerful motive. If he learned that Rosalind was betraying him with another man, how might he react? "If he was lying, he's a damn good actor. But find out more about him, Charlie. I wonder . . ."

"He has an alibi, Cap."

"I know. Check it."

"If you say so. Better hope he keeps quiet about what you told him, Cap."

"He will. His reputation's on the line." Matt turned the buggy onto a narrow unpaved street. Ahead lay the waterfront, bustling with people and traffic, and the police station. "We know he's not the baby's father, but that's about all we do know. Dammit, if we could just find out more about Rosalind—"

"Maybe you could ask Miss Cassidy again, Cap."

"Ha." Matt pulled the buggy to a stop in front of the police station, letting the horse dip his head into the stone watering trough. After this morning, Brooke likely wouldn't give him the time of day. And just who was Eliot Payson? "We'll have to find someone else," he said, walking inside.

"Cap," the desk sergeant called, and Matt turned. "Miss Cassidy's waiting for you in your office."

Matt stopped, and then turned, striding down the corridor. "Thanks," he called back, and entered his office. "Brooke. What do you want?"

"Good afternoon, gentlemen." Brooke smiled sweetly up at

them. She was sitting in the chair facing his desk, a mug cradled
in her hands, and she appeared not at all annoyed at his question. She wore black this afternoon, a dress of some shiny stuff,
and a ridiculous hat with several feathers perched upon her
head. That's right, the condolence call on the Sinclairs, Matt
reminded himself, pulling his mind back to essentials. "It's more
what I can do for you, Matt."

Matt paused in the act of sitting at his desk, looking at her
warily. "Oh? What have you been up to, Brooke?"

"Nothing very much." In contrast to her reserved demeanor
of this morning, now she sat forward, her shoulders braced and
chin up, the very picture of confidence, and something else. Triumph, Matt decided after a moment. "I paid a condolence call
on the Sinclairs today."

Matt waited. There was more to this than that. "And?"

"Have you found out yet where Rosalind got the maid's uniform?"

"We're working on it."

"Oh, I see. Working on it."

Her tone grated on him. "We'd be able to get more done
without all these interruptions."

"Oh? In that case, then, I'll leave." She paused at the door.
"I don't suppose you'd care to know . . ."

"What?" Matt said, when she didn't go on.

"That there's a uniform missing from Claremont. The girl
who owned it will be at Belle Mer tonight." She beamed at him.
"I just thought you'd like to know," she said, and walked out.

Matt reared to his feet. "Dammit, Brooke, get back here!"

Brooke turned in the doorway, biting back a smile. "Excuse
me?"

"What the hell do you think you're doing?" He came around
the desk toward her. "I told you not to get involved."

"I am involved." She raised her chin. "When my staff is
threatened, when a girl I know is killed—I'm involved, whether
I like it or not."

He stared at her for a moment. "Dammit, Brooke—"

"Please stop swearing at me, detective."

"Dammit—all right." He turned away, pulling out a crumpled packet of cigarettes. "Sit down," he added, indicating the chair across from his desk.

"Very well." Brooke sat gingerly in the chair, eyeing his already overflowing tin ashtray. "Must you smoke?"

"Yes. I must." Matt lighted the cigarette with quick, practiced motions. "Now, what have you been up to?"

"Nothing so very much." Brooke settled back, forcing herself to relax. He had a right to be angry, she admitted to herself. She'd interfered in police business. Yet, even now, she couldn't imagine doing things differently. "I decided to talk with Mrs. Dooley, the housekeeper at Claremont," she began, and went on to relate what she had learned.

"So the uniform was missing in New York," Matt said, when she had finished.

"Yes. Is that important?"

"It might be." He stood up, suddenly brisk. "What time tonight?"

Brooke rose, too. "Around nine, in the kitchen. If you stand in the butler's pantry, no one will know you're there."

"Good." He held his office door open for her. "I'll see you then."

"Very well," Brooke said, and at last moved away, compressing her lips in anger. Here she was, finding out information for him, and not a word of thanks had he given her, not a sign to show that she had helped in any way. Not that she should be surprised. Matt always had been stubborn. Pigheaded, she corrected herself, climbing into the Olmsteads' victoria. He hadn't accepted her decision to live with her aunt and uncle after her parents' death, all those years ago; he didn't accept now that she might be of help. Why was she bothering? she fumed, looking out the carriage window without seeing anything. Heaven knew she had enough to do without playing detective. Debutante detective. Hours later, that still rankled. Very well, then. She'd do as he asked, no, demanded, and leave solving the murders to the police. And it would be a long time before she helped Matt Devlin again.

* * *

"Come in. You're Molly?" Brooke said, holding the kitchen door of Belle Mer open that evening, to see two girls, both dressed in the black serge dresses and crisp white aprons of maids.

"Yes, mum." Molly, short and plump, came in, the other girl following reluctantly. One look at her tall, slender figure, and Brooke knew whose uniform Rosalind had worn.

"I'm glad you came." Brooke smiled reassuringly. "Come, sit down. I hope you didn't come alone."

"Mrs. Dooley sent a footman with us," the taller girl said, sitting down and surveying Brooke coolly. She had the unmistakable accents of Rhode Island, the broad, flat *a*'s and the non-existent *r*'s. She'd be more difficult to handle than Molly, who was looking around the kitchen anxiously, and yet what she had to say was important. "We didn't want to come."

"I understand. I promise you, no one at Claremont will hear of this from me." What Matt, listening in the pantry, would do with the information was another matter. "Molly, Mrs. Dooley told me you were Miss Sinclair's maid."

"I didn't have nothing to do with it!" Molly burst out. "Miss Sinclair, she did what she wanted, and I couldn't stop her."

"No one could stop her," the other girl said, glaring at Brooke.

"It's all right, Molly." Brooke reached over and laid her hand on Molly's arm. "I'm not accusing you of anything. Or you, either—what is your name?"

The girl stared defiantly at her for a moment. "Rachel."

"Rachel." Brooke nodded. "Molly, I'm sorry you lost your job over this. Do you have a chance at another?"

"Much you care," Rachel muttered.

Molly looked down, sniffling. "No, mum."

"Then I'll see what I can do here."

"Oh, mum." Molly raised her face, hope at last creeping into her pale, frightened eyes. "Do you mean that?"

"Yes. I'll speak with the housekeeper and see what we can do. What happened to you was unfair."

"Oh, it was, mum, and I didn't do nothing."

"Can you tell me about it?"

"They sacked me, mum."

"Yes, I know. How long were you Miss Sinclair's maid?"

"About a year, mum."

"And was she easy to work for?"

"No, mum." Molly looked at Rachel, who nodded. "Terrible hard to work for, she was, especially these last months. She was poorly in the mornings, you know, and if something wasn't just right, she let you know. Many's the time I caught the sharp side of her tongue! But she could be sweet as honey when she wanted something. Like when she wanted me to say she had a headache."

"Did she do that often? Why?" When Molly didn't answer, Brooke leaned forward. "That was when she would go out alone, wasn't it?"

"Oh, mum, I told Mrs. Sinclair I didn't know nothing about it! If she finds out I did—"

"I promise, she won't. How often did Miss Sinclair do that?"

" 'Bout once a week. Maybe more."

"In New York, too? Or just here?"

"New York, too, mum, but not that often."

"And you had no idea where she went."

"Oh no, mum, she wouldn't tell me that. But I wondered . . ."

"Yes?" Brooke prompted, when she didn't go on.

"If she wasn't seeing someone. A man," Molly added darkly.

"Why do you say that, Molly?"

"Dunno, mum. Something about the way she looked, sometimes, like a cat's got into the cream. But, like I said, she never told me nothing."

"No, she wouldn't. And when did you notice your uniform missing, Rachel?" Brooke asked, casually.

"First I noticed was March—who said my uniform is missing?" Rachel glared at her. "I'm wearing it, aren't I?"

"But it's a new one, isn't it?" Brooke said, gently.

Rachel rose so fast that her chair fell back. "Come on, Molly. We don't have to stay for any of this."

"Rachel." The smaller girl stood her ground. "I think we should tell her."

"Molly, are you insane? She's one of them."

"We can trust her. Rachel's uniform did go missing, mum, and a deal of trouble that made for her." Molly faced Brooke squarely. "It was after that I noticed Miss Rosalind having more headaches. If you know what I mean."

"Yes." Brooke nodded. Pleading a headache was a common lady's ploy to get out of doing something she didn't want to do. She had done the same this very evening, so that she could be here. "Did you see her with the uniform?"

"No, mum. But it must have been the one, don't you think? I mean, the way she was found, and all."

"I'm not taking the blame for that!" Rachel said.

"No one's asking you to," Brooke said.

Rachel glared at her again. "You think I don't know how your kind works?"

"Rachel—"

"It's not my fault, but I'll be blamed, anyhow."

"I'm not blaming you for anything, Rachel," Brooke said quietly.

Rachel glared at her for a moment. Something flickered in her eyes, the need to trust, perhaps, and then she turned sharply away, to the door. "Come on, Molly. We're leaving."

"Rachel!" Molly ran after her as she stalked out, and then stopped at the door. "Oh, mum, I'm sorry, but she gets like this sometimes."

"It's all right, Molly." Brooke hoped her smile was reassuring. "Come see me tomorrow. I'll let you know what we've decided."

Molly smiled, her plump face transformed into prettiness. "Oh, thank you, mum, I'm ever so grateful. Rachel will be, too, when she gets over her temper."

"I hope so. Good night, and be careful." Brooke stood for a moment as the door closed behind the two girls, and then turned away, her smile fading. "Well. I appear to have made an enemy there."

Matt ambled out from the butler's pantry, scribbling furiously in his notebook. "Does it matter?"

"Of course it does, Matt. No one likes having someone dislike them."

"Even servants?"

"Ooh!" Brooke braced her hands on the back of a chair and gazed up at the ceiling. "Why do you persist in thinking the worst of me?"

Matt looked down at his notebook. "Sorry. But you've changed, Brooke."

"Not that much." Her eyes searched his face. "Why won't you admit I can help?"

Matt's face hardened. "It's not your place. Thanks for this." He closed his notebook and shoved it into his pocket. "It was a help. But no more, Brooke. Is that clear?"

She stared at him in frustration. "Matt—"

"Well, well. And what have we here?" Henry Olmstead beamed at them from the doorway, and they looked at him, startled. "Entertaining friends, Brookie?"

"Uncle Henry." Brooke stepped away from Matt, brushing a strand of hair back from her face. "I thought you'd gone out with Aunt Winifred."

He winked at her and leaned against the table. "Tell you the truth, darlin', I didn't want to go to the musicale, either. Evenin', Devlin."

"Good evening, sir." Matt nodded at him. "I had some questions for Miss Cassidy about the staff here."

"Ah." Henry nodded. "I thought maybe you two were catching up on old times."

"Uncle Henry, it's nothing like that," Brooke protested. "Detective Devlin and I are acquaintances."

"Now, darlin', did I say different?" Taking an apple from the wooden bowl on the table in his right hand, he proceeded to peel it, using a silver-bladed knife. He wasn't wearing the cufflinks she'd given him last Christmas, she noticed irrelevantly. "Understand your father and Brooke's were partners."

"Yes, sir," Matt said, politely. "Maybe you could help me with something, sir."

Henry arched an eyebrow at him. "Oh?"

"Yes. I've been invited to dinner next week, by the chief. I'm not used to dressing up, and I was wondering. Should I wear a rose like yours in my lapel?"

Henry's face brightened. "Do you like roses, detective?"

Matt shrugged. "What I know of them. That one is a . . ."

"This?" He touched the tightly furled bud, light red in color, in his lapel. *"Rosa Gallica Aurelianensis.* La Duchesse D'Orleans. You won't find this at any florist. An old French rose. Not fashionable, but I like it." Henry reached up and pulled it from his lapel, handing it to Matt. "Here. Take it, my boy. Has a fine fragrance, has it not?"

"Yes." Matt handed it back. "I thought it was an American Beauty rose."

"No, no, that would be too big for a boutenniere. Come with me, Devlin." He set the apple down onto the table. "Let's go to the conservatory and I'll show you my roses."

"If it's not imposing . . ."

"No, no, though you might think I'm imposing on you. I like to talk about my roses, don't I, Brookie?" He winked at her.

"Yes," Brooke said, looking from one to the other. "He'll talk your ear off if you let him, detective."

"No matter. Thank you for your help, Miss Cassidy."

"I'm glad I could be of assistance, detective," Brooke said, and watched as the two men walked out, glad to see Matt go, and regretful at the same time. The easy friendship of their youth, which had once seemed as if it might develop into something more, was gone, and he wasn't above reminding her of it. Odd, though. In all the years she'd known him, she'd never once heard him express an interest in roses.

In the conservatory Henry pressed a switch on the wall, instantly flooding the room with light. "Nice," Matt commented, looking around. "We still use kerosene lamps at home."

"Look into getting electricity, my boy." Henry led the way into the room. "The way of the future. Had this built to my specifications. Got one in New York just like it." He waved his hand to indicate the room, which was large and semicircular in shape, constructed of cast iron painted white and huge windows that reflected their own images back at them. The scent of roses hung heavy in the air: dozens of them, hundreds of them, of all hues and sizes. Matt hadn't known there were so many roses in the world.

"My little hobby, you know," Henry went on, thus dismissing in a few words something Matt suspected would cost several policemen's salaries to maintain. "Some people think a conservatory should be on the south side of a house, but I prefer the north. Steadier light, you know."

"How many types of roses would you say you have?" Matt asked, standing still and trying hard not to be dazzled by the wealth of color.

"Don't know, my boy, I lost count a long time ago. Now, these, here, are the old-fashioned roses, the damasks." He led Matt down an aisle lined with tubs of flowers. "Notice how open they are, compared to the tea roses. Sweet fragrance, though. The teas are over here, and the hybrid teas."

"Mm-hm." Matt nodded as if he understood the difference. "Is the American Beauty a tea rose?"

Henry chuckled. "You're fond of the American Beauty, detective? Well, can't say I blame you, she's rather special. All my roses are ladies," he added, leading Matt to the center of the conservatory, where rose bushes grew in profusion. From here radiated aisles into other parts of the room, like spokes in a wheel. In the very center of the bushes was one spectacular bloom, huge and blood red in color. "There's your American Beauty, detective, though I think they're all beauties."

"It's amazing," Matt said, after a moment. "I didn't know roses grew that big."

"It's an art, my boy. Have to cut off the early buds so that one will bloom like this."

"Oh?" Matt looked up, sharply. "Then the bush produces more than just the one bloom?"

"It would produce many if I allowed it, but one must sacrifice something to beauty. It's called disbudding. All the plant's energy goes into producing the one bloom. I'm something of an expert at it, you know." He beamed as he led Matt to another bush. "This is a plant I'm allowing to grow without disbudding. Still fine flowers, though." He pulled out his pearl-handled knife and cut the offending bloom from the bush. "Here, detective. Your very own American Beauty."

"Thank you." Matt took the rose, aware of something subtly mocking in the other man's voice. "I see what you mean. Even this one is too large for a lapel."

"So it is. Well. These are my roses, detective. I could talk about them all night, but I suspect you have other things you should be doing."

Matt turned to walk with him down the aisle, toward the main part of the house. "As it happens, I still have reports to look over before I can go home."

"Ah. Then I won't keep you. Just one thing, detective."

Matt turned. Henry's usual genial, slightly befuddled look had been replaced by a sharp gaze. "Yes?"

"I don't want my niece involved in this. I don't know what you were doing here tonight, and no, I don't want to know. But I repeat. I don't want my niece involved in your investigation."

Matt paused. "I don't intend to involve her, sir."

"No?" Henry peered up at him, and then nodded. "Good. See to it." He crossed to the door and opened it. "Because if you do, I'll have to do something about it. Good night, detective."

"Good night," Matt said, and stepped outside, into the sea-scented darkness, lips pursed in surprise. He knew a threat when he heard one. He suspected he had just met the real Henry Olmstead, and he was not what Matt had thought.

Thoughtful, he climbed onto the safety bicycle he preferred to use when alone and rode off, down the tree-lined drive, gaslights flickering on either side, through the cast-iron, lacy gates that rose at least thirty feet high, to the street. The rose, wrapped now in his handkerchief, was in his pocket. It had been an interesting evening. He knew at last where Rosalind had obtained the maid's uniform she'd been wearing; he knew, as well, that she had planned her evening excursions as long ago as the spring, and as far away as New York. Which could mean that her death had been planned that long ago as well. The implications of that disturbed him, even if they did go to bolster his theory as to the culprit. And the rose. That was the most disturbing of all.

Still deep in thought, he pulled up before the police station, brightly lighted, though it was late at night. Something nagged at him as he went inside, the feeling that he'd seen something significant tonight at Belle Mer. Try though he might he couldn't remember what it was. It would come. This had happened to him before, when he was deeply involved in a case. He would just have to trust his memory.

The station house was only marginally quieter at night than in the day. Those the patrolmen arrested tended to be somewhat the worse for drink, and thus loud and disorderly. Matt skirted a group of young men in evening wear, one sporting a bruise high on his cheek and all arguing at once, stepped over a man who had decided to sleep it off on the floor, and headed for his office. With the door closed, it was relatively peaceful. Matt switched on the light and sat down. Check into getting electricity, indeed. Easy to say, when people could afford their own generator, as the Olmsteads did. Until the city could supply electricity to all its residents, and out to the country, where his parents lived, most people would made do with gas or lamp oil. Smiling grimly at Henry's ignorance, he settled down to read Rosalind's diary, which he had at last obtained from the Sinclairs late that afternoon.

A long time later, his hair rumpled and his suit coat long ago discarded, Matt tossed the diary onto his desk. Lord, he was tired. He leaned back, supporting his head on his hands and contemplating the peeling plaster ceiling. He knew a great deal more about Rosalind, who had been remarkably frank in her diary about some things, and reticent about others. He knew she hadn't liked her life, that she yearned for her parents' approval, and that she was baffled that people didn't like her. He also knew she'd been highly critical of people, which probably explained the lack of friends. Most importantly, he at last had confirmation that she had been slipping out to meet a man, while wearing a maid's uniform. Reading between the lines, Matt could almost pity her. Her lover had not only provided her with excitement and illicit thrills, but he had promised her love. Rosalind had been certain that any complications could be solved. After all, she had a plan, and she had written that she was going to put it into effect the following night. What the plan was, she didn't say. Nor did she once identify her lover, not by name or initials or even a pet name. Rosalind had taken that secret to the grave.

Matt flipped the pages back, and his mouth tightened. The last entry was dated the day before Rosalind's death. *Poor little girl,* he thought, as he had when he'd first seen her body. All she'd wanted was love. Well, he couldn't do anything about that, but he could, and would, do everything possible to catch her killer. That was a promise.

It was late. Rising, he stretched, and was reaching for his coat when his memory returned, with such clarity that he dropped into his chair again. He knew now what he had seen in the kitchen at Belle Mer. Henry Olmstead had peeled an apple with his left hand. Hunching his shoulders, Matt opened his desk drawer and withdrew from it a withered rose. An American Beauty rose, similar in size and hue to the one Henry had given him, and that troubled him. For the first time he had seen this particular rose had been yesterday morning. It had been lying by Rosalind Sinclair's body.

She knew something, she did. Something that no one else in Newport did. Something that might be important. She was not particularly honest and under other circumstances might not have noticed, or cared, that he'd asked her to lie for him. Said, if anyone, meaning the cops, came asking, he'd been with her that night, Friday night. That, and the other three nights when those maids had been killed. Not that she thought he'd killed them. No, she was no one's fool, and she wouldn't let a killer into her bed. He wouldn't have been with her all four nights, anyway. She'd had her monthly two weeks ago, and so what good would she have been to him?

Still, it made a body wonder, why he wanted her to lie. Course, he'd paid her well, better than if he had been with her. Ordinarily she didn't question such luck, but this time, it got her to thinking. Man like him, he could afford more if he wanted to, and maybe she could convince him that he did want to. After all, she wasn't getting any younger. Sooner or later he'd move on, and she didn't fool herself thinking she'd get another like him. She was on the downhill side of twenty-five, and rich protectors were few and far between. Time for her to start thinking of her future. She wasn't going to end up on the streets, no, not her.

She'd ask him, then, she thought, stretching voluptuous legs on the unmade bed and regarding her feet. He'd come tonight, since he'd missed Friday, and then she'd ask him. And he'd pay. He'd have to, if he wanted her to stay silent. After all, she thought, smiling like a cat, a girl had to look after herself. Who else would do it?

6

"Out!" a voice called from the tennis court, and the couple sitting on tall stools on the upstairs piazza at the Newport Casino glanced idly out.

"Iris is cheating again," Eliot Payson commented. "That ball looked in to me."

"She's a good player," Brooke said, sipping at her lemonade and trying to relax. She wasn't particularly fond of lawn tennis, but this excursion to the Casino with Eliot was exactly what she had needed, two days after the condolence call on the Sinclairs, two mornings after the meeting in Belle Mer's kitchen. It was the place to be on a late summer's morning, and had been since it had been built, an enormous, shingled building that contained, in addition to tennis courts, a theater, a ballroom, and a restaurant. On the Horseshoe Piazza, Mullaly's String Orchestra played softly, Offenbach's *La Belle Hélène,* in counterpoint to the slap of racquet strings hitting balls and the chattering voices of the cottagers. To Brooke it was all blissfully normal, a relief from tragedy and a reminder that life went on. She would forget about suspicion, about death. Most of all, she would forget about a certain policeman. That Matt would never approve of her seemed clear.

"Strong," Eliot agreed. "Vandenberg's making her run, too."

Brooke glanced out toward the court, where Miles Vandenberg and Iris Gardner were playing a particularly fierce game of tennis. Hampered though she was by long skirts and petticoats,

Iris was hunched over, her face a study in concentration, her hair coming loose, as she awaited the next shot. Miles, by contrast, seemed to hit the ball with no particular effort, yet it traveled fast and went exactly where he wanted it, almost as if he were toying with Iris. "Iris doesn't know any other way to play. She's competitive."

"Not a trait I admire in a woman," Eliot said.

Brooke looked back at him. "I know. You admire a woman's fortune."

Eliot's eyes widened slightly in surprise as he gazed at her over the rim of his glass, before his lids dropped into their habitual half-closed position. It gave him a sleepy look, but Brooke had known him long enough to know he was never less than alert. "If I didn't know better, I'd say you were jealous," he said mildly, draining the last of his gin and tonic and signaling to the waiter for another. "It's not like you to say something like that, Brooke."

Brooke sighed, looking out onto the court again. "I know. I'm sorry. I'm not in the best of moods, but I shouldn't take it out on you."

"What's wrong?" When she didn't answer, he pressed on. "I noticed you weren't quite yourself at your aunt's party."

Brooke gave a low, mirthless laugh. "I'd identified Rosalind's body that morning."

"Oh." He nodded at the waiter who set a full drink down before him. "Well, it was a bad experience, Brooke, but it's over."

"It's not over, Eliot. Not with whoever did it still out there." And not with the image in her mind that wouldn't fade, of Rosalind lying broken and still on the Cliff Walk. Matt would understand.

Eliot shrugged. "They were only maids."

"They were people," Brooke said, keeping her voice level with an effort. "Kathleen Shannon, Maureen Quick, Mary Manning—they were all people. So was Rosalind. And if you tell me again that she shouldn't have gone out alone in a maid's uniform, I will get up and walk out of here."

"Brooke, Brooke." He leaned toward her, smiling. "Why are

you so distressed over this? It doesn't concern us. Let the police deal with it," he said, draining his glass again and signaling for another drink. His third, she noted, and it wasn't yet noon.

Brooke shifted in her chair. In spite of the tranquillity here at the Casino, she felt anything but calm. The outside world and its problems weren't going to go away, she realized with a sinking heart. "Eliot, I don't know if—"

"Brooke." Eliot placed his hands on hers. "This doesn't concern us. We have more important things to discuss."

Brooke tried to pull her hands back, aware that they were the object of more than one veiled glance, but Eliot's grip stayed firm. She liked Eliot. He was the perfect bachelor escort, always available, always polite. He could be charming, with a delightful sense of the absurd. Best of all, he viewed society much as she did, with bemused detachment. Whether she would marry him was another story, though everyone seemed to expect it. Up until recently, so had she. "Eliot, please. People are staring at us and they'll talk."

"Let them." His voice was low, intense, making her look at him in surprise. This was a different Eliot from the man she knew. "Brooke, we haven't had a chance to talk lately."

"We're talking now."

"About us, Brooke. About our future. You know how I feel about—"

"Excuse me," someone said above them in a dry voice, and Brooke looked up to see Matt.

"Matt!" she exclaimed, jumping to her feet, her emotions jumbled. Relief at the timeliness of the interruption warred with embarrassment at what Matt must be thinking, and an odd joy. "What are you doing here?"

"Brooke?" Eliot uncoiled his long legs from the stool and rose, slouching back against the low wooden railing of the piazza, his hands tucked into the pockets of his white flannel trousers as he leisurely studied Matt. "Who is this?"

Brooke winced at the disdain in Eliot's voice. Matt looked out of place here, his celluloid collar and dark, square-cut sack suit, obviously off the peg, contrasting unfavorably with Eliot's impeccably tailored black and white striped coat. There was something about him that set him off, though, an air of vitality, of purpose that contrasted sharply with Eliot's affected languor. "Hello, Matt," she said, collecting herself. "I didn't expect to see you here today."

"Brooke." He nodded at her. There was something in his eyes she couldn't analyze as he glanced from her to Eliot. "Mr. Payson, I presume?"

"Yes." Brooke hastened to make the introductions. "Detective Devlin is with the Newport police," she added.

"Oh?" Eliot jammed his hands deeper into his pockets, and there was a look of such foolish amiability on his face that Brooke was immediately suspicious. "I was wondering when the police were going to get to me."

Brooke looked at him sharply. "Why?"

"They're questioning everybody, aren't they?" he said, mildly. "I assume you do want to question me, detective? Or did you come to see the tennis?"

Matt glanced out at the court, where Miles and Iris were just finishing their game. "I prefer baseball," he said, pleasantly enough. "And yes, Mr. Payson. I would like to talk to you."

"Ask away, then." Eliot sat down, lounging back in his chair. "I've got all morning."

Matt gazed at the other man steadily, and, try though she might, Brooke could get no hint of what he was thinking. "Is there someplace quieter where we could—"

"I still say you should try playing with your other hand, Miles," a woman's voice said. "Whew!" Iris dropped inelegantly onto the stool next to Brooke. "Hot one, isn't it? But a good game, I thought. Backhand's not as strong as I'd like, but then, Miles is the devil to play against."

"Did I hear my name?" Miles smiled as he sat across from Iris and signaled to a waiter. "You look nice and cool, Brooke."

"Thank you." Brooke was aware of Iris fidgeting beside her. Iris had her good points, but no one would ever accuse her of being dainty or cool. Strands of hair had come loose from the knot at the top of her head and were plastered to her face, while her straw boater, trimmed with blue flowers to match her full-skirted tennis ensemble, was definitely askew. Brooke suspected that Iris had left off her corset, so that she could move more freely, and briefly envied her, in spite of her dishevelment. Her own flared skirt and sailor-style jacket covered layers of constricting underclothes, and she had to resist the urge to pull at the high collar of her white shirtwaist. Hearty was the only word to describe Iris, though Brooke knew that under her gruff exterior lay a sensitive, and sometimes bewildered, heart. "I thought you both played well."

"Thank you." Miles held his glass up in a salute. Unlike Iris, he hardly looked as if he had just played a difficult match; his striped flannel jacket was unwrinkled, and he sat at ease, somehow managing to look his usual cool, urbane self. "Cheers. Did we interrupt something? I don't believe I know you," he said, smiling pleasantly at Matt. "Are you an acquaintance of Payson?"

"No." Matt shook his head. "Detective Devlin, of the Newport police."

"Oh. Miles Vandenberg." Miles held out his hand. "Is Payson in trouble for something?"

"Should he be?"

Miles smiled again. "No, no, just a little joke."

"Detective Devlin is here about the Cliff Walk killings," Eliot put in, an odd little smile on his face.

"Good." Miles sat down again. "About time something was done about that. Glad to see you're on the job, Devlin." He indicated a stool. "Care to join us, tell us what's going on?"

"Actually, Detective Devlin wants to question me," Eliot said.

"You?" Miles looked at him. "Ah, I see. The fight you had with Rosalind."

"Miles," Brooke protested.

"It's better discussed in private," Matt said, his face still impassive. "Mr. Payson, if we might go someplace else?"

"I suppose so." Eliot rose languidly to his feet. "Brooke, I'm sorry to leave you like this."

"Don't worry about it," Miles said. "I'll see her home."

There was a brief moment of silence. "Thank you, old man," Eliot said, finally, and turned. "Come, Mr. Devlin. We should be able to find a private room empty at this time of day and talk in peace."

Matt nodded. "Fine. Ladies, Mr. Vandenberg." He touched the brim of his hat, and turned. Brooke thought his eyes stayed on her for a moment before he left, but again she couldn't read the expression in them. She shivered. It felt as if a cloud had come over the sun, and yet the day was as bright as ever. The darkness was inside her. Reality had invaded her peaceful, normal day.

"Remind me never to cross you, Miles," Iris said in her gruff voice.

Miles smiled, leaning back and taking a sip of his drink. "Why, because I mentioned the argument? Common knowledge, my dear."

"Among us. Newport doesn't know of it."

Brooke emerged from the darkness, to find that the sun was still shining and that life went on about her. Iris was leaning forward, frowning, while Miles sat back, one arm thrown over the back of his chair, as if the discussion meant little to him. Iris was right. There had been no reason for him to mention the argument Eliot had had with Rosalind when she had broken their engagement. How well did she really know Miles? How well did she know any of the people she thought were friends? "I think Miles is right," Brooke said, slowly. "The police would have found out about it."

"But not from us," Iris argued. "In any event, what does it have to do with anything?"

Brooke looked away. "Nothing, probably." Nothing, unless Matt suspected Eliot. The thought made her shiver. It was all very well thinking that someone she knew might be guilty; it was another matter altogether to put a name to that person. Surely not Eliot.

"I heard the police talked to Paul Radley the other day," Miles drawled.

"Paul was in New York last Friday. He couldn't be involved," Iris said, her face getting red.

"No? He was engaged to Rosalind." An uncomfortable silence fell. True, they had been engaged. Before that, however, Paul Radley had been Iris's beau.

"Always pitied him that," Iris said, and the tension eased. Brooke couldn't help but admire the other girl. When Rosalind had captured Paul, she had done it in the most public, and insulting, way possible. Their unexpected engagement had been announced at a ball at Iris's house last winter. Nothing had been settled between Iris and Paul, but there'd been an understanding between them, until Rosalind had stepped in. Brooke wouldn't blame Iris for hating her. In fact—

Without meaning to, she focused on Iris's hands. They were long and broad and capable, strong enough for any game she might want to undertake. Strong enough to strangle a smaller girl? Brooke hastily looked up, to see Iris staring at her. In spite of the warmth of the day, she shivered.

"Paul didn't have anything to do with it," Iris declared, looking away, and Brooke's shoulders slumped in relief. "Doesn't have it in him. Had to be some kind of madman. Horrible thing, what's happening," she went on. "Don't care if it is only maids getting killed. I don't go out on the Cliff Walk alone myself anymore." She shrugged. "Horrible, but there it is."

Miles shrugged. "Who knows what someone is capable of?" he asked. "Not that I'm suggesting Paul did anything. In fact"—his smile turned devilish—"now that Rosalind's gone . . ."

"Wouldn't have Paul Radley on a silver platter," Iris announced, and rose. "Excuse me. See my mother over there. I'll go home with her."

The silence was thick in the wake of her departure. "Well," Miles said, his voice cheerful. "I think I've just been snubbed."

"You deserved it," Brooke said severely. "You said some nasty things."

"True." He nodded. "But Iris is so easy to bait. Of course Radley had nothing to do with it."

Brooke shrugged and set down her empty lemonade glass. Who knew the identity of the murderer? It could be anyone with enough strength. Why, even Miles—but everyone knew about the injury he had suffered in childhood, and the weakness it had left in his hand. "I think I should—"

"When are you and Payson setting the date?"

Brooke looked at him in surprise. He was smiling at her, turning his glass around and around, the condensation leaving little circles on the table. "We haven't decided. I must go," she said, rising, pulling on her gloves and checking that her boater hat was on straight. "Aunt Winifred is expecting me home to go visiting with her."

Miles rose and took her arm. "I'll see you home."

"That's not necessary, Miles."

"It will be my privilege." He smiled. "What do you think people will say if you go home alone?"

"As if I care about that." Nodding at acquaintances, Brooke allowed Miles to escort her through the Casino and down the broad staircase, with its elaborately turned balustrade.

"You should," Miles said as they emerged from the covered entrance onto Bellevue Avenue, shaded by striped awnings. The street was as crowded as usual, with summer people stopping into the exclusive New York or Paris shops that had their branches here, or going upstairs to the piazza; with ordinary people going about their business; with equipages of all kinds, from fine landaus to heavy drays, to the large horse-drawn drags which brought excursionists from out of town on tours of the city. "Have a care for your reputation, Brooke. Look who's here," he added, jerking his chin.

Brooke glanced across the street, where an inoffensive-looking young man in a gray suit watched them. She recognized him, of course; he was Robert Rowe, spy for the scandal sheet *Town Topics*. Doubtless the fact that she was with Miles would find its way into the next edition. It was also a foolish thing to worry about. "I am a Low," Brooke said, as if that excused everything, and Miles laughed.

"That sounded like something your aunt would say."

Brooke smiled. "Heaven forbid! But doesn't this all strike you as rather foolish, Miles?" She gestured with her free hand toward the people around them. "I've lived here all my life, did what I wanted to do, and no one ever said a word. Now I can barely move for fear someone will talk about it."

"Your life has changed, Brooke."

"So it has," she said, ruefully, as they strolled along the elm-shaded street. Away from the Casino, past the old Ocean House hotel, the traffic was lessening. "I was Big Mike Cassidy's daughter. Sometimes I forget that."

Miles gave her a startled look. "So that is why you are as you are."

"I beg your pardon?"

"I sometimes think, Brooke, that you are the smartest woman in Newport."

She glanced up in surprise. "Why do you say that?"

"Society doesn't fool you, does it?"

"No. But then," she said, thoughtfully, "I suspect it doesn't fool you, either."

"I see it differently. Living in Newport year 'round, I have a different life."

"How is your wife?"

"The same." The muscles of his arm under Brooke's fingers tightened. "There's a doctor in Germany I've heard of who might be able to treat her, but she won't leave Newport."

"I'm sorry," Brooke said, after a moment. Miles's voice was bitter, and no wonder, she thought. Though he came from an old New York family, he was tied to Newport, and his mansion out on the point, by an invalid wife. Not for him the life the rest of the cottagers led, of autumn in New York and springs spent abroad. Brooke sometimes suspected he resented the loss of his freedom.

Miles shrugged. "It's the way things are. Now, tell me." His voice became brisk. "Are you and Payson setting the date?"

She looked up at him again. "Why does that matter to you?"

"I'm curious, like everyone else. Of course, you wouldn't want to be tied to someone the police suspect of murder."

Brooke pulled her arm free. "I am not as easy to bait as Iris," she said, annoyed. "If you're going to continue being disagreeable, Miles, I'll go home on my own."

"No, no. Forgive me." Miles took her arm again. "Still, you

must admit it was a remarkable thing for the police to come to the Casino for him."

Why had Matt come to the Casino? Brooke wondered. Surely he could have met Eliot someplace else, someplace less public. Or was that the idea? "Eliot didn't do anything. At least—"

"What?" he prompted, when she didn't go on.

"No. He didn't do anything. I'm sure of it."

"Are you." He peered down at her. "You're concerned, aren't you? I was teasing just now, you know. I doubt Payson is involved in this."

"Yes. But," she said, taking a deep breath, "what if it is—one of us?"

"The Cliff Walk Killer? What a ridiculous idea."

"It could be," she argued. There. She'd said it aloud, the suspicion that had nagged at her all weekend. "The killings didn't start until we were here for the summer."

"Not enough victims," Miles said, promptly. "The man obviously goes after maids. There aren't many on the Cliff Walk in winter."

"Rosalind wasn't a maid."

"True, though she was dressed as one. I wonder why that was." He glanced at her as they turned onto a quiet, shaded side street, the blue water of the bay far ahead glistening in the sun. "Has your policeman friend said anything?"

"He's not—no. But I was wondering—Miles, do you think she was meeting someone?"

Miles was quiet for a long moment. "It's possible, I suppose," he said, finally. "Why would you think that?"

"Why would she go out in disguise unless she had something to hide?"

"I thought it was a lark." Miles spoke slowly, thoughtfully. "Sort of thing she would do, you know."

"Yes, it was, but—I think she was meeting someone, and it had to be someone her parents would object to," she said. It was a relief to voice her thoughts aloud at last, and to the one person who so far was taking them seriously. "Not Paul, obviously, he wasn't here. Not Eliot, either, I don't think. He was too angry with her."

"It gives him a motive, though."

"But surely not to kill three other girls!"

"That's the problem with your theory, Brooke. Who in our circle could have killed them?"

She shuddered. "I don't know. When you put it like that, it does sound like a madman."

"So it does. What does your policeman friend say?" he asked again.

"Very little, but then I don't expect him to. My father certainly wouldn't discuss a case with people he investigated."

"So he is investigating us, then."

"He has to. With Rosalind's death, we're involved."

"And you're doing some investigating of your own."

"No," she said quickly, wondering why she was denying it when she had done just that. "But I can't help being curious."

"No, of course not." They turned in at Belle Mer's gates and continued walking down the immaculate gravel drive. "I've enjoyed talking with you, Brooke. Promise you'll tell me what you find out."

She looked up at him as they reached the front door. "Why?"

"Life gets boring, you know. I find this fascinating. Terrible, of course, but fascinating. And who else would you talk to?"

Brooke opened her mouth to answer. Who, indeed? None of her friends took her concerns seriously, and Matt had made it quite clear he didn't want her help. It was gratifying to have someone listen to her. "Thank you, Miles. I'll do that. Perhaps we can figure this out ourselves."

"Perhaps we can." He held on to her hand for a moment longer than she thought necessary. "I'll be looking forward to it," he said, and turned, striding away down the drive. Brooke watched him for a moment before turning to go in. She felt oddly flat, and uneasy. Now that she had told her fears to someone, she wondered if she should have. Her father wouldn't have approved; nor, she suspected, would Matt. Yet what had she actually said? Nothing that other people couldn't figure out for themselves. She was worrying for nothing, she decided, and went inside, pushing the uneasy feeling away.

"Miss Cassidy," Hutton said in an urgent whisper as Brooke walked into the entrance hall. "Thank God you're home."

Brooke looked up from pulling off her gloves. "What is it, Hutton? Dear heavens." She grasped the edge of the marble-topped table. "Not another—"

"Dear me, no!" Hutton exclaimed, his narrow features pinched with shock. "No, not another murder. But there will be if Mrs. O. finds out."

Brooke frowned in a mixture of perplexity, concern, and amusement. For Hutton to speak so informally of his employer meant that he was rattled, indeed. "We can't have that," she said, briskly. "Very well, Hutton. What is the problem?"

"In here, miss." Hutton opened a door set to the side of the entrance hall, leading to the library. Ordinarily this room was used as a receiving room for male guests, while the sitting room on the other side of the hall was used for ladies. Brooke gave Hutton an inquiring look as she walked past him into the room, and then let out a gasp. Sprawled in an armchair, his head flung back, was her uncle Henry, covered with blood and as still as death.

7

"Uncle Henry!" Brooke ran into the room and fell to her knees beside the armchair. Close up, her uncle looked even worse, though he was, to her relief, breathing. One eye was blackened and swollen, several scratches ran down his cheeks, and his nose was encrusted with dark, dried blood. More blood stained his once-immaculate shirtfront, and his dinner jacket was torn at one shoulder. The same clothes he had worn last evening, Brooke realized, when he'd gone out with her and Aunt Winifred to dinner at Seaside, the cottage belonging to Octavius Low, Winifred's brother. "Dear heavens, what happened to you?"

"Hello, Brookie." Henry raised a hand to her hair and then let it drop, as if even that were too much of an effort. "You shouldn't be here, darlin'. This is something you shouldn't see."

Brooke looked up at Hutton. "What happened?" she demanded.

"I don't know, miss. He came in not half an hour ago like this."

"Half an hour—Uncle Henry, were you out all night?"

Henry raised his shoulders in a helpless shrug. "I suppose I was, darlin'."

"Oh, Uncle Henry." She sat back on her heels. "And after what happened in New York! Aunt Winifred will be furious."

Gingerly Henry touched his nose, and winced. "I was hopin', darlin'——"

"What?" She frowned. "That I'd distract her?"

"If you would."

"It would be for the best, miss," Hutton put in.

"I'm not so sure of that," Brooke muttered.

"I've put your aunt through enough, darlin'. She doesn't have to know about this."

Brooke looked from him to Hutton. Both men were regarding her hopefully. "I shouldn't, you know," she said. "I should let events take their course and let you pay for this."

Henry winced again. "Please, darlin', I've already paid. I'm not up to a scene with her."

"What did happen, Uncle?"

"I don't know, Brooke, and that's the truth." He gave her a sheepish smile. "Had a mite too much to drink, if you want to know."

"I'm not surprised. Well." Brooke rose. "I'll help you this time, Uncle, but not again. This has to stop."

"I know." He put his hand to his head. "Believe me, Brookie, the way I feel now, I don't want to feel again."

"I should hope not. You'll see him to his room?" she said to Hutton.

"Yes, miss, and see that his valet takes care of him."

"Good. We'll tell my aunt that Mr. Olmstead is out for the day."

"I already have, miss." His face was dour. "She wasn't pleased."

"No doubt. I'll go to her now. Is she in her room?"

"Yes, miss."

"Brookie." Henry caught at her hand. "Thank you, darlin'."

"Yes, well, just don't do it again, Uncle Henry," she said, and went out to distract her aunt while the staff got Henry to safety. The uneasy feeling she had had upon arriving home had intensified, as if some doom were hanging over her. On the outside Belle Mer presented an impressive, powerful front. Inside, however, was different. What else, Brooke wondered, climbing the stairs, was going to happen this summer?

* * *

Eliot Payson led Matt down the corridor from the piazza at the Casino and opened a door at random. "Good, it's empty. No one should disturb us here."

Matt ambled in, taking in everything, though his face showed nothing. The room Payson had chosen had obviously been set up for private conversation among men. Pairs of green leather chairs were grouped here and there on an Oriental carpet that enhanced the gloss of the floor, with ashtrays and spittoons of highly polished brass placed strategically about the room. Though the floor-length burgundy drapes were open, letting in the sun, the effect was comfortably dark and discreet, and very expensive. It was what Matt had always imagined a gentleman's club would look like. One thing about this case, he thought, choosing a chair at random. He certainly was seeing another side of life.

From his pocket he withdrew his battered pack of Richmond Straight Cut cigarettes, and tapped one on the mahogany side table. "Care for one?" he asked, holding the pack out.

"No, thank you." Eliot's lips pursed in distaste as he reached into his own pocket and pulled out a silver cigar case, his initials engraved on the front within a border of vines and leaves. From it he took out what Matt recognized as a fine Cuban cigar. "I have my own." He held out the case.

Matt shook his head. "Do you come here often?"

"Yes." Eliot lounged back, one leg crossed carelessly over the other. "Everybody does, you know."

"Even though you have invitations elsewhere?"

Eliot gazed at him through a cloud of smoke, his eyes calculating enough to belie his pose of foolish amiability. "Of course, one has invitations," he said, waving his hand languidly. The smoke, disturbed, swirled and eddied about.

"One does, does one?"

"Yes." His gaze narrowed. "Why do you ask?"

"You are a hard man to track down, Mr. Payson."

"I wasn't aware you were trying to find me."

"Oh, yes." Matt took out his notebook and turned the pages slowly, deliberately. "This season you are staying at Wayside, with the Dyers."

"But of course. Where else would I be?"

"With the Lelands, maybe, like last year? Or the Kernochans, like two years ago?"

"So boring." Eliot waved his hand again. "To stay with the same people too often. One doesn't want to impose."

"Especially when one doesn't have a fortune of one's own."

Eliot contemplated the tip of his cigar. "If you weren't a cop, I'd say you were mocking me."

"Would you." Matt made it a statement, not a question. "So you have no fixed address then, Mr. Payson?"

"Not in Newport, no. Hardly a crime," he added, swiftly. "You'll find many others who are merely guests here."

"And the rest of the year?" Matt asked, though he knew the answer.

"I have bachelor digs in New York."

"With no visible means of supporting them."

Eliot blew out another cloud of smoke, looking perfectly unconcerned, except for the narrowing of his eyes. "If you knew all this already, why did you need to see me?"

"You were engaged to Rosalind Sinclair."

"Not quite. We decided it wouldn't work before it got to that point."

"After her father found out about you and the Leland girl."

Eliot's eyes widened, but, again, that was his only reaction. "You have been busy, haven't you," he stated, reaching over to crush out his cigar in a crystal ashtray. Matt noted it wasn't quite half-smoked. "But that was ancient history. Rosalind knew about poor Miss Leland and her unfortunate attraction to me." He sighed. "Poor girl, I let her down as easy as I could."

"Did Rosalind also know her father offered you money to leave her alone?"

"I didn't accept," Eliot said, his voice clipped. "I'm not that much of a cad. In any event, it was Rosalind who broke off our attachment, not me." His eyes narrowed. "How did you find out all this?"

"I asked questions." Matt flipped another page of his notebook, looking down to hide his amused triumph. Over the past two days, he had kept the telegraph lines to New York busy, requesting information about the few suspects he had so far. He hadn't known, however, that Sinclair had tried to buy Payson off, not until this moment. Since that had been the rumor about Payson's attachment to the Leland girl, it had seemed a good guess, but only a guess. Until Payson himself confirmed it.

"You were born in Cleveland, Ohio," he recited, glancing only occasionally at his notebook. "Not exactly the social center of the world. After leaving high school you decided to make your fortune, first in Philadelphia, then in New York. Did okay on the stock market, but got out before the market crashed in '93. With, as it happens, your money intact." He looked up. "Wonder how you knew the crash was coming."

Eliot returned the stare, unblinkingly, as if unaware of the rumors about him concerning insider trading. "Luck."

"Huh. By then, however, you'd discovered society, and society discovered you. You're a popular man, Mr. Payson." Matt slapped the notebook shut. "Tailors pay you to wear their clothes, and Delmonico's always keeps a table open for you, as long as you keep bringing people there. You know all the right people, and you get invited to the right parties. Am I correct so far?"

Eliot reached for his cigar, glared at the tip of it as if just now realizing what he had done, and dropped it into the ashtray again. "What of it?" He shrugged. "It's not a crime."

"Where were you last Saturday morning between midnight and six A.M.?" Matt asked, in the same casual tones he'd used in reciting Eliot's past.

"I was—" Eliot began, and then stopped. Slowly he pulled another cigar from his pocket, snipping off the end with silver clippers attached to his watch chain. He lighted the cigar with the same deliberate movements. Matt let him do so in silence, even though he knew Eliot's mind was racing ahead to the consequences of answering the question. Eliot Payson wasn't quite what he seemed. But then, Matt wondered, was anybody in this case?

"That was the night Rosalind was killed," Eliot said, finally. Matt didn't answer, and Eliot looked at him sharply. "So. Am I a suspect, then?"

Again Matt let the silence spin out. Let it go on too long, and the person being interviewed would talk. He'd learned long ago it was almost inevitable. "Am I a suspect?" Eliot demanded, his voice rising. "Because, damn it, I didn't do it!"

"I'm not saying you did, Mr. Payson," Matt said, and Eliot's mouth snapped shut. "Where were you?"

"Friday night." Eliot leaned back, recovering some of his poise, though he was still pale. "There was a party at the McCormacks'. Dreadfully dull affair. They're parvenus, you know. From Dorchester, of all places. Trying to buy their way into society. I don't believe I stayed much after two."

"How late do you stay for a good party?" Matt muttered.

"Pardon?"

"Nothing. After that, Mr. Payson?"

"After that I was in my bed. The Dyers' butler can vouch for me coming in."

Matt grunted, noting down Eliot's words. No doubt the butler would verify Eliot's story. That didn't mean, however, that Eliot had stayed in the house after that time. "Why did you and Rosalind quarrel?"

Eliot drew on his cigar, very cool, very poised. "Who says we did?"

Matt stubbed out his cigarette with the same deliberation Eliot had shown earlier. "It's common knowledge. You and Rosalind quarreled last winter. The way I heard it, she broke it off, and you didn't agree. Can't say I blame you." Matt contemplated the end of the fresh cigarette he'd taken from the pack. "Must have been tough, seeing all that money slip out of your hands."

"You think you know everything, don't you?" Eliot said, his voice contemptuous. "For your information, I cared a lot about Rosalind."

"All the more reason to be angry with her."

"Oh, I was angry with her," he agreed, and then, as if realizing what he had said, glanced away.

"Why?" Matt pressed. "Because you need the money. Because you did care about her. Because she laughed at you, and—"

"She was seeing someone else, damn it!" Eliot threw down his cigar and rose, pacing toward a window. "She was seeing someone else."

Matt let the silence lengthen. This time, the trick didn't work. "Who?" he asked, finally.

"Radley. Who else?"

"Huh." Interesting. Paul Radley had named Eliot as a possible suspect; Eliot had returned the favor. "Why do you think that?"

"It's obvious, isn't it? They became engaged not long after. I suggest," he said, turning, "you ask him where he was last Friday night."

Matt picked up his notebook. "On July 6 you claimed to be attending a party at By-The-Sea. On July 13, another party, this one here at the Casino. And on July 19, there's no account of your activities at all."

Eliot stared at him. "So?"

"Those dates don't mean anything to you?"

"Should they?"

"Three other women have been found dead beside Rosalind, Mr. Payson. Maybe they were only maids, but that doesn't make what happened to them any less wrong. Those dates are the days they were killed."

"My God." Eliot stared at him. "You think I'm the Cliff Walk Killer." Matt stayed silent, and after a moment, Eliot let out a disbelieving laugh. "This is unbelievable. How even you could think such a thing. Well, I'm not the killer, Devlin. I'm not."

"Can you account for your whereabouts during those times?"

"I've no idea. I can look in my diary, of course, and my valet can probably verify where I was. Look, Devlin." He leaned forward. "If I were guilty, don't you think I'd have covered myself? Give me credit for some intelligence."

Matt shrugged. "Or you could count on looking innocent simply because you have no alibi."

"I say!" Eliot said, staring at him. "So now I am guilty because I look innocent?"

"I didn't say that, Mr. Payson."

"It sounded like that." Eliot rose. "Are we through? I have a luncheon appointment I'd rather not miss."

Matt regarded Eliot for a few moments, and had the satisfaction of seeing his face twitch. So the calm Mr. Payson wasn't so calm, after all. "All right. You can go. But, Mr. Payson," he said as Eliot turned away. "Don't leave town."

"Leave Newport in summer? Of course not, old man," Eliot said, and sauntered out, looking not one bit the worse for the encounter.

Matt quickly made some notes about the interview and then went out himself, far less jauntily. Payson was a possibility. He could have murdered Rosalind; he'd been angry enough for it. How that fit in with the deaths of the other girls, Matt wasn't yet certain. Killing in anger was one thing; killing in cold blood quite another. He was beginning to think there was a cold mind behind the deaths. But then, no one was quite who he seemed in this case. Eliot Payson would bear watching.

Matt glanced out as he passed the piazza, scanning the tables. Most of them were empty. It was nearly noon, and people had left for luncheon, Brooke apparently among them. Just as well, he told himself, turning away and squelching an irrational feeling of disappointment. True, she did know the people involved in this case. True, she could ask them things he couldn't. He could not, however, involve her in an investigation. Best to stay away from her completely, he thought, and set out for the station.

"Cap," Charlie called as Matt walked into the station. "These telegrams just came."

Matt took the sheaf of yellow papers Charlie handed him, without breaking stride. "From New York?"

"Yeah." Charlie grinned. "All the background information you asked for. I told them they should ask about the household staff, as well."

Matt stopped. "Don't tell me there are maids dead there, too."

"No. Somethin' else, though. One of our possibles got himself into trouble a few years back. Seems a maid who worked for him found herself pregnant and caused a ruckus." His grin widened. "Sued him for paternity. Didn't win, but it caused a hell of a scandal."

Matt let out a silent whistle through his teeth. "Good work, Charlie. Who was it."

"Well, that's the thing, Cap." Charlie's grin faded. "We already have evidence against him, but I don't think you're going to be too happy."

Matt went still. "Who?" he asked again, but he knew already. "Don't tell me—"

"Yeah." Charlie nodded. "It was Henry Olmstead."

"Miss," Annie called as she crossed the lawn. "That policeman fellow is here again."

Brooke, a paintbrush placed crosswise in her mouth, looked up from her easel. "Which one is that?"

"The one that's sweet on you." Annie stopped a few paces away and squinted at the canvas. "Nice. I like this one, Miss Cassidy."

"What do you mean, the one that's sweet on me?"

"What? Oh. Detective Devlin. Thought you knew."

"He is *not* sweet on me, Annie." Brooke slammed the paintbrush down on the edge of the easel, annoyed. "Heaven knows that's the last thing he is."

"I don't know. Seems to me, the way he looked at you last time he was here—"

"What does he want, Annie?"

"He wants to see you. Actually, miss," her hands twisted in her apron, "he asked to see Mr. Olmstead. Hutton sent me out here to tell you."

"Hutton told him Mr. Olmstead's not at home, didn't he?"

"Yes, miss, but now he's asking for you." She waited. "Should I tell him you'll be in?"

Brooke glanced toward the easel. "Yes—no. Tell him to come out here," she said, and turned back to her work. The light was behind the hydrangea bush, just the way she wanted it. If she waited even a few more days, the flowers would have faded and she'd lose her chance to paint them. Besides, Matt had not been eager for her help in the last few days. Why should she jump to his bidding now? Still, she wished she wasn't wearing a paint-spattered smock over her skirt and blouse, and that her hair was neater. She wished she knew where her uncle had been last night. Lying to Matt was going to be difficult.

"Brooke," Matt called as he crossed the lawn, and she turned again. As Annie had, he stopped a few paces away, staring at the canvas. "I didn't know you painted."

"I took it up after I went to live with my aunt and uncle." Picking up a turpentine-soaked rag, she wiped her brush. "Is there something I can do for you?"

"Mm. I like it." He moved to the side, studying the painting. "It looks like something I saw in Boston once. By a French artist, what was his name? Monet."

"Thank you," she said, surprised both by his knowledge and the compliment. "I don't consider myself his equal, but I like it. It keeps me busy." She concentrated on dabbing paint in just the right place. "Why are you here, Matt?"

"Came to see your uncle." Hands in pockets, he moved to stand behind the easel, so that she couldn't avoid seeing him. "I understand he's out."

"Yes." Brooke frowned at the canvas, not looking at him. "I don't know where he is."

"I see. Any ideas?"

"Have you tried the Reading Room? I think he was there this morning."

"Yes, I tried the Reading Room, and no, he hasn't been there today." He eyed her steadily, making it difficult for her to concentrate. "Why do I have the feeling you know something you're not telling me?"

She did look up at that. "You didn't want my help, or have you forgotten?"

"Maybe I was wrong."

"What?"

"I can't get you involved, Brooke." He moved closer to the easel. "You're a civilian, a cottager, and a woman. Under those circumstances I can't involve you in an investigation."

"What do you want, then?"

"Did Eliot tell you anything about this morning?"

Brooke set down the brush, at last giving up any pretense of painting. "Matt, surely you don't think he has anything to do with the murders?"

"I don't know." His eyes were somber. "How close was he to Rosalind?"

Brooke opened her mouth to answer, and then closed it again. "I don't think I can tell you that."

"You're protecting him," he said, flatly.

"He's my friend."

"So am I."

"You were," she retorted. "A long time ago."

"And whose fault was that, Brooke?" He thrust his face forward. "My family would have taken you in after your parents died, and you know it. And with what there was between us . . ."

"What was there between us?" she challenged, her hands on her hips. "I don't recall your ever saying anything to me about it."

"How could I, with all this?" His gesture encompassed Belle Mer and all it stood for. "All of a sudden you were a cottager. How could I say anything to you?"

"So it's my fault? If you'd given me any kind of sign—"

"You left, damn it."

"I needed family," she said quietly. "Do you have any idea what it was like for me, losing both my parents at once? Not only that, but I lost my home, and all my friends, too. Once I was a cottager, they weren't comfortable with me anymore. I needed something, Matt. I needed family."

"And are you happy?"

"Happy enough." She busied herself with putting her paint-box in order. "I have relatives in New York, and new friends. I'm content."

"How much do you know about these new friends, Brooke?"

"Enough to know none of them are capable of murder," she said, ignoring the fact that she had voiced that very fear aloud to Miles just that morning.

"How do you know? No one really knows what someone else is capable of. Rosalind Sinclair seems to have annoyed quite a few people."

Brooke closed her paintbox. "Let's say for the sake of argument that someone I know did kill Rosalind. Why would he kill three other women, too?"

"Maybe he didn't. Maybe he took advantage of the fact someone's murdering maids to make it look as if the same person killed Rosalind. I don't think so, though. I think we're dealing with one person."

"Then, why—"

"I think the same person killed all four women. I think he knew Rosalind dressed as a maid—you found that out easily enough yourself—and he took advantage of that fact. He needed to get rid of her, for some reason, and her dressing up as a maid gave him a way to do it."

"But, the others—"

"Were killed so it would look as if Rosalind was mistaken for a maid and was chosen at random. Their deaths weren't important in themselves. Rosalind was the primary target."

She stared at him in horror. "But that would mean he's a madman!"

"Or someone very cold-blooded." His face was serious. "Do you understand now why I don't want you involved? If it is someone you know and you start asking questions, you could be in danger."

"But—dear heavens." She groped her way over to the low stone wall that enclosed the garden and sat down, staring blindly ahead. She had better reasons for staying out of the investigation than he knew, if Eliot or her uncle were involved. "It's monstrous, Matt."

"It is." He stood before her. "Are you all right?"

"I—yes. I'm just stunned. Who would ever think of such a thing?" She gazed up at the house, not really seeing anything. Her safe little world suddenly seemed menacing, no longer a haven. If her uncle were involved . . . "I have to go. My aunt will expect me to see to things for dinner—we're having guests, you know—and my uncle—"

"Yes? Your uncle?" he said, when she didn't go on.

"N-nothing. I should warn him about the guests, when he comes home, that is, he doesn't like playing host, and—"

"Detective!" Charlie called from across the lawn, running toward them.

The sight of him made Brooke stiffen. "Why is he here?"

"I don't know." Matt held his hand palm out to Charlie, gesturing for him to stop, all the time keeping his eyes on Brooke. "Brooke, is there something you want to tell me?"

"Detective," Charlie said again. "I've got to talk to you."

"Not now, sergeant."

"Yes, sir. Now."

Matt at last looked away, and Brooke let her breath out in a silent sigh of relief. One more minute, and she might have blurted out all her worries about her uncle. "What is it?" he asked in clipped tones.

"Got something to tell you, Cap. It's important."

Matt glanced back at Brooke. Her face was pale, but otherwise composed. Damn the interruption, he thought. He had the feeling that she had been about to tell him something important. "Dammit, Charlie," he said, but he walked over to him. He listened in silence to what Charlie told him in a low voice, his shoulders stiffening in surprise at the news and his face getting grimmer. "Damn. All right, Charlie, I'll be there in a moment. Brooke." He turned back to her. "I have to go. Remember what I said."

Brooke stood with her hands folded before her. "I won't do any investigating, detective."

"Good." He walked a few paces away, stopped, and then continued on. Whatever Brooke had nearly said would wait; he doubted she'd tell him now, anyway, unless he questioned her. And he didn't have time for that, not with the news Charlie had brought him. Another body had been found. The Cliff Walk Killer had struck again.

8

"We don't have her name yet, Cap," Charlie said, as they climbed the stairs leading from the Bell and Anchor saloon on Thames Street to the rooms above. This was a different world from the mansions on Bellevue Avenue, this dusty, unpaved street that ran along the waterfront and was the heart of the city's business district. Here were shops and wharves and offices, and the saloons that catered to working men; here the voices of the people were louder, and the smell of fish pervaded everything. "One thing's for certain, she's not a maid."

"No uniform?" Matt said.

"Not much of anything. You'll see."

Charlie opened a door off the landing and Matt went in, taking in the room in one quick, comprehensive glance. The victim definitely wasn't dressed as a maid; she was not, in fact, dressed at all. Her nude body sprawled, face down, across the unmade bed, half-on, half-off, one arm dangling limply down. Her face was turned away from Matt, a fall of thick, curly red hair hiding her features, but Matt had the impression she had been young. She had also been stabbed, more than once, and left to die a messy, undignified death.

Dr. Chandler was already there, crouching by the bed and examining the victim's hand. "Anything?" Matt said.

"If you want time of death, I can't give it to you yet," Dr. Chandler said brusquely. "Looks like she was killed here, but until we move her I can't say for sure. Look at this, though." He pointed to the hand, and Matt crouched beside him, careful to avoid the blood which had pooled on the floor. It was a small hand, soft and white, its nails buffed and polished and shaped to perfect ovals. Like Rosalind's, he thought, and the sight evoked the same pity in him. "She fought her killer. See this nail? Almost torn off."

"Then she might have left scratches."

"Possibly. If you find a suspect, I'd look for marks on him. Look at this, too."

Matt looked closer at the hand. At the base of the fourth finger the skin showed white in a narrow band. "Looks like she usually wore a ring there."

"That's what I was thinking."

"Mm." Matt got up, glancing around. So far he'd seen nothing to contradict his initial impression, that this was a prostitute who had been killed by her last client. The missing ring added robbery to the crime. It was very different from the murders he'd been dealing with, and yet it bothered him. Five deaths in five weeks. It didn't matter that this death broke the pattern. Its timing was coincidental, and he didn't like coincidences.

"Cap," Charlie called from across the room, where he and a patrolman had been going through the woman's clothes, lying in a heap on a chair. "Come look at this."

"Any identification?" Matt asked.

"None, Cap. Her purse is missing, and there's nothing in the pockets. But look at this." Charlie held up a shirtwaist. "This is good quality for this part of town."

"Mm." Matt examined the shirtwaist. Of white lawn, it was trimmed and tucked and edged with soft, cobwebby lace that had been stitched on by hand. Not exactly what the usual prostitute wore. The remainder of the clothing, the tan serge skirt, the houndstooth man-tailored jacket, and the silk underthings, were of similar quality. "Is this how you found them?" he asked the patrolman, who had been first on the scene when the body had been reported. He snapped to attention at being addressed.

"No, sir. At least, not all of them. The skirt and jacket were hanging in the wardrobe, there." He jerked his thumb back at the pressed oak wardrobe in the corner. "When I came in, the landlady was throwing things on the chair. I stopped her and made her leave." He grimaced. "She's a tough one. She carried on about getting what was owed her. Whoever rented the room didn't pay her."

"So everything was hung up?"

"That's what the landlady said." He glanced over at the body and his face turned white, so that his freckles stood out. "Can I go, sir? I've got to finish patrolling my beat."

Matt nodded. There were enough other policemen around to secure the area that this man wasn't needed. "Go ahead. Good work, officer," he added, and the patrolman, saluting, went out. "Don't know if I've seen him before. Who is he?"

"Pat Harrington. He's new. Good, though." Charlie, too, looked over at the body. "Far as I know, this is his first murder, but he handled it okay."

"Did he talk to the landlady at all?"

"Only to keep her out of the room. That'll be your job, Cap."

"Huh." Hands in pockets, Matt turned around, studying the room. It was small, bare, anonymous, with an iron bedstead and a plain oak washstand in the corner. That, along with the wardrobe and the straight chair, were the room's only furnishings. The only touches of color were provided by a threadbare carpet, now unalterably stained, faded red flocked wallpaper, and a floral-painted frosted glass globe on the gas wall sconce. Not a pleasant place to die. "I assume the landlady found the body?"

"Yeah."

"All right. I'll talk to her later."

"I'm ready to turn the body over," Dr. Chandler said, and Matt moved to his side. "Rigor's well established," the doctor said, grunting a little as he maneuvered the still, stiff body onto its back. "I think you can safely say she was killed here. See the lividity? Can't give you a better estimate than twelve to twenty-four hours."

Matt nodded. She had been pretty once, he thought dispassionately, looking at the body as an object and not as someone who had once been alive, breathing, living. It was easier that way, easier to note the lividity Dr. Chandler had pointed out, the discolored skin on the body and the side of her face where the blood had pooled, showing that she had been in that position since dying; easier to count the numerous stab wounds. "Any idea what the weapon was?"

"No, not yet. Large blade, by the size of the wounds. Sharp, too. See?" He pointed to one stab wound. "Edges are clean. I'll know more after the autopsy."

Matt nodded and turned away. He'd seen all he needed. "Oh, by the way." He stopped and turned back to the doctor. "Would whoever have done this get blood on himself?"

"He'd have to. No way to avoid it, the way she was cut." He clapped his hat back on his head. "Look for a bloodstained man with scratches on his face and you've got the culprit. Are you done with the body?"

"Yes, you can have it. Come with me, Charlie," he said, heading for the door. "Tell me about the landlady."

"You know her, Cap," Charlie said, as they clattered down the stairs. "Julia Perry. You arrested her yourself a time or two."

Matt stopped. "I remember, but not for prostitution."

"No. Back when the state was dry, you brought in her and her husband for running a kitchen bar."

"I remember now." Matt nodded. "And if I'm correct, she's also been accused of running a brothel."

"Claims she doesn't know what her tenants do in the rooms, but yeah, that's right. We've raided the place now and then when the citizens start pushing us to clean up vice."

"Sounds like she hasn't changed." Pushing open a door, they emerged from the stairway onto the street. Beside them was the Bell and Anchor, closed now because of the events upstairs. The patrolman standing guard at the door saluted as Matt walked in.

"Well, Julie," Matt said, stopping and looking around. The smell of stale beer and old dust tickled his nose. "Up to your old tricks again, I see."

"Who're you?" The woman behind the bar peered at him. "Devlin, ain't it? I remember you."

"I thought you might. I need to ask you some questions."

Julia stayed behind the bar, her face sullen. "I didn't do nothing."

"No? I could take you in right now for running a house of ill repute. In fact, I'd say that'd be grounds for taking away your license to sell liquor, wouldn't you, Charlie?"

"Yeah, I'd think it's a good reason."

"Oh, hell." She came out from behind the bar, a short woman running to fat, her apron none too clean. "Sit down. I'll talk to you. But I want you to know I had nothing to do with what happened upstairs. I run a clean house."

"I'm sure you do," Matt said, with no trace of irony in his voice. "Who was she?"

"Dunno. I don't, I swear," she went on, when Matt looked at her. "Gave her name as Nellie, that's all I know."

"Then she wasn't one of your regulars?"

She shrugged. "Once a month, maybe."

Matt looked up, his pencil poised over his notebook. "Even in the winter?"

"No, not in winter. She told me that after last night she might not be back."

"Why was that?"

"Well, I dunno. She was awful mysterious about it. But she said she'd never have to worry about being poor again. Said she was gonna get what was comin' to her." Her face screwed up in what might have been a smile. "Guess she did."

"Huh." What she had coming to her. Money, by the sound of it. Matt rubbed a finger over his mustache. What would her client be paying her for, besides her services? "Who was her client, Julie?"

"Now that, I don't know. Never laid eyes on him."

Matt sat back, one arm flung carelessly over the back of his chair. "That's a thumper, Julie," he said. "Don't lie. Do you really expect me to believe you didn't look just once?"

"She came when it was busy," Julie argued. "Couldn't leave the bar, could I? But I remember once."

"What?"

"Seems like a while back, it was." Julia's face screwed up in concentration. Like the body upstairs, she, too, had once been pretty, in a superficial way. Her face was hard now, though, raddled with wrinkles and the rigors of her life, and there was no warmth in her narrow, shrewd eyes. "She did tell me he was a gent."

Matt and Charlie both sat up straighter. "What else did she say, Julie?"

"Not much. Said he liked to come here once in a while, like to feel he was living dangerous."

"And you never saw him."

"Well . . . I might've, once. Had to go out one night, get one of my customers into a cab. He sure weren't in no shape to walk home. That's when I seen him."

Matt leaned forward. "What did he look like?"

"Well, it was dark, you gotta understand that. And I only seen him for a minute, going in. But Nellie was right, he was a gent. I noticed 'cause you don't usually see his type around here. Dressed all in black, and his coat had tails on it. Had on a top hat, too."

"Was he tall? Short? Dark?"

She considered for a moment. "Medium, I'd say. As to what he looked like." She shrugged. "He was going up the stairs. I looked, but I couldn't tell. Tell you the truth, he might not have been Nellie's at all. He could've been seeing one of the other girls."

Matt let that pass by. Julia was cooperating with him, so he wouldn't charge her with prostitution. Not this time. "Could you tell how he got here?"

"No." She pursed her lips. "Now I think on it, though, I got the impression he come in the same cab I put my customer in. Don't know why I thought that. I remember once, though. Nellie came downstairs with a rose in her hair. Said he gave it to her."

Matt's head jerked up. "What kind of a rose?"

"Dunno. Red, I think. Smelled nice, I remember that."

A gent with a red rose. Matt made himself concentrate on his notes, so that he wouldn't give away his reaction to that bit of news. "All right." He rose. "That's all we need right now. Keep yourself out of trouble, Julie."

"I'm not the one causing trouble!" She glared at them, hands balled into fists on her hips. "And who's going to clean up upstairs, that's what I want to know?"

Matt shrugged. "I guess you will," he said, and went out. Her shriek of outrage followed them out to the street.

"Whew!" Charlie said. "She's a shrew. Want me to check for any violations, Cap?"

"Not this time." He glanced at the door that led upstairs as they passed it. "We need to find the cab driver who brought Nellie's gent here. Get someone started on that."

"Right. How about finding out who Nellie is?"

"We'll ask around. If that doesn't work, we'll just hope someone reports her missing. If she's local, she might have family." He climbed up into the buggy. "I'm more interested in who her gentleman friend was."

"If he was a gent. Strange place for them to meet, don't you think?"

"Mm. Also, find out where Henry Olmstead and Eliot Payson were last night. Also Paul Radley."

Charlie let out a whistle between his teeth. "So you think it's connected to the Cliff Walk killings?"

"Don't you? Sounds to me like Nellie was blackmailing someone. And a gent with a red rose is a little too much of a coincidence for my taste."

"The chief's not going to like it."

Matt pulled the buggy up before the police station and jumped down. "He'll like it even less if someone else gets killed. Get on it, Charlie."

"Right, Cap," Charlie said, and they went in, Charlie to begin implementing Matt's instructions, Matt to talk to the chief. He had a bad feeling about this. He very much feared they hadn't seen an end to the killing yet.

The death of a prostitute in a waterfront saloon made no stir in New York; neither the *New York Times* nor Joseph Pulitzer's more sensational *World* chose to print a story about it. In quiet, placid Newport, however, it caused a furor. In a town that prided itself on its low murder rate, even the killing of a prostitute was too much. Editorials blared the outrage, and the mayor held meetings with concerned citizens' groups and the chief of police. Something had to be done, and quickly, to restore a sense of safety to the town.

Matt sat at his desk, rubbing his eyes. On his desk were reports, and more reports: on the possible murder weapon, which had not been found; on bloodstained clothes found in an alley several blocks from the scene of the crime, a rough overcoat and corduroy trousers; on interviews with cab drivers; on women reported missing in the area and the subsequent efforts to locate the dead woman's family and learn her identity. All important, but the words blurred together before his tired eyes. Lord, it felt as if this investigation had been going on forever. He could hardly remember what the inside of his room at Mrs. O'Malley's boardinghouse looked like, so long had it been since he'd slept there, and he sometimes felt he would kill for a home-cooked meal. The last few nights he had spent on a cot in the dormitory in the back of the station house, grabbing what sleep he could; meals consisted of sandwiches, hastily eaten and as quickly forgotten. Yet while the murderer—or murderers—remained at large, he couldn't rest. He had to solve the case, and soon.

"Mr. Devlin." A large, raw-boned man stood in the doorway. "They told me you're the one I should see."

Matt stood up. "Yes? And you are?"

"William Farrell." He held out a large, work-hardened hand. "From Providence. I think it's my daughter you found yesterday."

"Do you. What makes you think that, sir?"

Mr. Farrell shook his head. "The name, and the description. Our Ellen, she has a head of red hair like her mother's. We ain't heard from her in a while, but we know she's in Newport. Leastwise, she was last we heard."

"When was that?"

"Some months back." He swallowed, and his Adam's apple bobbed. "Is there—do I have to see her?"

"We need someone to make an identification." Matt pulled

on his jacket. "I'm afraid the body is in the morgue at the hospital. I warn you, it's not a nice sight."

Mr. Farrell stood up. "Guess I can stand it if you can."

"All right, then. Come with me."

A while later, the two men sat in Matt's office again, Matt holding a cup of strong, bitter coffee, Mr. Farrell with a tumbler of whiskey clutched in his shaking hands. His face was ashen, and his large frame seemed shrunken. But then, Matt thought, not without compassion, it had to be hell seeing your daughter laid out on a slab in a morgue.

"I don't know where we went wrong," Mr. Farrell said, suddenly. "We tried to bring her up right. Didn't spare the rod, no sir, not like some other people. Read the Bible every day, our Nellie did, and went to church on Sundays. We did right by her." His eyes were bewildered. "She always was a wild one, though, couldn't do a thing with her once she got to a certain age, but to see her end up like—this." He took a deep gulp of the whiskey. "There are those who'll say she deserved it, but I don't agree. No, sir. Not my Nellie. No matter what she did, she didn't deserve that."

Matt nodded. No one deserved what had happened to Nellie Farrell in that bare room above the Bell and Anchor. "Do you know who she was seeing, sir?"

"No." He shook his head. "Nellie never told us that. Knew we wouldn't approve. She told her sister, though." His voice was tinged with bitterness and anger. "Said she'd caught herself a live one. Those were her exact words. A live one. A real, live gent, she said."

Matt's pen poised over his notebook. "When was this?"

"Let's see. I disremember—last October? Or was it November? Yes. November."

Matt looked up in surprise. "November? Are you sure?"

"Yes. I remember thinking we didn't have much to be thankful for, with our youngest living in sin."

November. Matt stared blankly down at his notebook, which now contained the scanty details of Nellie Farrell's life. She'd left home at sixteen, a sometime prostitute who eventually found better things. But, November? It didn't fit. Not with the cottagers gone back to New York by that time. "She gave you no idea who it was?"

"No. Wanted to tell Josie, that's her sister, but Josie's a God-fearing woman and would have none of it." Mr. Farrell stood, putting his hat on his head. "I have to get home. Have to tell my wife. She's going to take it powerful hard, even though Nellie's been dead to us for years. Our Nellie." His eyes suddenly grew shiny, and he looked away, clamping his mouth into a straight line. "You've been kind, Mr. Devlin. I'll remember you in my prayers for the evil you see each day."

"Thank you, sir," Matt said, seriously, and walked the man to the door. Evil was not too strong a word for what was happening in Newport, and at the moment he felt powerless to stop it. Someone had to, though. It looked like he was the only person who could.

"Charlie," he called, rising and pulling on his jacket.

Charlie appeared in the doorway. "Yeah, Cap?"

"Get a buggy for us. We're going to go find out where Nellie Farrell lived."

Matt stood in the cluttered parlor of a small Gothic Revival cottage tucked away on a quiet side street, making note of everything he saw, touching nothing. Nellie Farrell's house, an odd dwelling in this neighborhood of neat colonial homes. It wasn't quite what he'd expected. The parlor looked as if it belonged in any proper, middle-class home, with its piano covered by a silk paisley shawl, the top littered with silver-framed photographs; the heavy, burgundy-colored horse-hair furniture; the whatnot in the corner, crammed with geegaws and curios and souvenirs; the velvet drapes with lace curtains beneath. It was spotlessly clean, with not a speck of dust to be found, and, in spite of the clutter, every object had its place. Nellie had apparently been house-proud.

Other police were in the house, searching the kitchen, the sitting room, the bedrooms upstairs. If there were any clue as to who Nellie's lover had been, they'd find it, but Matt doubted there was. A quick glance at the bedroom had shown that someone had been there before them. The signs were slight, and yet jarred with the fastidiousness of Nellie's housekeeping; a table drawer not quite closed, a frock slipped from a hanger in the wardrobe to lie crumpled upon the floor, underwear in a jumble in the bureau. Someone was going to great lengths to protect himself.

"She bought the house in August last year," Charlie said, reading from his notebook and squinting against the rays of the early evening sun streaming into the room. A search at the Registry of Deeds had turned up Nellie's ownership of the house, and the agent who had helped her purchase it. "Free and clear, one thousand dollars cash. No going to a building and loan association for our Nellie. The agent remembers because it was so unusual."

Matt nodded, remembering what they had learned that afternoon from the agent. It wasn't enough. Not nearly enough. "And where would a girl like Nellie get so much money?"

"From a man, Cap," Charlie said, though Matt's question had been rhetorical. "Where else? Only thing is, she never told anybody which man."

"No. But, August. That means she probably was seeing him for some time." Hands in pockets, he turned. "Certainly before November, when she told her sister about him."

"You really do think it's one of the summer people, don't you, Cap?"

"Yes. Don't you?"

"Yeah," Charlie said after a moment. "Eliot Payson was at a musicale last night, but he left early. Said he was going to a ball at Beechwood, but no one remembers seeing him."

"What about Radley?"

"At home, stayed in his room reading, but again no one saw him most of the night. He could have snuck out."

"And Mr. Olmstead?"

"Also claims he was home. At least, his butler did. Mr. Olmstead apparently is sick." He frowned. "Funny thing about that, though, Cap. I got the impression the butler was nervous about something."

"Excuse me, detective." A patrolman walked into the room.

Matt turned. "Yes?"

"We're finished upstairs, sir."

Matt walked toward him. "Find anything?"

"Not much, sir. No diary, no address book. There's a photograph album with some pictures missing, looks like they were just torn out, and these."

Matt took the scraps of paper the patrolman handed him. "Ticket stubs for the New York steamer."

"Yes, sir. Looks like she traveled to New York a few times."

"Mm." Last October, December, and April, to be precise. Another fact to bolster his theory. "Anything else?"

"Just this, sir. Found it under the bed. It looks like it rolled there."

"Huh." Matt took the object from the patrolman. "Well, what do you know."

"What is it, Cap?" Charlie said, crossing to him.

"A cuff link." He held it up so that Charlie could see it, a man's heavy cuff link of gold and onyx. Embossed on the onyx were the letters *H* and *O*.

"Jeez. That looks like—"

"Yes." Henry Olmstead's. "I think we have to ask Mr. Olmstead a few questions."

"Jeez," Charlie said again. "Splinters'll fly when the chief hears that."

"I know." The chief of police wouldn't be the only one upset about such questioning, Matt thought grimly, and looked once more around the room, hoping against hope to find evidence of someone else's involvement. His gaze settled on the whatnot. Dresden shepherdesses competed for space with more photographs, and a china plate with the Statue of Liberty painted on it. And on the top shelf—. Matt's gaze sharpened. On the top shelf was a vase holding a drooping red rose.

"Detective," a voice called from the hallway.

"Just a minute." He crossed the room. The vase was silver, etched in a distinctive scrolled design of vines and grapes, reminding him of something he'd seen recently; the rose was, as he'd feared, an American Beauty. It didn't have to mean anything, but he very much feared it did.

"Detective," the voice said again, and this time Matt turned.

"What is it?" he asked the patrolman who came into the room, a paper in his hand.

"Thought you should see this, sir." He handed over the paper. "I've been talking to cab drivers."

Matt looked up. "You found the one who brought a fare to the Bell and Anchor?"

"No, sir. This is something else. One of the drivers brought a man home."

"This morning," Matt muttered. He scanned the report, and then sucked in his breath. "Dammit."

"What now, Cap?" Charlie asked.

"The man had a black eye, scratches on his face, and a bloodied shirt."

"Could be our man."

"When the cab driver asked what had happened, the man said he'd been in a fight. It goes on to say that the passenger was a gentleman, probably a summer resident."

"Jeez, Cap. Who is it?"

"It doesn't say." Matt looked up, his face bleak. "But the cabbie brought him to Belle Mer."

Chief Read did lose his temper when Matt talked to him the next day, but after listening to Matt's reasoning and the evidence he had found, he agreed there was probable cause to make an arrest. "But you'd better be right about this, detective," he warned, as Matt rose to leave the office. "It's your neck on the line for this, not mine."

Matt stared back at him, his face expressionless. That the chief wouldn't support him should the arrest prove to be false was disappointing, but not surprising. The chief held his job through political connections. If he angered those connections, he'd be out. "I'm certain of it, sir," Matt said, and went out. Oh, he was certain of his facts, and of his case. He only wished he weren't.

As he turned the buggy into the drive at Belle Mer, Charlie by his side, Matt reviewed his case yet again, marshaling to-

gether the facts that had been collected since Nellie's body had
been found. Henry Olmstead had returned home yesterday
morning, his face scratched and bloodied; they knew Nellie had
probably scratched her killer. Olmstead had been in Newport
several times this past winter, without his wife, supervising the
building of his mansion, and discreet inquiries at the Muenchinger-King Cottage showed that, while he had stayed there, he
had come and gone as he pleased and no one had taken any
notice. He could easily have spent time with a mistress. There
was the fact that Nellie had intended to blackmail someone, as
well as too many other things that tied Henry to the Cliff Walk
killings. Red roses, his left-handedness, his obvious preference
for maids, all added up to make Matt suspicious. Nor could
Olmstead account satisfactorily for his whereabouts at the times
of the murders. Most damaging of all was the cuff link found
under Nellie's bed. His facts were right, Matt thought. He was
probably about to make an arrest that would solve five murders,
and there was no joy in it.

The butler who opened the door to them told them that Mr.
Olmstead was unavailable, and began to close the door. Matt
grabbed it before it could close completely. "Then we'll see
Miss Cassidy. If she's available."

Hutton glanced into the house, and then stepped back. "This
way," he murmured, leading them across the Italian Hall to the
loggia. "Miss Cassidy, someone to see you."

Brooke looked up. She had been sitting in a white wicker
chair on the loggia, *Harper's Weekly* lying unread on her lap as
she gazed across the lawn toward the sea. "Matt." She rose,
dropping the magazine. "And Sergeant Sweeney. Is there
something you need?"

"Brooke." Matt nodded. "I need to talk to your uncle."

She hesitated. "I'm sorry. He's—"

"Indisposed. I know. Regardless, I need to see him. Will you
bring him to me, or do I have to go look for him myself?"

She frowned. "Is this official, Matt?"

"It is."

"Oh." Her hand went to her throat, and the fears that had
kept her company for the past few days crowded in on her,

threatening to smother her. "Very well. I'll get him," she said, and went into the house.

A few moments later she was back, Henry and Winifred following. Henry looked better than he had; the swelling in his nose had gone down, but his eye was still discolored and the long scratches on his cheeks stood out against his skin. "Good afternoon, gentlemen," he said, his voice crisp. "What is this about?"

"That's a nasty bruise on your eye, sir," Matt said.

"Yes." Henry sat down, regarding him steadily. "What do you want?"

"Where were you the night before last?"

"He was with me," Winifred declaimed. "We had dinner at my brother's. Really, Henry, I don't see why we have to let these men badger you like this."

"Brooke." Matt turned. "Was he?"

The sudden question caught her off-guard. "Y-yes."

"Then why, sir," Matt swung back to Henry, "did you come home yesterday morning in a cab?"

"What?" Winifred exclaimed. "He did no such thing."

"Where were you that night, sir?"

Henry's gaze remained steady. "I don't think that's any of your business, sir."

"Oh, Henry. Have you gotten yourself into another scandal?" Winifred wailed.

"Hush, Aunt!" Brooke took her arm. "I'm sure these are just routine questions."

"You won't tell us where you were, sir?" Matt said.

"No." Henry's voice was clipped. "I won't."

"Then I'll tell you." He opened his notebook. "You were at a saloon on Thames Street, where you met a woman named Nellie Farrell." He looked up. "Sound familiar?"

"Never heard of her."

"No? She's dead, Mr. Olmstead. Murdered."

"Henry!" Winifred wailed again.

"I assure you, Devlin, I had nothing to do with that."

"No? Does this look familiar to you?" Matt held out the cuff link, and Henry squinted at it.

"Looks like one of mine," he said, after a moment.

"It was found at Nellie Farrell's house." Behind him Brooke let out a gasp, but he pressed on. "Now how did it get there, Mr. Olmstead? And were you there yesterday morning?"

Henry stared at him for a moment, and then his shoulders sagged. "I don't know, detective. For the life of me, I don't know where I was the night before last, or what I did."

"Matt, he couldn't have done anything," Brooke said.

"I'm sorry." Matt's voice was brusque. "Mr. Olmstead, you are under arrest for the murder of Nellie Farrell."

"No!" Brooke cried, and Winifred fainted.

9

"Brooke, my dear, I came as soon as I heard." Eliot crossed the marble floor in the Italian Hall and took Brooke's hands. "Is it true?"

"That my uncle killed someone? No." She pulled her hands free and turned away. Outside, past the loggia and the lawn, daylight was fading, and the setting sun cast a pink glow onto the ocean.

"But he was arrested—"

"Yes." She swung back, her eyes flashing fire. "Oh, yes, he was arrested, and if I could have five minutes alone with Matt Devlin—"

"Whoa." Eliot held up his hand, retreating a pace. "I'm on your side, Brooke."

She gazed up at him a moment and then turned away. "I'm sorry, Eliot. Of course you are. But everything's been so upset here."

"I can imagine."

"With Uncle Henry in jail—they won't let me see him, can you imagine that?"

"It's only right," he said staunchly, putting an arm around her shoulders. "Come and sit down. A jail is no place for a lady."

Brooke shrugged off his arm, but she did sit. "I practically grew up at the police station. I should be there."

"Your uncle wouldn't want you to see him there, Brooke," he said, gently.

She gazed up at him, and her shoulders slumped. "You're right. Of course he wouldn't. And I am needed here." She glanced away as the doorbell rang, echoing sonorously through the hall. "Aunt Winifred is quite prostrated, of course, and she calls for me every other thing. And we seem to have had a great many callers. I'm sure they're all very concerned about my uncle's well-being," she added, bitterly.

"I'm sure they are, and yours, too. I know I am."

"I'm sorry," she said after a few moments, her gaze averted. "I didn't mean to include you. Of course you're concerned. But it does make me angry, Eliot." She struck her knees lightly with her fists. "This is just another sensation to them, while my uncle—"

"Brooke." He reached over and laid a hand on hers. "Let me help you with this. Let me take care of things for you."

It was tempting. Very tempting, to take her problems and place them on his shoulders. Let him deal with Matt and the forces he had brought to bear against Henry. It wouldn't ease her anger at the injustice that had been done, however. Nor could she quite imagine Eliot squaring off against Matt. In any contest between them, physical or otherwise, she suspected Matt would win. "Perhaps you could talk to the lawyers," she said, slowly. "They don't seem to want to listen to me."

"Of course not." Eliot patted her hand. "You're only a woman."

"Eliot!"

"Calm down. I meant that is the way they see you. They're more likely to listen to a man."

"True," she admitted grumpily. Matt would listen to her, she thought, or he would have, once. But Matt was her enemy now. Foolish ever to think he could be otherwise.

"What do you want me to tell them?"

"That he didn't do it, of course."

Eliot paused. "Brooke, is there a chance he did?"

"No!" She jumped to her feet. "I know my uncle, Eliot. He has his faults, but he couldn't have done it. Never that."

"Calm down, Brooke," he said again, reaching out to clasp

her wrist. She pulled away. "I had to ask. They'll have to find a way to exonerate him, that's all."

"They'll have to find out where he was and they won't," she burst out. "I told them who to ask about where he really was, and they just smiled at me."

"Who would they ask?"

"The servants."

Eliot eyed her askance. "The servants? Really, Brooke—"

"They know everything," she insisted. "I'm willing to bet there's someone in this town who knows exactly where my uncle was that night and can prove it."

"And the other nights?" Eliot said, quietly.

"What other nights?"

"The night Rosalind was killed, for one."

Brooke stared at him for a moment, and then sank her face into her hands. There it was, the fear she had been trying to avoid facing. Would Henry be charged with the Cliff Walk killings as well? "I don't know," she said, admitting the unthinkable. With things as they were, he might very well be charged with the crimes, and she couldn't let that happen. She couldn't. She raised her head, making up her mind. This was different from the bit of investigation she had done earlier. This was serious. Her uncle's life was at stake. If no one else would question the servants, then she would. She had to.

"Is it true she was stabbed twenty-two times?" a reporter yelled.

"What about Olmstead?" another called out over the din of reporters milling about near the front desk at the Newport police station. "Were his clothes bloody?"

"How did Olmstead meet her?"

"Were they lovers for long?"

"Is he a suspect in the Cliff Walk killings?"

"Gentlemen." Chief of Police Read held up his hand, and the room quieted. It had been his idea to let the press in; they had been clamoring for information since the arrest. The news that Henry Olmstead was suspected of the murder of a sometime prostitute was sensational, and every newspaper that could be represented was here, from the local *Mercury* to the Providence *Journal* and the New Bedford *Standard*, as well as the scandal sheet *Town Topics*. Tomorrow the New York newspapers would likely arrive in force. "One at a time, please."

"How did he meet the victim?"

"What clues made you arrest him?"

"What is the evidence?"

"Is he a suspect in the Cliff Walk killings?"

Chief Read handled each question with aplomb and dignity, but at the last one, he hesitated. Matt, who had stayed silent, hands clasped behind his back, stepped forward as the Chief gave him a look. "Not at the moment, no."

"Then he might be in future?" the reporter persisted.

"We can't answer that yet," the chief put in. "Any other questions?"

"Detective," a patrolman hissed at Matt's side as the clamor increased again. "There's someone in your office to see you."

Matt didn't take his eyes off the reporters. Like sharks, they smelled blood, and they wouldn't be satisfied until they had it. "I can't leave. Who is it?"

"Miss Cassidy, sir."

Matt glanced at the patrolman in surprise, and then back to the reporters. The chief was leaning forward, hands braced on the table, and was answering questions forcefully and straightforwardly. He could handle this. No one else, however, could handle Brooke. Lips tight, he slipped through the door to his left, into the relative peace of the hallway.

"Brooke," he said, walking into his office. She stood in the middle of the room, hands clasping her purse. "You shouldn't be here. We're surrounded by reporters."

"He didn't do it." She regarded him steadily. "You know he didn't."

Matt let out his breath and ran a hand over his hair. "Brooke, there's evidence—"

"I don't care!" She set her hands on his desk, leaning forward. "I don't care what the evidence is. My uncle could not have committed murder."

"Sit down, Brooke," he said, his voice tired but firm, and, looking slightly surprised, she did so. "You know yourself your uncle came home the other morning in suspicious circumstances. You were there."

"Suspicious, yes. I'll be the first to admit that my uncle has not lived a blameless life, as you probably know, but he could not commit murder. He simply could not."

Matt looked away. "I'm sorry, Brooke."

"Sorry. Ha." Silence stretched between them. "Is he a suspect for the Cliff Walk killings, too?"

That made him look back at her. She was regarding him with the same steady gaze, and, in spite of the circumstances, he felt a reluctant flash of admiration for her. She was Big Mike Cassidy's daughter, all right. If she were a man, she'd make a fine police officer. "We have to consider it, Brooke," he said, finally. "There is evidence."

"I see." Lips tight, she rose. "May I see him?"

"Brooke, I don't think that's advisable."

"May I see him?"

"Damn. All right. But only for a few moments."

"And only because the chief is busy elsewhere?" she inquired with exaggerated sweetness, pulling her elbow away from the hand he placed there. "I know the way, detective."

"I know you do," he said through gritted teeth. "I'll have to speak to the officer in charge."

"Thank you," Brooke said, and swept out into the hall before him.

The cells were in the back of the police station. Brooke's father had rarely let her see this part of his work, preferring to protect her from it. Uncle Henry's lawyers had explained to her that he would be staying here only temporarily. Tomorrow there would be a preliminary hearing in District Court, where Henry would probably be given bail. If not, he would be housed in the Marlborough Street jail to await trial. Brooke was determined that that wouldn't happen.

The mingled odors of disinfectant and too many people

crowded together assailed her nostrils as she walked down the narrow corridor, Matt by her side. Earlier, she'd wanted nothing to do with him; now she was glad of his presence, as though he could somehow protect her. She was aware of prisoners looking out at her from the cells on either side, though she resolutely ignored their muttered comments and catcalls. Her relief at reaching her uncle's cell was brief. Ahead lay a different kind of ordeal.

"Mr. Olmstead," Matt said through the small barred window in the cell door.

"Matt, couldn't I go in?" Brooke whispered.

"I'm afraid not. Sir, you have a visitor."

"I heard you, young man." Henry frowned at them from the other side of the bars. "What did you let her in here for, Devlin?"

"I insisted. Oh, Uncle Henry—"

"Brookie." A smile briefly touched Henry's lips, never reaching his eyes, before he abruptly turned away from her. "Devlin, get her out of here."

"Uncle Henry," she called, leaning forward to the bars. "You have to tell us where you were that night."

Henry stopped, standing still in the center of his cell. The harsh light of the gas lamp on the wall set his features in stark relief. "I told you, Brooke. I don't remember."

"You must have some idea. Matt." She turned. "Can't you leave us alone for a few moments?"

He shook his head. "I'm afraid not."

"What do you think I'm going to do?" She glared at him. "Help him escape?"

"No." He considered her for a moment. "All right. I'll go to the end of the corridor. But just for a few minutes."

"Thank you. Uncle Henry." Her whisper was urgent as she turned back to the door. "Please. You must talk to me."

Henry kept his back turned to her. "Go away, Brooke. I don't want you involved in this."

"I'm already involved. Don't you see? I'm your only chance of getting out of here."

He did turn, then. "I didn't do it, Brooke."

"I know that. But did you know they're thinking of charging you with killing Rosalind Sinclair?"

Shock crossed his features. "I didn't do it," he repeated, at last coming over to her.

"Of course you didn't. But they know about the maid who sued you in New York. Uncle, listen. I know how the police work. They have to solve this case. If you fit, they may not look any further."

He opened his mouth, and then closed it again. "I can't tell you anything, Brooke."

"There is someone, isn't there?" she pressed. "You have been meeting someone."

"I can't tell you." His smile was sad. "I gave my word."

"Your word!" Her mouth snapped shut in astonishment. "Uncle, your word might send you to prison."

"I know. But I can't do it, Brooke. I can't."

"Then I'll have to find her myself."

"Brooke," Matt said at her side.

"Brooke, don't do anything," Henry began.

"I love you, Uncle Henry," she said. "We'll get you out of this."

"Brooke," Matt said again, this time touching her shoulder. "It's time."

"Oh, yes, detective, it's time." She wheeled around, her chin up, and stalked down the corridor. It was high time something was done about this. If no one else would do it, she would.

Belle Mer was dark and quiet when Brooke stepped out of the victoria, except for the light in the entrance hall. Mrs. Olmstead had gone to bed, Hutton informed her as she walked into the house, resting with the aid of a sleeping draught administered by the doctor. Brooke nodded, drawing off her gloves and removing her hat. With all that had happened, she was now in charge of running the house. "Thank you," she said. "I'm going to my room, too. Oh, and Hutton." She turned back.

"Yes, miss?"

"Send Annie to me, please."

"Of course, miss."

In her room, Brooke stood patiently while a maid unhooked her dress and loosened her corset, and then slipped into a be-frilled cotton wrapper. A cool, damp breeze blew in through the window, and she glanced out, to see a quarter moon rising over the sea. A lovely night. If only the day's events hadn't been so dreadful.

"Miss?" Annie said, knocking on the door. "You want to see me?"

Brooke turned back. "Yes, Annie. Come in." She nodded at the other maid, dismissing her, and then gestured Annie to a chair. Annie sat on the edge of it, looking distinctly uncomfortable, while Brooke took the blue velvet wing chair across from her. "You know everything that goes on in this house, don't you?"

"Pretty much. Is there somethin' wrong, miss? Somethin' else, I mean."

"No. You're not in any sort of trouble, if that's what you mean, Annie." She leaned forward, elbows on her knees and her hands clasped. "I need to know who my uncle was seeing."

"What? I mean, I don't know what you mean, miss."

"I think you do." Brooke's voice was soft. "We both know my uncle has a mistress. He always has had one. We also both know she's probably a maid somewhere, because that's what he prefers."

Annie squirmed. "I'm sure I don't know, miss."

"Don't you?" Brooke sat back, watching her, letting the silence spin out. She'd noticed Matt doing that when he'd come to the Casino, and that Eliot had spoken first, just to end the silence.

"No, miss, why would I?" Annie said, after a moment. "I've things to do, miss. Can't I go?"

Brooke leaned forward again. "Who is it, Annie? You have to tell me," she went on, as Annie opened her mouth and then closed it again. "The time has passed for protecting anyone. My uncle has been charged with a murder he did not commit and he'll likely be charged with the Cliff Walk killings, too."

"Oh, no, miss! They can't do that."

"They can and they will, unless I find out where he really was."

Annie's hands twisted together. "Oh, miss, I don't know—"

"I do. Tell me."

"I don't know for certain that he was there, but . . ."

"Yes?"

"Her name's Nora Kelly," Annie said in a rush. "She works at Belcourt."

"Good heavens. For the Belmonts?"

"Yes, miss. Oh, miss, she'll be in dreadful trouble for this."

"She already is," Brooke said, her tone grim, as she rose. "She may as well come forward. Thank you, Annie."

"Yes, miss. I hope I did the right thing."

"You did." Brooke nodded. "Go, now. I've some thinking to do." She sat for a few moments after Annie had gone out, closing the door behind her, and then rose, leaving the room and slipping down the back stairs. In the back hallway she hesitated for a moment at the wall telephone, the only telephone in the house. This had gone beyond what she could handle herself. With her uncle due to appear in court tomorrow, she had to share what she knew with his lawyers. Who did the actual questioning didn't matter, as long as her uncle was set free. Squaring her shoulders, she lifted the receiver of the telephone.

"All rise," the clerk called as the black-robed judge swept into the courtroom, and Brooke rose along with everyone else. Beside her stood Winifred, her face pale and stony and a handkerchief clutched in her hand. Before them was a table where Henry now stood with his lawyers; behind them were reporters and the curious, cramming the room. More were gathered outside the State House, where court was held. Pushing through them to get inside this morning had been an ordeal she didn't want to face again.

"Be seated," Judge Baker rumbled, picking up a paper on the bench and peering over his reading glasses at his courtroom. "This is a preliminary hearing into the death of one Ellen Farrell. Counsel, please rise and identify yourselves."

Brooke's hands clutched her purse so tightly that her knuckles showed white. This hearing might be the only way to free her uncle, but it was frightening. She watched as the lawyers rose, Mr. Putnam representing Henry; Colonel Sheffield, the city solicitor, for the state of Rhode Island. "We've entertained Colonel Sheffield at Belle Mer," Winifred hissed in Brooke's ear. "Such ingratitude!"

Brooke quickly placed a hand on Winifred's arm. "Hush, Aunt. It will be all right."

"At this time, your honor," Jonathan Putnam was saying, "I would like to move that all charges against my client be dismissed."

A buzz of whispers and conversation broke out in the courtroom, and the judge banged his gavel sharply. "Quiet! On what grounds, Mr. Putnam?"

"Your honor," Mr. Sheffield broke in, "the case against Mr. Olmstead is quite clear. We have proof that two nights ago he did deliberately and with malice aforethought stab to death one Ellen Farrell."

"We have a witness, your honor, who will definitively state that Mr. Olmstead was elsewhere at the time he supposedly committed such an act," Mr. Putnam put in, shooting an annoyed glance at Sheffield.

"Your honor, I must object," Sheffield said. "We have no knowledge of such a witness."

"Her identity became known to us only last night. There was no time to inform our esteemed colleague. Your honor, if you would—"

"Quiet!" The judge held up his hand. "Very well. This is a preliminary hearing, Colonel, and we will hear all the witnesses, including those you don't know about. Mr. Putnam, call your witness."

"Thank you, your honor." Without the least hint of triumph he turned to the bailiff. "Call Nora Kelly to the stand," he said, and Henry suddenly sat up straighter. To Brooke it was the first indication that he actually was involved with the girl. She watched him closely as Nora, a slim, dark-haired girl dressed in a plain navy blue frock, took the stand. She looked remarkably

poised as she was sworn in, in spite of the seriousness and ceremony of the proceedings, in spite of the reporters scribbling
furiously in their notebooks and the newspaper artist quickly
sketching her features, to appear in the next edition of every
paper in the area. Brooke doubted she herself would be so composed under such circumstances.

"Now, Miss Kelly," Mr. Putnam said, approaching the
stand. "I have just a few questions to ask you."

"Who is she?" Winifred whispered, clutching at Brooke's
arm. "Is she Henry's mistress?"

Brooke placed her hand on top of Winifred's. No matter
what happened, this was going to be an ordeal for her. "I'm
sorry," she whispered back.

"Where were you on the night of July 29, Miss Kelly? Three
nights ago."

"Yes, sir, I know when that was." Nora sat very straight and
very still. "I had an unexpected night off, sir. Usually I have
Friday nights, but this week the Belmonts are giving a dinner on
Friday and I'll be needed. I had Monday night instead."

"And did you stay at the Belmonts'?"

"No, sir. I was at a lodging house on Spring Street."

"Alone, Miss Kelly?"

"No, sir." She faced him steadily. "I was with a friend."

"Is that friend in this room?"

"Yes, sir. It was him," she said, and pointed at Henry.

To Brooke it seemed as if the courtroom erupted with
amazed speculation. "Quiet!" the judge shouted over the din,
banging his gavel. "One more outburst like that and I'll have
this room cleared. Is that clear? Good. Proceed, Mr. Putnam."

"Thank you, your honor," Putnam said, smoothly. "Let the
record show that the witness pointed out Henry Olmstead.
Now, Miss Kelly, I realize this is difficult for you, but can you
tell the court what you were doing there?"

"Yes, sir." Nora took a deep breath, the first sign of any agi-
tation, and began. "Mr. Olmstead and I would meet there, sir.
We were lovers. We have been since last summer."

"Were you together all night?"

"Most of it, sir. I arrived at ten o'clock, and he came in around eleven."

"Very good. May I remind the court that Ellen Farrell didn't arrive at the Bell and Anchor saloon until close to midnight?"

"Yes, yes." Judge Baker waved a hand. "Get on with it."

"Yes, your honor. What happened next, Nora?"

"Well, we—went to bed. Do I have to say?" she asked, suddenly appealing to the judge.

"You say you were lovers, Miss Kelly?" the judge asked.

"Yes, sir."

"And it was with that purpose that you went to that room?"

"Yes, sir."

"I believe we can infer what happened next. Continue, counselor."

"Thank you, your honor. Nora, will you tell the court, in your own words, what happened that evening?"

"Yes, sir." Nora kept her eyes fixed on him, her hands folded in her lap. "We went to sleep. Sometime later, I don't know what time it was, someone knocked on the door. It was my brother Patrick." She swallowed, hard. "He had told me that if he ever heard of me doing such a thing with a man, that he'd do something about it."

"What did your brother do, Miss Kelly?"

"He began hitting Mr. Olmstead. I yelled at him to stop, but he wouldn't."

"Where did your brother hit Mr. Olmstead?"

"Everywhere, sir, but mostly in the face, in the eyes and the nose. He gave Mr. Olmstead a bloody nose."

"Thus accounting for the blood on his shirt."

"Objection!" Sheffield called.

"Withdrawn. What did you do, Miss Kelly?"

"Well, I couldn't let Patrick do that, so I tried to stop him. I took his arm, and then I tried to scratch him. But he moved, and I scratched Mr. Olmstead instead. Then the landlady came up, and she made Patrick leave. She wanted us to leave, too, but Mr. Olmstead was hurt. She let us stay."

"For how long?"

"All night."

"All night," Mr. Putnam said musingly. "What did you do in the morning, Miss Kelly?"

"I helped Mr. Olmstead get cleaned up, sir, and then I found a cab for him. Then I returned to Belcourt."

"Good. One last question, Miss Kelly. You say you usually have Fridays free. What do you do on those nights?"

For the first time, Nora ducked her head. "I meet with Mr. Olmstead."

"Every Friday?"

"Yes, sir."

"Thank you, Miss Kelly, that will be all. Your witness," he added to Sheffield, as he sat down next to Henry.

"I cannot believe it!" Winifred hissed. "How he could embarrass me by going with that common—girl!"

"Shh!" Brooke said urgently. "The judge is talking."

"Colonel Sheffield. Do you have any eyewitnesses that place Mr. Olmstead at the scene of the crime?"

"No, your honor, but at the victim's house was found—"

"And do you have anyone who saw the victim and the accused together?"

Colonel Sheffield swallowed. "No, your honor."

"We are prepared to call Patrick Kelly to corroborate Miss Kelly's story, and the landlady," Mr. Putnam put in.

"That won't be necessary. In fact, I need to hear no more witnesses. I am ready to rule on your motion, Mr. Putnam." Judge Baker removed his glasses again. "I find that the case against Henry Olmstead has no basis and therefore I am dismissing it. Mr. Olmstead, you are free to go."

Pandemonium broke out in the room. Even the judge's banging his gavel couldn't stop the rush of reporters out of the room to get their stories in, or the press of people forward to congratulate Henry. The ordeal was over. Brooke, relaxing for the first time in what felt like years, released herself from her uncle's embrace and turned, smiling, to encounter Matt's gaze.

Instantly her smile faded. He stood across the courtroom behind the prosecution's table, his face grim. The noise in the courtroom seemed to fade as his eyes held hers, and she felt a shiver run down her spine. It wasn't over. Uncle Henry was free, but nothing else had been settled. The Cliff Walk Killer was still at large.

10

"The best I can do for you is suspension," Chief Read said, not rising from behind his desk. "I warned you about this, detective."

Matt stood before the desk, stiff and still, at attention. "Yes, sir. You did."

"It was poor police work. I'm surprised that you, of all people, made such a mistake."

Matt stared straight ahead. "The evidence was there, sir."

"But not enough of it, apparently. Now—"

"I would still like to know how Olmstead's cuff link ended up in Nellie's bedroom."

"You're lucky Olmstead decided not to press charges against you for false arrest," the chief retorted. "Now I suggest you go out of town for a while. Let this die down. In the fall, when the cottagers are gone, you can come back. Maybe." The chief's face was grim. "If I still have my job by then."

"I hope so, sir." Matt continued to stare ahead. The political uproar caused by Henry Olmstead's arrest had yet to subside. Bad enough that an innocent man had been arrested, the editorials blared; worse when he was someone such as Henry Olmstead. The cottagers might be capable of excesses, but murder surely wasn't among them. That was a lower-class crime. Already the mayor had received more than one demand from state lawmakers to name a new chief of police. The mayor's refusal to do so said more about the conflict between the Democratic city government and the Republican legislature than it did about his faith in Chief Read. Someone had to be sacrificed to appease the protesters, though. That someone, it appeared, was Matt. "Who will be taking on the case, sir?"

"You'll hand your files on the Cliff Walk killings and on Nellie Farrell over to Tripp before you leave."

"Tripp!" Matt's eyes blazed, and he slammed his hands down on the desk, leaning forward. "The man's a bloody incompetent. You know that as well as I do."

"Nevertheless, he'll be taking charge of the case. He's the only detective we have left. You'll cooperate with him, Devlin, or maybe there won't be a place for you here in the fall. You follow?"

"Tripp." Pushing his fingers into his hair, Matt paced the room. "You'll never see either case solved. You realize that, don't you?"

"I don't expect him to make another false arrest."

"Not of a cottager," Matt shot back. "But of some poor worker who doesn't have political friends to call on, yes, that he'd do. I'm willing to swear that Nellie Farrell was being kept by a wealthy man."

"If that's the case, Tripp will handle it. He deals better with the cottagers than you do, and that's the truth."

"He licks their boots," Matt muttered.

"You've no choice in this, detective," Chief Read said sharply. "If you want any chance of coming back you'd better play along. You follow?"

"Yes, sir," Matt said, after a moment.

"Good. I'm sorry about this, Matt." The chief came around the desk, clapping a meaty hand on Matt's shoulder. "You're a good cop. But this is the way things have to be right now."

"I know."

"Now go and give those files to Tripp. And don't show your face around here for a while. You'll be told when to come back."

"Yes, sir," Matt said, and went out, striding toward his office. Patrolmen walking toward him opened their mouths to speak, only to be stopped by the sight of his grim face. The atmosphere in the station house was uneasy. Most of the patrolmen liked

Matt, thought he was a good cop. Most also owed their jobs to patronage, in one way or another, and didn't want to jeopardize their own positions. On the other hand, none of them looked forward to taking orders from Detective Tripp.

Matt smelled the distinctive aroma of pipe tobacco even before he reached the door of his office, but it still didn't prepare him for what he would find there. Tripp was perched on the edge of his desk, studying the wall chart that Matt had put up to keep track of the various suspects. Matt detoured around him to sit down. "What are you doing here?"

"Seems to me you missed several suspects," Tripp said mildly, indicating the chart with the stem of his pipe. "First thing I plan to do is take them in for questioning."

"This isn't your office, Tripp," Matt said through gritted teeth.

"No, but it is my case." Tripp bared his teeth in what Matt supposed was a smile. "As it should have been all along. I want the files."

Matt glared at him. He had always disliked Tripp, but never more than now. Smug and arrogant though the other man was, Matt had no choice. Opening a desk drawer, he took out a thick stack of paper and tossed it onto the desktop. "There. I'd wish you luck, but we both know you're not up to this."

"And you were? I'm not the one who arrested the wrong man." Tripp rose, hefting the papers. "Think I'll get started on these. Oh, and Devlin." He stopped in the doorway. "I'd wish you luck, too, but we both know you deserved this."

Matt surged up from his chair, knocking it over, but Tripp was gone, only the smell of his tobacco remaining. Damn him! Matt righted the chair and sat down, aware of a vein throbbing insistently in his forehead. The hell of it was, Tripp was right. By rushing to make an arrest, Matt had brought his fate upon himself.

This wasn't doing any good. If he had to go, then he had to go. Rising, he grabbed his hat from the rack and stalked out, looking neither to right nor left, discouraging any conversation. Better to make a clean break, even if he was leaving a place that had been his second home for as long as he could remember.

But he would be back. He had to hold on to that belief. This was only temporary.

"Matt," Charlie called, as Matt swung onto his bicycle and started to ride away from the station. "Wait."

Matt stopped, one foot still on the pedal and the other on the ground. "Aren't you afraid of being seen with me, Charlie? God know what they'll do to you."

"They've already done it. They've got me guarding prisoners. Jeez! Do you believe it? I'd rather be pounding a beat."

For the first time that day Matt felt like smiling. "So would I, Charlie."

"What are you going to do, Cap?"

"God knows." Matt glanced down the street toward the harbor, though he hardly saw anything. "Probably go to my father's. Maybe take up fishing. Maybe . . ."

"You're not giving up, are you?" Charlie demanded, and Matt's gaze came back into focus.

"No. Are you?"

Charlie wouldn't look at him. "I'm off the case. Anyway, I couldn't work with Tripp."

Matt snorted. "No one could. Listen, Charlie." He swung his leg off the bicycle and began walking, Charlie by his side. Around them swirled crowds of people, going into shops or heading for the ferry landing. Market Square was one of the busiest places in the city. He'd miss the bustle, Matt realized. "You're right. I'm not giving up. But if I'm going to do anything, it means I won't have any help from the department. I can't do it alone. I want you to help me."

Charlie looked away. "I don't know if I can, Cap. Tripp won't give me the time of day, never mind let me know what's going on."

"You'll hear things, though, Charlie."

"Yeah, I will. But I don't know, Cap—"

"Look. We both know Tripp's not going to solve this thing. That means he'll still be out there, Charlie. Whoever did the killings is still out there."

Charlie looked off into the distance. "I'll let you know what's going on, Cap," he said, finally, "but quiet, like. If it gets out that I'm talking to you, we'll both be in trouble."

Matt nodded. It was one thing jeopardizing his own career; it was another to ask Charlie to jeopardize his. That didn't allay the strange sense of urgency he felt, however. He didn't think they'd heard the last of the Cliff Walk Killer. "All right, Charlie. We'll work it out so no one will know."

"Yeah. Good. Listen, Cap, I've got to get back."

"I know." Matt held out his hand. "Been a pleasure working with you, sergeant."

"An honor working with you, detective." The two men shook hands, and then Matt turned away, mounting his bicycle again and riding off. Where he would go, he didn't know. He only knew that the case, and his part in solving it, wasn't done yet.

The air was sultry, humid, heavy. Brooke blew a strand of hair out of her face and wished that the high-boned collar of her dress weren't quite so constricting. She tugged at it as she slipped through the gates that led from the grounds of Belle Mer to the Cliff Walk. At least there was a damp breeze off the water here, ruffling her hair and stirring her skirts. Brooke stood still, taking in deep breaths of the pungent, salty scent, and feeling as if she'd just escaped from prison.

Uncle Henry was safe. She had helped prove conclusively that, not only had he had nothing to do with the Farrell woman's murder, but that he wasn't involved in the Cliff Walk killings, either. The cost, however, was high. Society delighted in scandal. When it was thought that Uncle Henry was a murderer, the Olmsteads had been shunned. Now that it was proved that he was merely a philanderer, people were visiting in droves. Allegedly they called to offer commiseration, but Brooke wasn't fooled. She had seen avid curiosity in too many eyes in the past to believe words of sympathy now. Since Aunt Winifred was, for the most part, still prostrate from shock, Brooke had had no qualms about telling Hutton not to admit any visitors.

Thankfully, the flow of visitors had dwindled to a trickle. It was midafternoon, time for the daily promenade on Bellevue Avenue and the Ocean Drive. That meant the Cliff Walk and the rocky shore were empty, except for a few fishermen in the bay, checking their lobster pots. Today was the first time she'd walked here since—since seeing Rosalind's body. Amazing to think that had been less than a week ago, so much had happened since. And yet, the image of what she had seen remained sharp and clear, as if Rosalind's body still lay on the bend in the path, crumpled and still. . . .

A foot appeared in her vision. Gasping, Brooke jerked her head up. A man stood there, silhouetted against the sky, perhaps the murderer, come to gloat over his victim—but no, it was only her imagination, playing tricks on her. It was Matt who stood there. Only Matt.

They stood staring at each other for a moment, and then he glanced away. "Hello, Brooke."

"Matt," she said, equally polite, though a thousand questions crowded into her mind. What was he doing here? "I—it doesn't look as if anything ever happened here, does it? There's not a trace of it."

Matt glanced down, and she wondered if he were seeing the same image she was. "No." He looked back up. "Are you all right, Brooke?"

"Yes." She straightened. "Why wouldn't I be?"

"And your aunt and uncle?"

"What do you expect?" She allowed bitterness to creep into her voice. "Uncle Henry hasn't stirred from his hothouse since he came home, and Aunt Winifred has locked herself in her room. Except for when we first came home and she quareled with my uncle."

"I'm sorry." Hands thrust into his pockets, he turned, looking out to sea. "I didn't want to disrupt your life, but—"

"But you did," she said, crisply. "What do you want here, Matt? Hoping to find another victim?"

"No. God, no." He shook his head. "I've been taken off the case, Brooke." At her silence, he looked up. "That doesn't surprise you, does it."

"No, not really. I remember what happens when a policeman annoys the wrong people. My father did it once or twice."

"I've been suspended, Brooke." He looked out to sea again. "I'm not only off the case, but I'm off the force."

Brooke reached out her hand, and then pulled it back. He was no longer any friend of hers. "Surely not forever?"

"Probably."

"What will you do?"

Matt shrugged. "I don't know. I didn't expect this—"

"Well, you should have!" she exclaimed, anger boiling up within her. "It was criminal of you to arrest the wrong man."

"And of course everyone knows that a man in your uncle's position couldn't commit such a sordid crime."

"That's not what I meant, and you know it! How could you have made such a mistake, Matt? My father once told me that after a while he could tell if someone was guilty. How could you think my uncle—"

"There was evidence, dammit!"

"What, a cuff link? Have you found anything else that links him to the Farrell woman? Have you?"

"No, dammit, but he's got to be stopped. Whoever's doing the killing has to be stopped."

"So you let that pressure you into arresting the wrong man? Matt, how could you? When you had to know my uncle had nothing to do with it."

"How could I know that? The evidence was there, Brooke. I didn't like it anymore than you, but it was there. The fact that he prefers maids, his inability to tell us his whereabouts, he's left-handed, the roses—"

"The roses?" Brooke said, when he didn't go on.

"Nothing," he said, waving his hand in dismissal.

"No, it's not nothing," she persisted at the look on his face. "You meant something by that."

He turned away. "I can't tell you."

"Oh, no, you don't, Matt Devlin!" This time she did reach out to him, clutching at his sleeve. "What do roses have to do with this?"

Matt looked down at her hand, and very carefully pulled away. "Dammit. Will you forget I said anything?"

"No." She crossed her arms on her chest. "I think you owe me an explanation, Matt."

"Brooke." He rubbed his finger across his mustache. "All right. There was a rose found by every body on the Cliff Walk. There was also one at Nellie Farrell's house."

Brooke frowned. "I don't understand. Roses are common enough in the summer."

"This was a special rose. An American Beauty rose." He hesitated. "Like the ones your uncle grows."

Brooke drew in her breath, remembering the other night, when Matt and Uncle Henry had gone off together to the conservatory. "So that's why you were asking about roses."

"Yes. Brooke, I want you to keep this to yourself."

"But Matt, other people grow American Beauty roses."

"Other people didn't have other evidence against them." His eyes met hers, grave and solemn. "I made a mistake, Brooke. I was eager to solve the case and I moved too fast. But the evidence was there."

"I wonder . . ."

"What?"

Brooke's brow furrowed in thought. "If there were such strong evidence, could someone have perhaps manufactured it?"

"I thought of that."

"And?"

"What can I do about it now?" His voice was bitter. "I'm off the case, remember?"

"But whoever's taken it over—"

"Detective Tripp? Ha. He can't see beyond the end of his nose."

"Then why in the world has he been given the case?"

"Because he won't offend anyone." Matt jammed his hands in his pockets. "Do me a favor. Don't mention the roses to anyone. We want to keep that secret."

"I must admit this is the first I've heard of it. Or that the murderer's left-handed."

"Damn." Matt turned. "Did I say that, too?"

"Another secret?"

"Yes."

"I won't tell anyone." The breeze whipped at her skirts, and she looked up at the sky, dark with heavy, threatening-looking clouds. "If the new detective is as bad as you say, the murders may never be solved."

"Not if I have anything to say about it."

"Matt." She paused. "If someone set up the evidence against my uncle, it has to be someone I know."

"Don't think of it!" Matt swung toward her. "Don't even think of doing anything on your own."

"But I can help! Look what I found out, about the missing maid's uniform, and what Annie heard on the Cliff Walk, and where my uncle actually was—"

"No! Dammit, Brooke, this person has already killed five times. Do you want to be the sixth?"

"N-no." She stared at him. "You think it might come to that?"

"Yes."

"I'd be careful."

"No, Brooke." His face was stony. "If you keep on with this, I'll see to it that you're put into protective custody."

"You wouldn't!"

"Don't try me, Brooke."

She turned away, biting her lip. He'd do it. Of that she had no doubt, and it meant she was powerless. There wasn't anything she could do to restore safety to her world. It was a terrifying thought. "It looks like rain. I'd better go in."

"Brooke." His voice stopped her as she began to turn, and her eyes met his, serious and as brooding as the lowering sky. "I don't want anything happening to you. You do know that?"

"Yes." This time, she forced herself to turn away. "Goodbye, Matt," she said, and hurried off, back to Belle Mer, back to her peaceful, normal life. Nothing had changed. Matt was just a policeman doing his job, and once the furor had died down, things would go on as they had before. Except, she thought, fear clutching her throat as she stepped onto the loggia and into shelter, that the Cliff Walk murderer had yet to be caught. Dear heavens. Would this nightmare never end?

11

Out past Sachuest Beach, the old man stood on rocks shiny with waves and expertly cast his fishing line far out, past the line of breakers near the shore. The rain that threatened had yet to fall, but the sky was darkening by the moment and the surf was incessant, angry. Carefully picking his way across the wet rocks, Matt cursed under his breath and considered calling out a greeting. He'd have to shout to be heard, however, and it likely would startle the old man, intent as he appeared to be on his fishing. He'd probably fall, then; with his bad leg it was a miracle he'd gotten out onto the slippery, treacherous rocks. The old man. Matt's father.

"Well, boyo, don't sneak up on a man," Sean Devlin said before Matt had quite reached him, displaying again the heightened awareness of his surroundings that had made him a successful cop.

"Hello, Da." Hands in pockets, Matt balanced himself on the rocks. "Fish biting today?"

"Nothing good. Blues aren't running and no stripers to be found."

"What are you doing out here, Da? You could fall on the rocks."

"Fall? Ha. Never fallen in me life, boyo, and don't you think it. Only place I can come to get some rest from your ma. A dear soul, she is, but she does like to talk."

Matt smiled. Since the first death on the Cliff Walk he'd had little chance to visit his parents, who now lived in a cottage in

Middletown, the town next to Newport. Growing up in the Fifth Ward, Newport's Irish neighborhood, Matt had known two things. His father loved his work as a policeman, and his mother, missing the hills of Ireland, longed for a home in the country. It was ironic that the end of his father's career had meant the realization of his mother's dream. "Ma's well?"

"That she is. She'll be talking to her grave." Sean twitched the fishing rod, but there was no response on the line. "Haven't seen you for a while, boyo. Heard your arrest went bad."

Matt's shoulders hunched. He'd long ceased to wonder about his father's sources of information. The preliminary hearing had been just that morning, yet his father already knew about it. "Worse than bad. I've been suspended, Da."

"Happens to the best of us." Sean reeled in his line. "Think I'll quit for the day. Haven't had a catch this past hour."

"Be careful, Da." Matt took Sean's elbow as the old man turned on the rocks.

"Don't coddle me, boyo." Sean shook off the hand. "I've gotten around without your help all this time."

"Da," Matt protested, but without heat.

"If you want to help, take the bucket."

"Yes, Da." Matt picked up the battered wooden bucket in which sat three small fish. He wrinkled his nose. He hated the smell of fish. Hated fishing, come to that. If that were all he had to fill his days, he'd go mad. He frowned. What if he didn't get back on the force? "Thought I'd spend a few days with you and Ma," he said, as they clambered over the rocks toward shore. "If it's all right."

"So it's givin' up you are, boyo?"

"No. At least—hell, I needed to get out of Newport. For a few days, anyway."

Sean threw him a shrewd look from under bushy eyebrows that were the same snowy white as his hair. "Well, come along home, then. Your ma'll be glad to see you. Still riding that fool contraption, I see."

Matt pushed his bicycle by the handlebars as he walked beside his father on the sandy road, lined with marsh grass and scrub pine. "It's decent transportation."

"Oh, will you listen to the boy, now? Well, if you want to waste your money that way, that's your problem." He glanced at Matt again. "So they suspended you, eh?"

"They had to." Matt stared straight ahead. "I made a mistake. Someone had to pay for it. As it is, the chief'll probably lose his job."

"That's what happens when you deal with the cottagers. They'll do you over every time."

"I made a mistake," Matt repeated.

"So you did. Took Big Mike's daughter to set it right, too, from what I heard."

Matt stopped. "Who told you that?"

"I hear things. Come along, boyo, this fish isn't gettin' any fresher."

"Stubborn old man," Matt muttered under his breath, but he began walking again, catching up with him. "What do you think about what's been happening, Da?"

"Think you're better out of it. Anytime you get involved with the nobs and the swells, you're likely to come out of it bad."

"I had to do my job." Matt's voice was mild. If he disliked the cottagers, his father's feelings verged on hatred, and with good reason. A carriage driven by the son of a wealthy banker had run Sean down, ending his legendary career. Sean's leg had been so badly broken that he had been forced to retire; his fellow officers had taken up a collection to provide a pension, and Matt himself donated to his parents' income. Adding insult to injury, the driver, though arrested for drinking illegally, since liquor was prohibited in the state at the time, had escaped with only probation. He had not even had to pay a fine, nor had he ever proffered an apology. It was no wonder if Sean were bitter. No wonder, too, if he had passed his attitude to his son. Matt felt strange now, defending the cottagers and their point of view.

"So you did," Sean said, breaking Matt out of his thoughts. "So you think it's a cottager who did it?"

"I did. I still do. If Olmstead's innocent, someone took pains to make him look guilty. It has to be someone who knows him."

"And not a servant, because of the Sinclair girl. Or do girls like her walk out with servants nowadays?"

"Apparently not. Not this girl anyway." He hesitated, and then made up his mind. His father was his mentor, his ideal; he was the reason Matt had become a cop and that he had so easily gotten onto the Newport force. Who could Matt trust, if not him? Quickly and concisely, omitting no details, he told his father about the investigations of the last month.

Sean was silent when Matt had finished, his only comment a nearly inaudible whistle as they walked along. They had left the beach behind and were now walking through a valley, past tidy farms. "Sloppy police work, there at the end," he said, finally. "You rushed things, Matt."

Matt scowled, not liking the reminder of his mistakes. "I know, Da, but there was a lot of pressure to solve the case." He looked off across a field growing high with corn. "Guess I wanted to get it over with, too. I didn't like arresting Olmstead."

Sean threw him the same shrewd look he'd given him earlier. "You've got circumstantial evidence, boyo, but nothing solid."

"I know. Still, it adds up, Da."

"So it does. You realize what that means, don't you?"

"What?"

"You have to stay on it."

Matt stopped. "You seem to forget it's not my case anymore."

"No, I'd not be forgettin' that, boyo. But how do you think you're going to get your job back? No one's going to do it for you. They're all too busy protectin' themselves."

Matt opened his mouth to speak, and then stopped. It was true. The chief was a good man, but if he had to sacrifice Matt to keep his job, he would. It was up to Matt to clear his name. "I'm going to keep on it, Da."

"Good for you, boyo, and I can help."

"Da—"

"Told you, I hear things, didn't I? I'll find out what's going on."

He would, at that, Matt thought, and with Charlie's help

Matt would likely know everything that was going on in the investigation. There was also someone else who could help, someone who'd already proved her worth as a detective. Brooke. After the events of the last few days, though, she'd likely want nothing to do with him. "It could work."

"It could. Somethin' else you need to think on, boyo," Sean said as they stopped in front of the Devlin cottage. "Big Mike's daughter might be in danger."

Matt looked up as he leaned his bicycle against the wall. "Why do you say that?"

"If what you think is true, she thwarted someone's plans. Better watch out for her."

Matt looked hard at his father. There was a twinkle in Sean's eyes that he immediately mistrusted. He didn't think Brooke was in any danger. Not really. "I'll do what I can, Da. The sooner this is settled, the better."

"Good lad." Sean clapped Matt on the shoulder. "Come on inside, now. We'll talk about what you should do over supper."

"We must have a party," Winifred declared, setting down her teacup on the white and gold table in the morning room, and Brooke looked up in surprise.

"A party? But Aunt, we just had one—"

"That was different. We cannot stay in hiding any longer."

Brooke sipped at her tea to cover her expression. "I wasn't aware that we were," she murmured, glancing out the window. The morning room was one of the most comfortable rooms in the house, situated so that it caught the rays of the sun as it rose over the ocean, and furnished with antique chairs upholstered in pink or crimson brocade. Here Brooke and Winifred met most afternoons to discuss their plans for the evening. This, however, was one of the most outrageous ideas Winifred had ever had.

Several days had passed since Uncle Henry had been set free, and life was returning to normal. The disclosures in court had caused a scandal, as Brooke had expected, and gossip still swirled around them. Yet every day Henry went to the Reading

Room or attended meetings of the Clambake Club; every morning Brooke and Winifred could be seen at the Casino or Bailey's Beach, and every afternoon they joined the coaching promenade on Bellevue Avenue. It was not what she considered being in hiding.

"A party," Winifred went on, as if Brooke hadn't spoken. "It is the only way. Why, look at Alva Vanderbilt."

"She's divorced," Brooke said, remembering the scandal that had ensued the previous spring when the William K. Vanderbilts had divorced.

"Precisely. But wasn't she at church on Sunday? And hasn't she opened Marble House again? And," she added, her tone smug, "I hear she's planning a ball for her daughter at the end of the month. She is not in hiding. The only way to face scandal is to brazen it out."

Resignedly, Brooke picked up her notebook, which she carried with her always when around her aunt. Perhaps a party wasn't such a bad idea. "What would you like me to do?"

"Let me see." Winifred tapped her cheek with a fingertip. "The first thing to do is to make certain that we choose the right date. It would be disastrous if someone else was having an affair the same evening."

"I'll look into it."

"Naturally. Then we must think of a theme. Let's see, what hasn't been done lately? We need something spectacular. It wouldn't do to have people thinking we're moping about."

"Not at all," Brooke murmured.

Winifred ignored her. "Of course, you could do something to ensure the party is a success."

Brooke looked up from the notebook. "What?"

"You could announce your engagement to Eliot."

The notebook fell to the floor with a clatter. "My engagement!"

"Why, yes." Winifred beamed at her. "You are going to marry him, of course. It's only a matter of time. Yes." She leaned back. "If we could announce your engagement, everyone would know that we have risen above our circumstances."

Brooke bent to pick up her notebook. "Aunt, I'm not sure I want to marry him."

"Don't be silly. He is eminently suitable for you."

"But—"

"You are not getting any younger, Brooke. You are twenty-three years old, and every year girls are being presented who might just catch his eye. You cannot afford to miss this chance."

"Am I so unappealing that I'll never have another chance?" Brooke retorted.

"Of course not. You are a Low, after all. But that means you must choose someone special."

"I'm not sure that Eliot's so special, Aunt."

"Why, of course he is. A most charming young man—"

"But what does he actually do? Nothing," she rushed on before her aunt could answer. "Oh, I know. He plays tennis. He's excellent at polo. He's the perfect extra gentleman, and he was made to wear a dinner jacket."

"Is there anything wrong with that?"

"No. But has he ever done anything else? Has he ever done anything useful in his life? And he drinks too much," she added.

Winifred peered at her over the top of her reading glasses. "I told your mother it was a mistake to raise you middle class."

"You were raised middle class."

"Yes, but I overcame it. Here you are, Brooke, with all the advantages, and a man who can support you. What more do you want?"

"I don't love him," Brooke said, voicing aloud for the first time her real objection to the match. "Don't tell me that love doesn't matter, because it does. I saw what my parents had."

Winifred's lips thinned. "And in the end it killed your mother. If she hadn't been with him the day his carriage went off the road—"

"It's past. But I would like what they had, Aunt."

Winifred slowly removed her glasses and fixed Brooke with a piercing gaze. "We're talking about that Devlin person, are we not? Are you seriously telling me you would choose him over someone like Eliot Payson?"

"Excuse me, ma'am," Hutton said from the doorway of the

sitting room, saving Brooke from answering. "There is a, er, gentleman here to see you."

Winifred glared at Brooke a moment longer before turning. "Who is it, Hutton?"

"His card, ma'am."

Winifred took the small pasteboard square and frowned at it. "William Tripp? Do we know him?"

"Detective Tripp," Brooke said in surprise. "It must be."

"From the police? No." She thrust the card back at Hutton. "We are not at home."

"He requests only a few moments, ma'am. He says it's important."

"I think we should see him, Aunt," Brooke put in.

"Well, I do not! We are done talking with the police."

"Ahem." Hutton cleared his throat. "He told me, ma'am, that he wishes to reassure you about the investigation."

"Reassure me?"

"Yes, ma'am. That it won't inconvenience you any further."

Brooke's gaze caught Hutton's at that. "Inconvenience?" she queried. "A strange way to put it."

"But true. Very well, Hutton," Winifred said. "We shall see him. But only for five minutes, mind."

"Very good, ma'am," Hutton said, and withdrew.

"Another policeman." Winifred frowned. "I thought we'd seen the last of them."

"I'm glad he's called," Brooke said. "I hope he can tell us what's been happening."

"Oh, you do, do you?" Winifred glared at her again. "Don't think this ends our discussion, Brooke, because it doesn't. If you think I'll allow my niece to marry a common policeman—"

"Mr. Tripp, ma'am," Hutton said at that moment, to Brooke's immense relief. She looked up to see a man of medium height bounce into the room. Her first impression of him was that he was too dapper and jaunty to be a policeman. It wasn't just his clothes, the tweed jacket, fine wool trousers, and felt derby; they were carefully tailored, but not of the very first quality. Nor was it the malacca walking stick, or the carefully waxed ends of his ginger-colored mustache. It was something in the way he held himself, something about his shallow blue eyes. They didn't immediately survey the room, its furnishing and occupants, as her father's would have, as Matt's would have. Nor did he have that look in his eyes of having seen more than his share of the world's pain. He was not, in short, like most policemen she'd known.

"Ladies." He executed a faultless bow. "Forgive me for intruding on you like this. I am Detective Tripp." He held out his wallet to Winifred. "My credentials, madam."

Winifred barely glanced at the badge. "Good afternoon, detective. Is there something we can do for you?"

"No. I hope, however, I can do something for you. May I sit?"

"Please." Winifred gestured him toward a pink brocade chair. He sat down, looking not at all out of place, as Matt would have in such feminine surroundings. "Hutton, bring a cup for Mr. Tripp, and more tea."

"Have you any news of the investigation?" Brooke asked as Hutton withdrew.

"Nothing to worry you, Miss Cassidy." He smiled at her, a toothy grin that was not at all comforting. "I understand you've had a dreadful time of it. Devlin didn't handle matters well at all."

Brooke set her lips to hold back her protest. "Detective Devlin was doing his job."

"Oh, no, no, to involve someone such as yourself in the investigation? Not well done of him at all."

"As I have said, Brooke," Winifred said. She was eyeing Tripp with distinctly more approval than she had shown a moment ago. "Mr. Tripp is obviously a gentleman."

Tripp took a sip of his tea and then set the cup down. "Ah. Lapsang souchong?"

"Why, yes." Winifred's expression thawed even more. "You know your tea, sir."

"The only civilized drink." He took another sip and then turned to them, his face more serious. "With your indulgence, madam, why I've come is to apologize for any pain my colleague might have caused you."

"Thank you." Winifred nodded graciously. "It was a dreadful thing to endure."

"I'm sure it was. Rest assured, something like that will not happen again, now that I'm on the case."

"Thank goodness. It was ridiculous to think that one of us could ever have been involved in such sordid crimes."

"Have you any ideas on the murders, detective?" Brooke asked, finally setting her cup down.

He smiled at her. "Many, I assure you."

Brooke leaned forward. "Do you think you're close to making an arrest?"

His smile broadened, though it didn't reach his eyes. "As it happens—I trust I have your confidence, ladies?"

Winifred leaned forward, too. "Oh, yes. We won't breathe a word, will we, Brooke?"

"Well." He sat back, brushing at the ends of his mustache. "This must be kept absolutely quiet, but at this very moment a suspect is being investigated."

"Who?" Brooke burst out.

"Now that, dear ladies, I cannot tell you. Suffice it to say I think you'll be pleased at the results."

"It's not one of us, then, sir?" Winifred asked.

"No, madam. It is definitely not a cottager."

"But . . ." Brooke's brow furrowed into a frown. "Surely there's evidence that it was."

"Faulty." Tripp dismissed the evidence Matt had struggled so hard to garner with a wave of his hand. "These crimes could not have been committed except by someone of the lower class."

"He was heard, and his voice was definitely upper class."

"Was he?" Tripp's face went blank, and then he nodded. "Ah, yes. One of your maids, I believe? She mistook what she heard."

"But—"

"Brooke, pray don't pester the man so," Winifred put in, frowning. "I am sure he knows his business."

"I do. Rest assured, ladies, I will do all I can to bring the villain to justice. In the meantime, Miss Cassidy, don't worry your pretty head about it."

Brooke stared at him. "I beg your pardon!"

"Leave it to me." Reaching over, he patted her hand, and in that moment Brooke conceived an intense dislike of dapper, red-haired men. "I will see to it that all is settled, and you may enjoy your season as before."

"But—"

"I have taken up enough of your time, ladies." He rose and bowed. "I hope I have set your minds at ease."

"But I still think—"

"Yes, you have," Winifred said at the same time, shooting Brooke a look. "Thank you for coming to us."

"The least I can do, madam. In fact, I will be speaking to all the cottagers as soon as I can." He executed another bow. "Good day, madam. Miss Cassidy," he said, and, turning, left the room.

Brooke remained on her feet, her hands clenched. "I didn't know anyone talked like that outside of books," she muttered.

"Sit down, Brooke," Winifred said, sharply. "I am mortified at your behavior. Mr. Tripp was a perfect gentleman."

"Gentlemen don't solve crimes," Brooke shot back. "He patronized me, Aunt."

"Did he? I'm sure he didn't mean to. Brooke, dear, ring for Hutton. This tea has gone quite cold."

Brooke's face wore a mutinous look, but she pressed the button that was set into the wall molding, signaling for the butler. "He'll never solve the case."

"That is hardly our concern. Now, as to our party," she said, and Brooke stared at her. It was hopeless. There was no one in this house who took what had happened as seriously as she did, no one she knew. Except Matt. And oh, how she missed him now.

Annie hurried through the remainder of her chores and then clattered up the back stairs to her attic bedroom. Tonight was the night she'd looked forward to for weeks, and she didn't want to waste a moment. Pulling off her starched maid's cap and apron, she hastily splashed water on her face and then dressed, buttoning the white cotton shirtwaist with fingers made clumsy by excitement. The blue serge skirt and matching jacket followed. Looked just fine, she did, she thought, studying herself in the mirror. The walking suit couldn't touch the outfits Miss Cassidy wore, it coming from Mr. Sears's catalog and all, but it was as close as Annie could manage. Styling her hair in a topknot looser than she usually wore, she carefully set a feather-bedecked hat upon her head, skewering it in place with a large hatpin. There. Done up all proper, she was, and ready to enjoy tonight's Grand Illumination.

Fog drifted in from the sea as she hurried away from Bellevue Avenue, down the narrow side streets that led to the waterfront. She cast an anxious look toward the sky. Couldn't rain tonight, could it? Not when there'd been so much planning and so much excited speculation about tonight's events. The Illumination had been planned to welcome the return of the New York Yacht Club, an annual event that always caused excitement, though never quite this much. On Thames Street and Washington Square people were decorating, with Chinese and Japanese lanterns, or more grandiosely, with incandescent lights. Shopkeepers and homeowners alike vied to outdo each other, while on the harbor there was to be a parade of all kinds of crafts, all illuminated. Except for the awful events on the Cliff Walk, the Illumination was all anyone had talked about for a week. Annie was overjoyed that it was happening on her evening free.

Behind her a rock clattered, as if it had been thrown. Startled, Annie turned to look behind. Nothing, 'cept a buggy driving the other direction. Horse must have kicked up a rock, she thought, turning to go on her way. Though the sun had not yet set, the fog made everything dim, and this section of Coggeshall Avenue, near the new Vanderbilt stables, was lonely. She wasn't certain if she'd seen someone behind her or not, but, if so, it was nothing to worry about. Likely he was heading for the waterfront, like herself. Annie's spine tightened and spasmed, and she hunched her shoulders against it. Silly, she scolded herself as a trolley clanged past her. This wasn't the Cliff Walk, after all, lonely and deserted in the fog. This was a busy city street, with neat, tiny dwellings pressing together and people about. She was perfectly safe.

The fog didn't seem to hamper anyone's enthusiasm, Annie noted when she at last reached Thames Street. Forgetting her momentary scare, she plunged into the crowd of sightseers, good-natured and jostling. Newport was crowded for this event; there'd been special trains bringing excursionists from Fall River all day, and she'd heard there wasn't lodging to be found anywhere. She could understand it. Mouth agape, she wandered down the street, staring at the displays that would soon be lighted, feeling excitement rise within her. And, glory be, the fog was lifting. It was going to be a clear night, after all.

The clock in the Trinity Church tower clanged the time. It was as if a starting gun had been fired, for, suddenly, electric lights blazed out, gas jets flamed, and shopkeepers scurried about, lighting the candles in their lanterns. Annie let out a gasp of sheer delight. The Grand Illumination had begun.

He stalked her like a panther, through a jungle of arms and legs and vinelike strings of electric lights. Not ten feet ahead of him her hat with its jaunty feathered plume bobbed up and down, and yet she wasn't aware of him. He'd thought she'd spotted him back there on Coggeshall Avenue, when, intent on his pursuit, he'd stumbled on a stone, but apparently she hadn't. Nor would she spot him now. He looked entirely unremarkable, in rough trousers and shirt that were an affront to his dignity, and the heavy work boots he found so clumsy, but oh, so useful. No one knew who he was. Only she did.

Not for the last time, he cursed the bad luck that had put her near the Cliff Walk when he'd been there, and the breeze that must have carried his voice to her. Not for the last time, he raged, inwardly, against that cop, Devlin, who had kept such crucial information to himself. Thank God Tripp was a different sort altogether, amenable to sharing details of his investigation with a willing listener. Foolish, but useful. Because of

Tripp, he knew he had one more obstacle to overcome, before he could be free.

He disliked killing. He really did. It was messy and disgusting, and he regretted the necessity of it. Not that he was sorry. Oh, no. Rosalind had had to go. It was a pity about Nellie, though. He'd rather liked her. But she had been foolish, threatening to tell what she knew about him. Smart of him to put her off, suggesting meeting the next night at that saloon, rather than at her house. There was nothing to tie him to her death. Nor would there be anything to tie him to this one.

Electric lights blazed above him at that moment, making him blink. Temporarily blinded, he squinted, enraged at the thought of losing his quarry. Had he—no, there she was, staring with open-mouthed wonder at the display stretching across the front of a building and making him hastily turn away, lest she see him. He had to be careful. In eliminating one loose end, he didn't want to start any others.

Her pace had slowed as she stopped to look at each display. It made his blood thrum in his head, made his fingers itch with impatience. Get it done and get out, he thought. Do it. Carefully, keeping his eye on her and standing well back in the crowd, he edged around her. Ahead was an alleyway, dark and narrow, where even the lights of the Illumination didn't reach. Perfect. He'd make his move there, and then he'd be free.

The Illumination was stunning. Annie drifted down Thames Street, gawking at everything. Flags were hung along the multi-armed telegraph poles, and there were garlands of Japanese lanterns strung across storefronts and homes alike. There were gas jets arranged to form special displays, or to spell out words. There was even a model sailboat, decorated with lanterns and suspended across the street, from one building to another. The electric light displays, however, were the ones that drew her eyes. Alternating red and white lights were twined maypole fashion around the flagpole at the *Daily News*, while, not to be outdone, the *Herald* had put together a display that read WELCOME YACHTSMEN 1895 and stretched across the street. She wished Sam was here, he who she kept company with, but he worked at Beaulieu and couldn't get tonight free. It was her one regret about this magical night, that she had to experience it alone.

"Annie," a voice whispered, and her head jerked around. Who was calling her? In all this vast crowd of people she could see no one she knew. Either she'd imagined it, or someone had called to another woman named Annie. It was a common enough name. Still. . . . Her spine contracted as it had back on Coggeshall Avenue, when she'd thought she was being followed. Ridiculous. She was safe here.

"Annie." There it was again, stronger now, and somehow familiar. Again she glanced around, uneasy, alone in a crowd of strangers. It almost sounded as if it had come from the alley opposite her, but that was silly, wasn't it? Besides, she knew better than to go looking into some dark alley. Better to get away from here. She stepped back, bumping into a man who let out a yelp and then doffed his hat, as if in apology. It distracted her for a moment and made her fears seem foolish. Until, looking down, she saw the toe of a sturdy work boot protruding from the alley.

"Annie," the voice said, still a whisper, and it came together in her mind, that voice, and where she'd heard it before. She knew who it was, and she had to get away, had to escape—

But before she could run, before she could even scream, the Cliff Walk Killer had grabbed her and dragged her into the alley.

12

The fog had cleared. Brooke, leaning on the varnished rail of the Burnhams' yacht, sipped from the crystal flute of champagne in her hand. Thank heavens. Perhaps the evening would be bearable, after all. Even as she had the thought, she was aware of the irony of it. Wearing an evening gown from Worth, the Paris couturier, drinking champagne and nibbling at goose liver pâté spread on toast, she was one of the privileged who was seeing the Illumination from a yacht in the harbor. With her were the best of society, her aunt and uncle, of course, and Eliot Payson, the eminently suitable young man who wanted to marry her. What girl wouldn't want to change places with her? Yet, at the moment, she thought of Annie McKenna, who had chattered about this event for days and even now was probably having a grand time, seeing all the sights in perfect freedom. She envied Annie that.

Eliot came up behind her, setting a hand on her shoulder. "The fog's lifted," he remarked, and though Brooke had had the same thought a moment ago, she felt irritated at its banality.

"It will be a fine night," she replied, smiling at him a little more cordially than she had planned, to make up for her annoyance.

"Very fine." His hand slipped from her shoulder to her waist. She would have stepped away, except that she stood between him and the yacht's rail. There was nowhere to go. "Dashed romantic, this." His upward glance indicated the gaudily col-

ored lanterns hanging from masts and along the deck house.
"Clever of Burnham to rig electricity to them."

"Safer, too, I'd think, than candles," she agreed. The scene
was magical. Every craft in the harbor was decorated, from the
smallest dinghy to the majestic boats of the Fall River Line,
twinkling with rows of electric lights. The Goelets' launch *Bea-
trice* even had red fire in her smokestack, reflecting eerily against
the low, overhanging clouds. Not to be outdone, the ships of the
Navy were decorated at masts and yardarms with lanterns and
flags; Fort Adams was ablaze with lights; and the Torpedo Station stood out in a brilliant display. Faintly across the water the
music of the Newport Band, on a lighter near the Torpedo Station, reached them, playing waltzes and marches. It was a magical night. Brooke only wished she had someone to share it with.

"Even better being out on the harbor," Eliot said, and she
started. She wasn't alone, though she felt as if she were.

"Yes." Her voice sounded rusty, so she cleared her throat. "I
wish the buildings didn't block the land displays, though. All we
can see is the Ocean House."

"Never mind. We have our own illumination here." His
hand curled around her waist, and Brooke glanced hastily
around. Eliot's voice was steady, his eyes clear, and yet she
knew him well enough to know that he'd already had too much
to drink. In this state, he'd be difficult to deal with. Fortunately,
no one was paying them any attention, though a great many
people had been invited aboard the yacht. White-jacketed waiters with trays holding champagne or canapes circulated among
the guests, who were dressed in evening jackets or fine gowns.
Everyone was either talking to someone or, as she and Eliot
were doing, looking at the decorations. Still, it wouldn't do to
allow him to take such liberties. Pushing back from the railing,
she slipped away from him.

"Brooke." He was right behind her as she headed forward,
sounding hurt. "What was that for?"

"You should be more discreet, Eliot, don't you think?" she
said, without turning.

"No one's paying us any attention. Besides"—his breath was
warm on her neck—"everyone knows we're engaged."

That made her turn, so quickly she would have lost her balance if he hadn't caught her by her arms. "Everyone knows— Eliot, we're not!"

"As good as," he said, matter-of-factly. "Don't pretend, Brooke. You know it as well as I."

"I do not."

"Yes, you do."

"You've had too much to drink."

"Maybe." His smile was crooked. "But I'm right about this. Why else have we been together so much this summer? Or this spring, for that matter? I almost proposed to you in New York. You know that, don't you?"

Brooke didn't answer. Oh yes, she knew it. She remembered the moment well, when they had slipped out of a ball for some air, and her frustration when her aunt had followed them as a chaperon. Because, if Eliot had indeed proposed at that time, she would have agreed. "That was then."

"Nothing has changed, Brooke."

Oh, but everything had changed, couldn't he see that? Or had it? She suddenly had the sensation that she was standing a great distance away, watching them talk and seeing herself objectively. She was the one who had changed, the one who had been horrified enough by the deaths on the Cliff Walk to do something about them. In so doing, she had found a sense of purpose. Only one man appreciated that, and it wasn't Eliot. "I've changed, Eliot," she said, quietly.

"No, you haven't. Not really. I think what happened," he went on, as she started to protest, "is that old memories came back to you, of when you used to live here. But those days are gone, Brooke." His voice wasn't without sympathy as he laid his hand on her shoulder. "You can't bring them back."

"I'm not sure I want to," she said, struggling with an idea that was new to her, foreign. For if her life had changed in the past five years, she had changed, too. The girl she had once been was long gone. And yet . . . "I don't know . . ."

"This is your life now, Brooke." He placed his hand on her other shoulder, and though his grip was gentle, she felt imprisoned. "We belong together. Surely you know that? We care about each other."

"Yes," she said, because it was true. She did like Eliot. She just wasn't sure it was enough.

"Plenty of marriages in our set have started with less. We'll be happy, Brooke. You'll see. And your aunt and uncle will be pleased."

"Yes."

"Is that a 'yes, they'll be pleased,' or a 'yes, you'll marry me'?"

"You haven't asked," she said, and then wanted to kick herself.

"Well, I'm asking now. Will you marry me, Brooke?"

"Oh, Eliot. I just don't know—"

"What will you do otherwise?" he interrupted her. "Marry the man who arrested your uncle?"

Her spine stiffened. Eliot was right. Knowing her, knowing how she would feel, still Matt had gone ahead and put her uncle in jail. If she'd ever had a chance of a future with him, it was gone now. "Yes, Eliot," she said, turning, her shoulders squared with resolve. "I'll marry you."

In the alley the noise of the crowd was lessened and the light was dim, alerting the senses to other stimuli, the smell of garbage and the scuttling of rats. Annie was aware only of the hard pressure of a hand over her mouth and the metallic taste of fear. Oh, sweet Jesus, if she could only get away, but his grip was strong and her petticoats hampered her efforts to kick her attacker. A hand was at her throat, squeezing, squeezing, the thumb pressing hard. Stars danced at the edge of her vision, and in one panicky moment she knew what that meant. With a mighty effort she threw her arm up, roughly dislodging the hand from her mouth. Her attacker grunted, in surprise or pain, and the pressure on her throat lessened, just long enough for her to draw a deep breath. "Help!" she shrieked, her voice raspy and shrill. "Help! Murder!"

He didn't waste time telling her to be quiet; he simply

slammed his hand over her face again. This time she couldn't breathe, and though she continued to struggle, she could feel her limbs growing weaker. Oh, sweet Jesus, she was going to die in the alley like all those other poor girls. . . .

"Here, what's going on?" a gruff voice said, and a light shone into the alley. As abruptly as she had been seized, she was released, flung away to land against the brick wall of a building. Her legs too weak to support her, she slumped to the ground, vaguely aware of footsteps running away. Her attacker was escaping. She didn't care. She was, thank God, alive.

"Now, what's all this, then?" A light shone in her face, and she looked up, squinting, into a lantern. Instinctively her hand went up, shielding her eyes, and she made out a burly shape beyond the light, dressed in blue, with a shiny helmet. A cop. Oh, thank God.

"The Cliff Walk Killer." It came out as a croak. "He tried to—he ran that way—aren't you going after him?"

"The Cliff Walk Killer, is it?" The cop sounded amused as he reached down and pulled her to her feet with a beefy hand under her arm. "Now, that's a new one. What are you doing workin' the streets on a night like this?"

"Working—!" Leaning against the building for support, she stared at him. "You think I'm a—"

"Prostitute. Haven't seen you on my beat before, but I suppose there's a first time for everything, isn't there? Come along, now." He strode out of the alley, and she stumbled behind, unable to resist the strength of his hand.

"But I'm a good girl," she protested as he pulled her through the crowds to a side street. "I am!"

"Yeah? Well, tell that to the sergeant. In with you." Before she could protest further he shoved her up a narrow step and into cavernous darkness. She stumbled, falling into something soft, and then tumbled to the floor.

"Hey, watch what you're doing!" a voice said above her, and the cop outside chuckled.

"Behave yourself," he admonished Annie, as she pushed herself to her knees. "And keep quiet."

"But—" She scrambled to her feet, banging on the door as it slammed shut. "But I didn't do anything."

"Ah, shaddup," a voice called out of the darkness, making her jump.

"You see that? Fell right on me, she did, but does she apologize? No," another voice said.

"You might as well get up off the floor, honey." This was a woman's voice, whiskey sultry and world-weary. "They're not being too good to us working girls tonight."

Dazed, Annie turned, trying to see the people around her in this small, dark space. "Where are we?"

"Oh, honey, you are green, aren't you? Haven't you been in a black maria before?"

A black maria. Annie's knees went weak, and she sank down onto the bench at her side, feeling the other occupants shift to make room for her. She may have been rescued from the killer, but her troubles were far from over. Sweet Jesus, she had been arrested. "But I didn't do anything," she said, bewildered. It was too much. Overcome by the night's events, she lowered her head and broke down into sobs.

"Who've we got this time?" Charlie Sweeney asked, coming out of the station house just as the doors of the paddy wagon opened and the human detritus it held tumbled out.

"The usual," Officer Eccleston said. "Mostly drunks, but we caught us a pickpocket this time and a couple of whores."

"Watch your language," the whiskey-voiced woman said as she stepped down.

Eccleston grinned at her. "All right, Jewel. Streetwalker, if you prefer."

"Streetwalkers, my foot. That little girl in there isn't on the streets."

"Little girl?" Charlie said.

"Get inside, Jewel. Yeah, this is a new one. Claims her client was the Cliff Walk Killer."

"The Cliff Walk—" Charlie turned back to the wagon in time to meet the frightened eyes of Annie McKenna. "Annie?"

"Oh, Sergeant Sweeney!" She tumbled down the step. "I didn't do nothin', I swear!"

"Annie? What the hell?" He looked down at her in the flickering gaslight, taking in her disheveled clothes and the bruises around her throat, and his face grew hard. "What happened to you?"

"Oh, Sergeant Sweeney!" She threw herself into his arms, to the vast amusement of Jewel and Eccleston. "It was him! The Cliff Walk Killer."

"Jeez!" Awkwardly, he held her away. "You sure?"

"Yes," she sniffled. "Heard him clear as I hear you. It was him."

"Jeez." He looked at Eccleston. "Is Tripp around?"

"Upstairs sleeping, I think. You're not taking this seriously, sarge?"

"Damn right, I am. This girl's no streetwalker."

"Sarge, I caught her in the act—"

"Release her."

"But—"

"Anyone gives you any guff, you tell them to come to me."

"All right," Eccleston said after a moment, clearly reluctant. "But it's your funeral."

"I'll worry about that myself. Come on, Annie." He took her arm in a far gentler grip than Eccleston had. "I'll see you home."

"You're not arresting me?" she sniffled.

"Nah. You didn't do anything. Now, keep quiet like a good girl. You can tell me everything at home."

"Hutton told me there's a problem—Annie!" Brooke gasped, coming to a dead stop just inside the kitchen doorway at Belle Mer, later that evening. "Oh, no, what happened to you?"

"I'm sorry to cause such trouble, miss," Annie said, her voice a croak.

"Oh, Annie, your neck—oh no, you weren't on the Cliff Walk, were you?" Brooke sank into the chair next to Annie, whose throat was wrapped with cold towels. Gone were her jaunty hat and neat appearance; her jacket was dusty and torn at the shoulder, and the bruises on her face stood out in stark relief against her pallor. Brooke stared at her in horror for a moment and then looked up, somehow unsurprised to see Charlie Sweeney here. "Sergeant?"

"Not the Cliff Walk, no," he said, his voice grave, his hand resting reassuringly on Annie's shoulder.

"I went down to the Illumination, miss," Annie began, and at that moment there was a knock on the kitchen door.

Brooke's head jerked up. "Who in the world could that be, at this hour?"

"I'll get it." Charlie pushed past the housekeeper to open the door, and Matt Devlin stepped in.

Brooke's breath caught in her throat, though one part of her wondered why she was so surprised. It seemed inevitable that he would be here. "Matt?" she said.

"I sent for him, Miss Cassidy," Charlie said, almost apologetically.

"Oh." She didn't ask why Detective Tripp hadn't been notified as well; she was just as glad he wasn't here. "I don't understand."

"I heard him again, miss," Annie rasped.

"Who?"

"The Cliff Walk Killer."

Brooke gasped, and Matt pulled out a chair. "Tell me about it, Annie," he commanded.

"Oh, sir, it was awful," Annie said, and went on to relate the events of the evening. And to think, Brooke thought irrelevantly as she listened, that for a time tonight she had envied Annie her freedom.

"You're sure it was him?" Matt said when Annie had finished.

"Oh, sir, I couldn't never forget that voice, long as I live. To hear him calling my name like that." She shuddered. "It's lucky I was that cop came along when he did. Even if he did think I was a streetwalker."

"Did you get a good look at the man who attacked you?"

"No, sir. It all happened so fast, and it was dark in the alley. I—ow." She put her hand to her throat. "Hurts, it does."

"Here, drink this." Mrs. Smith bustled over, a glass of honey and lemon mixed with water in her hand. "It will help."

"Thanks." Annie grimaced as she sipped at the mixture.

"Let me see your bruises, Annie," Matt said.

Mrs. Smith glared at him. "Can't you leave the poor girl alone?"

"Mrs. Smith." Brooke rose, going over to the housekeeper and putting a hand on her arm. "Why don't you go to bed? I'll see to Annie."

"And leave you alone with these—men?" Her sniff told exactly what she thought of Matt and Charlie. "I don't think so, miss."

"Mrs. Smith." Brooke fixed her with a stern look. "Go to bed."

To everyone's surprise, Mrs. Smith turned and walked out of the kitchen without a word of protest. "Well," Brooke said, bemused, "that's the first time she's ever listened to me."

"You sounded like Mrs. Olmstead, miss," Annie said.

"What? Good heavens. Well, never mind." She sat down. "Matt, what do we do now? Should I notify Detective Tripp?"

"No," Matt and Charlie said at once, making the women look at them in surprise. "No," Matt went on. "How do you think our culprit found out about Annie?"

Brooke's eyes widened. "Do you mean Mr. Tripp—"

"He's been going around talking with all the cottagers, hasn't he?"

"Yes, but how do you know that?"

"I know that we didn't tell anyone outside the department that Annie heard anything. But Tripp . . ." He snorted. "I wouldn't be surprised if he's told a lot more than he should."

"But that's terrible! It could have gotten Annie killed."

"It nearly did. Remember, though, he doesn't think a cottager did it. Now." Matt leaned forward. "Let me see those bruises, Annie." Annie unwrapped the towels and he studied her neck. "Hm. A little darker on this side." He pointed at the left side of her neck, and she flinched. "Sorry. When he grabbed you, where was he? In front or behind?"

Annie closed her eyes, as if trying to remember. "In front at first, because I looked down and saw his feet. But once he grabbed me, he was behind me."

"So his hands were around your neck like this." Matt demonstrated on his own throat, and Annie shuddered. "And the left side is darker."

"Does that matter?" Brooke asked.

"Yes. I wish we could have Dr. Chandler look at these, but—what do you think, Charlie?"

"They look the same," Charlie said. His voice was even, but his face was red with anger. "Dammit, if I could catch him I'd—"

"Now, Charlie," Matt said mildly. "We'll get him. Looks like you're right, Annie. It was the Cliff Walk Killer."

"Dear God," Brooke said. "If he knows about her, then he knows where she lives. She can't stay here. She'll be in danger."

"But miss, where would I go?" Annie protested.

"My parents would take you in," Matt said. "Unless . . ."

"Unless what?" Brooke prompted.

"You're the only witness we have, Annie." He faced her directly. "The only one who can identify the Cliff Walk Killer."

"So she has to be kept safe."

"Yes. Except that all she knows of him is his voice. If she stayed here . . ."

"Matt, you're not suggesting giving the killer another chance!"

"No," Charlie said at the same moment. "We're supposed to protect civilians, not put them in danger."

"Dammit, Charlie, it's all we have. If she can identify him—"

"I won't put her in danger. If you go on with this, detective, I'll have to tell the chief."

The two men glared at each other. "Doesn't anybody care what I think?" Annie said, her voice small in the tense silence. "I think Mr. Devlin's right."

"No," Charlie barked at her. "You could be killed. I won't let that happen."

Annie tossed her head, and then winced. "Well, it's my life, isn't it, sergeant?"

"Annie, you don't mean that you'd want to stay here," Brooke said. "Not when the killer knows where you are."

"Oh, miss. Scares me to death, it does. But"—her chin was outthrust—"he's got to be stopped. If I can help, I want to."

"Matt, you can't do this. You're not even on the force anymore."

"I'm still a cop." Matt's face was grim. "I'm not walking away from this. Look, Charlie." He leaned forward. "The man is getting desperate if he'd follow Annie and attack her in a crowd."

"I don't like it." Charlie's face was stony. "If he'd do that, what's to stop him from coming to Belle Mer?"

"He probably has," Brooke said. "If he's a cottager, he's been here."

"That's a good point. He couldn't do anything here, not if he's well known."

"It's a big estate," Charlie argued. "Plenty of places he could go without being seen. He'll come after her."

"And then she can tell us who he is. She's our only chance—"

"No. She can't stay here. I won't let her."

"It's not your decision, sergeant," Annie said, her raspy voice startling them. "Mr. Devlin's right. If I'm the only one who can identify him, then I have to do it."

Charlie leaned forward. "I don't want you to be hurt, Annie."

Annie's gaze softened. "I'll be fine, sergeant. I'll stay inside where he can't get me."

"The place is guarded," Matt put in, "and you could arrange for more protection, Charlie."

"Dammit." Charlie glared at him. "Yeah, I could, but I don't like it." He looked back at Annie. "You sure?"

"Yes." Annie rose. "If no one minds, I think I'll go to bed now."

"No, do go, Annie," Brooke said, walking with her to the

door. "You must be exhausted. I'll talk to Mrs. Smith about letting you take it easy for a few days."

"Oh no, miss. I'll carry on as usual." She looked back into the room. "Good night, miss. Mr. Devlin, sergeant."

"Good night, Annie." Charlie remained standing, gazing after Annie. "She's a brave woman."

Matt's eyebrows rose at that, and Brooke, sitting down again, frowned. "Yes. I hope you know what you're doing, Matt."

"So do I." Charlie's gaze sharpened. "If she's hurt, detective, it'll be on your head."

"She won't be, Charlie," Matt said, his voice surprisingly mild. "Thanks for letting me know about this. We might solve this thing yet."

"Yeah. Well." Charlie picked up his helmet. "I'd better get back to the station before they start wondering where I am."

"Charlie," Matt called after him. "Not a word to Tripp about this."

"Do you think I'm stupid?" Charlie said, and went out.

Silence fell in the kitchen in the wake of his departure. "Heavens, what a night," Brooke murmured.

"Yes." Matt rose. "I'd better go, too. The fewer people who know I've been here, the better."

Brooke accompanied him to the door. "What will happen if you're found out?"

"God knows. Dismissal from the force, at any rate. But I can't let this go."

"I know. Neither can I."

"Brooke." His voice was abrupt. "I'm sorry about what happened with your uncle. You do know that, don't you?"

"Yes. I know you did what you thought was right."

Matt nodded, his eyes never leaving hers, an intent look that she knew too well. It drew her in, that blue gaze, and shook her at the same time. Too much, on top of all that had happened tonight, too much for her to deal with, and much too late. She stepped back. "It's been a long evening," she said, wearily brushing her hair back from her face and evading his eyes. "If you'll excuse me, Matt—"

"What is this?" Matt caught her hand and stared at it, his gaze sharp now.

"Matt—"

"A diamond ring." He looked up at her. "I gather congratulations are in order?"

"I—yes." She pulled her hand free. "It just happened tonight."

"Payson?"

"Yes."

"Dammit, he's a suspect, Brooke."

"He was on a yacht in the harbor tonight, with me," she retorted. "Or do you think I'd lie to protect him?"

"No." He turned away. "No, of course not. My best wishes, Brooke."

"Thank you," she said, her voice stiff.

"I'll be in touch with you about Annie."

"Of course."

"Well." He hesitated, as if about to say something, and then reached for the door. "Good night, then."

"Good night," Brooke replied, and closed the door after him, utterly weary, utterly dispirited. The long night was over, she thought as she headed for her room. God only knew what tomorrow would bring.

Detective Tripp breezed into the servants' sitting room at Claremont, the Sinclairs' cottage, and the people who had gathered there for midmorning tea or coffee looked up in surprise and suspicion, cups arrested halfway to their lips, conversations halted in mid-breath. "Well." Tripp beamed at them, hands clasped behind his back as he rose up on the balls of his feet and then settled back, again and again. Behind him stood a tall, burly patrolman, and Claremont's guard, looking as concerned as the staff. "So here you all are."

Graves, the butler, recovered first. "Is there something we can do for you, sir?" he asked, rising, his demeanor as unruffled as the tails of his morning coat.

"Sit down." Tripp's voice was sharp. "I shall ask the questions. Now." Hands still behind his back, he prowled about the room. "I've had my eye on you all a long time. You." He spun around and pointed to a maid. "What's your name?"

"M-me, sir?"

"Yes, you. Stand up. Are you deaf? Stand up."

"That would be Rachel, Mr. Tripp," Mrs. Dooley, the housekeeper, said. "There's no need to go bullying her."

"When I want your opinion I shall ask for it. Now, Rachel. Was it your uniform Miss Sinclair wore?"

Rachel's head was up, her eyes defiant. If she were remembering a similar interview several weeks earlier at Belle Mer, she gave no sign. "No."

"No?" He gave her a piercing look, which she met steadily. "I think you're lying, but I'm not here for that. Not today." He let the silence stretch out before he turned. "Which one of you is Thomas Pierce?"

An uneasy silence fell over the room, and from the back there was a shuffling sound as Tom rose. "That's me."

"Is it? Slacking off, are you?"

"No, sir." Tom's gaze was stolid, though he twisted his cap in his hands. "I always come in for coffee at this time."

"That's right." Tripp paced back and forth in front of him. "I knew that, see? I know everything about you."

Tom swallowed. "Sir?"

"You're a gardener, aren't you?"

"Yes, sir."

"Know something about roses, do you?"

"Roses? Well, yes, I guess I do."

Tripp wheeled around, stopping directly before Tom, and though Tripp was shorter, he didn't seem at all intimidated. "Of course you do. What is this?"

Thomas pulled his head back to look at the withered flower Tripp held up. "Looks like a rose, sir."

"Looks like a rose, does it? Of course it's a rose, you idiot."

Thomas reared back again, this time from the scorn and menace in Tripp's voice. "Yes, sir."

"Now, Mr. Tripp," Graves said from the other side of the room. "What's this about?"

"Be quiet," Tripp barked. "I am conducting an interrogation. Unless you want me to take you in for obstructing justice? No? I didn't think so. Now. You, Pierce, were keeping company with Maureen Quick."

Thomas's face grew even more stolid. "Yes, sir."

"And you cannot account for your movements the night of her death."

"I was here, sir."

"Were you?" Tripp sneered. "No one remembers seeing you."

"I was here."

"What about the others, eh? The other maids." He paused for what seemed like a very long time. "Miss Sinclair."

"Mr. Tripp, I must insist," Graves began.

"Be quiet! Now. I didn't come here today to chat. I came to make an arrest."

Gasps went up around the room, and conversation broke out in anxious whispers. "An arrest, sir?" Graves said.

"Yes," Tripp said, and spun around. "Thomas Pierce, I am arresting you for the killings on the Cliff Walk."

13

Annie burst into Brooke's room as Brooke was finishing dressing for luncheon at Beechwood, with Mrs. Astor. "Oh, miss, did you hear? There's been an arrest!"

Brooke turned from the mirror, scattering combs and hairpins about. "What? Who?"

"Tom Pierce, miss, him that's gardener at Claremont."

"A gardener! But why?"

"For the Cliff Walk killings, miss." Annie put a hand to her throat. The bruises there were nearly covered by her starched uniform collar, but those that showed had turned a rainbow of colors. "He was keeping company with one of the girls who got killed, see, and I guess with that and working at Claremont—"

"But he didn't do it."

"I know. Oh, miss, what do we do?"

"I don't know." Brooke sank down on her dressing table stool. "Oh, this is terrible. That poor man." She looked up. "Where did you hear this?"

"Everyone knows it, miss. I—"

"Have you heard the good news, Brooke?" Winifred sailed into the room, her chihuahuas tumbling behind her, barking. "They've finally arrested the Cliff Walk Killer."

"Yes, Annie was just telling me."

"Imagine, a common gardener! And that Devlin person had the nerve to arrest your uncle."

"Aunt, what if Thomas Pierce didn't do it?"

"Didn't do it? Of course he did. Pray don't talk nonsense, Brooke. Now. Are you nearly ready to go?"

"Yes. Just let me do my hair."

"If you would let a maid do that, it would get done faster. And neater." Brooke, her mouth filled with hairpins, couldn't reply, and so Winifred went on. "Well! Now we can be assured that our ball will be a success."

Brooke started. The ball. With all the excitement she had forgotten about their upcoming ball, and what it was to celebrate. The ring on her finger was a visible reminder. She had a sudden urge to pull it from her finger and throw it across the room. "Yes. Aunt, I don't think—"

"Good. Don't think. It will make you late. I shall wait for you downstairs," Winifred said, and sailed majestically out of the room.

Brooke stared after her, torn between amusement, exasperation, and annoyance, all underlaid by unease. An ordinary gardener couldn't have done the killings on the Cliff Walk. He couldn't have. He certainly wouldn't have been the man Rosalind had met in disguise. Brooke caught Annie's gaze, reflected in the mirror, and her unease grew. This wasn't over.

The Cliff Walk Killer had been found! Newspaper headlines blared the news, but even before that the story flew across the city. He'd been caught and put in jail, and everyone in town breathed in relief. No longer would decent citizens have to fear for their safety. And of course, the cottagers assured each other, they'd known all along he had to be a servant of some sort, since only someone from the lower classes would commit such a crime. Thank heavens that was over. Life could go on as before.

The police station was besieged by reporters demanding to know the details of the arrest. Detective Tripp, twirling the ends of his mustache, was happy to oblige. He was equally happy to stand up in court the following day when Thomas Pierce was arraigned, in front of a crowd even larger than the one which had come to see Henry Olmstead. Chief of Police Read, relieved that an arrest had been made and that his job was safe, received the congratulations of the mayor and of local politicians. And, quietly and without any publicity, Matt Devlin returned to his job at the police station.

His office had a musty air, even though he'd been gone just over a week. The charts he had so painstakingly constructed to keep track of the Cliff Walk killings suspects still hung on the wall, but his desk was free of its usual litter of papers. That would change soon enough, once he got back into the rhythm of the work. It was good to be back, he thought, looking about the small, square room. He only wished the circumstances were better.

An odor of pipe tobacco warned him of who was coming. "Well." Tripp stood in the doorway, hands on hips, pipe clenched between his teeth. "Heard you were back."

Matt leaned back in his chair. He was not going to let Tripp annoy him, no matter what he said. "As you see."

Tripp went to stand in front of the charts, studying them with his hands clasped behind his back. "You won't be needing these any longer."

Matt picked up a pencil and then let it drop, once, twice. "Maybe."

"Maybe?" He looked over his shoulder at Matt. "Didn't you hear, old man? I solved the case."

"Maybe," Matt said again, still toying with the pencil.

"No maybe about it. Solid police work, that's what I used. Found out all I could about Pierce—you did know he has a record for assault, didn't you?—and he fit what I was looking for to a T. None of your guesswork for me. Nosiree. Solid police work, as I said."

"Except that you arrested the wrong man."

Some of the glow went out of Tripp's grin, but he put his head back and laughed, anyway. "The wrong man! That's rich, coming from you. Ha, ha, the wrong man. Well, the chief doesn't seem to think so, and neither does the attorney general. We've got our man, Devlin, the right man."

"What about Nellie Farrell?"

"What about her? That had nothing to do with this. No,

mark my words. I'll solve that case, too, and if I'm not mistaken, there'll be a promotion in it for me."

Matt let the pencil drop again. "Maybe."

"Stop playing with that damned pencil!" Tripp braced his hands on Matt's desk and leaned forward, all cordiality gone. "You'd better listen to me, Devlin. One of these days I'm going to be in charge around here, and I'll be watching you. One mistake, Devlin, just one, and you'll be gone. Understand?" Matt stared unblinkingly back at him, still toying with the pencil. "I said, do you understand?"

"Detective?" someone said at the door.

"What?" Tripp barked.

"Come in, Charlie," Matt said at the same time. "I believe he means me, Tripp."

Tripp snorted and straightened, glaring at Charlie. "What do you want?"

"The lieutenant told me to report to Detective Devlin, sir," Charlie said, sounding innocent. "You have something for me to do, sir?"

"Yes." For the first time since Tripp had come in, Matt smiled. "We're back on the Nellie Farrell case."

"What!" Tripp yelled. "But that's my case—"

"Take it up with the chief," Matt said, leaning his head back on his linked hands. "And don't make me tell you again. Get out of my office."

"Don't think I won't talk to Chief Read. You'll be hearing from me, Devlin," he blustered, and stormed out.

Charlie grinned. "Good to have you back, Cap."

Matt returned the grin. "Good to be back, Charlie. Now." He straightened. "Where do we stand on Nellie Farrell?"

"It's gone cold." Charlie straddled a chair, his arms folded on the back. "You don't think Pierce did it, do you?"

Matt gave him a look. "No, I do not. I don't think Pierce did anything." He let the pencil drop once more and then pushed it away. "How is Annie McKenna?"

Charlie's face brightened. "She's fine. I saw her last night."

"Oh?"

"Just to make sure she was all right."

"Of course." Matt's tone was dry. "She hasn't received any threats?"

"No. But she's scared, Cap. Real scared."

"We'll find him, Charlie. Tell her that. And stop calling me Cap." He grimaced. "After this last disaster, I'll probably never make captain."

"Maybe not. Listen, Annie was telling me something last night. There's going to be a ball at Belle Mer next week."

"Oh?"

"Yeah. To announce Miss Cassidy's engagement." He hesitated. "You knew about that, didn't you?"

"Yes. So the killer will probably be there."

"Probably," Charlie agreed. "Annie's certain she'd know his voice if she heard it again."

"Good." Matt drew some paper forward. "All right. We'll get something up for that night. Quiet, though. And in the meantime we'll take another look at Farrell."

"Where, Cap? We looked everywhere we could."

"We'll look again, and we'll look harder. Ask around, that kind of thing. There's got to be some way to find out who her lover was. And once we find him, we've got her killer."

"All right." Charlie stood up. "I'll get right on it. Anything else?"

"No. Yes," Matt said as Charlie went to the door. "I want to see all the reports from the Cliff Walk investigation."

"Thought you would. I already got 'em together for you."

"Good. Good work, sergeant."

"Thanks, detective." Charlie grinned. "Glad you're back," he said, and went out.

"Me, too." Matt leaned back, again resting his head on his hands. It was good to be back. Like being home. Or it would be. Determinedly Matt pulled paper toward him and began making notes. He would not rest until the true Cliff Walk Killer had been found.

Belle Mer rose high against the sky, the early evening sun making a nimbus about it. Matt looked at the house for a moment more and then resumed his scrutiny of the barren patch of earth on the Cliff Walk. This was where it had all begun. Not the killings themselves, but the realization that the tenor of the case had changed. This was where Rosalind Sinclair's body had been found.

Matt closed his eyes and the scene burst into his mind as if it were still happening: the sprawled body, undignified in death, with the gulls, squawking, flying above; the curious bystanders and the ashen face of the girl who'd found the body; and the red rose, whose significance still eluded him. Apparently it didn't elude Tripp, Matt thought, opening his eyes and blinking in mild surprise at the tranquility of the day. He had to give Tripp credit for something. Linking the rose to a gardener was actually rather smart, or would be, if the roses were an important clue. Matt doubted they were.

Sometimes studying again the place where unsolved crimes had been committed suggested new ideas to him, new plans of action. Not today, however. The Cliff Walk was as it always had been, and this section was bare, anonymous, a convenient spot for dispatching a victim. He'd do better sitting in his office and sorting through the mountain of reports Charlie had dredged up for him. He turned and was about to go, when a scuffing sound behind him made him turn.

The man walking toward him was dressed casually, but among other things Matt had learned from this case was how to spot expensive tailoring. He knew this man, too; a memory flashed into his mind of him standing, at ease and supremely self-confident, at the Casino, a tennis racquet in hand. "Mr. Vandenberg," he said, by way of greeting.

"Detective Devlin." Miles ambled over to him, hands in pockets and shoulders set in a fashionable slouch. "It is still detective, isn't it?"

Matt kept his smile pleasant, refusing to be goaded. "It is. You live around here, Mr. Vandenberg?"

"Near enough." He pointed south, where the Atlantic stretched to meet the horizon. Silhouetted against the rich blue sky was an enormous gabled house, dark and somehow ominous-looking. "At the Point. Don't tell my friends, but I enjoy taking a stroll on the Cliff Walk."

"Why wouldn't you want them to know that?"

He shrugged. "So plebian, isn't it? But then, I appreciate Newport." From an inner pocket he withdrew a silver cigarette case and proferred it to Matt. "Care for a smoke?"

"Thank you." Matt took a cigarette, noting as he did the distinctive etched design of grapes and vines on the case's lid. Somewhere, sometime, he'd seen something like that. "That's an unusual case," he commented, as Miles snapped it shut and slid it back in his pocket.

"You have a good eye, detective. Yes, it is unusual. One of my ancestors was a vintner. This is my own design. Tiffany made it for me. The cigarettes, however, are ordinary Cameos." He took a long drag. "Yes, I appreciate Newport. More, perhaps, than any of my friends."

Matt cast him a shrewd look. "Is that why you never leave, then?"

"Been checking on me, detective?" Matt shrugged in response. "Then you must know that my wife is ill and it's been recommended that she stay in one place."

"The dampness here doesn't bother her?"

"No."

"And you don't miss New York?"

Miles tossed his cigarette down and ground it out with his heel, though it was barely half-smoked. "Is this an interrogation, detective?"

"No. Just curiosity. I'm from Newport, myself. I have to tell you I wouldn't mind seeing someplace new. Yet you—the cottagers—seem to take all this"—he turned and gestured toward Belle Mer—"for granted."

"Some do, detective. I, on the other hand, appreciate what I have. I rarely go anyplace else. New York, especially." Absently he withdrew another cigarette, tapped it on the case, and lighted it. "This is where Rosalind Sinclair's body was found, wasn't it?"

"Yes."

"Hmm. If I may ask you a question, detective? The killer has been caught, hasn't he?"

Matt smiled again. "I'm just tying up some loose ends, Mr. Vandenberg."

"Ah. Then you're not happy about the arrest, either."

Matt shot him a look. "Don't you think Thomas Pierce did it?"

"A common gardener? Hardly." Miles discarded the second cigarette, this time tossing it over the cliff. "There's a bit too much élan to the crimes for him, don't you think? Besides, I can't see Rosalind consorting with him."

"She didn't have to," Matt said, wondering about Miles's comment. No one else thought the crimes at all stylish.

"Ah. You subscribe to the madman theory, detective? Then why was she dressed in a maid's uniform?"

"I don't know." Matt kept his smile bland. "Why was she?"

"To meet someone, of course. I suggest you look a little harder at the people she knew, detective."

"Oh? As you pointed out, the case is closed."

"Mm. But I do wonder, you know, why Paul Radley said he was on the steamer from New York that night."

"Do you," Matt said, casting his memory back. They had established that Radley had been on the steamer as he'd said, hadn't they? "Why?"

Miles shrugged. "Curiosity. And I'm not unfeeling, detective. I'd like to see justice done as much as anyone." His face hardened. "This is my town. I don't like what's happening here."

"Neither do I."

"I didn't think so. If you'll excuse me now, I'll continue with my walk. Good day, detective."

Matt nodded in reply, watching for a moment as the other man strode along the path toward his house, in contrast to the casual stroll he'd displayed earlier. A man of contrasts was Miles Vandenberg, Matt thought, turning and walking away himself. A man of secrets, with more going on inside than he probably let on. Was he really happy living in constant isolation at the Point, splendid though it was? Matt doubted it. That Vandenberg had probably lied about that wasn't what bothered him, however, Matt conceded, as he reached the Forty Steps and turned off the Cliff Walk, onto the street. Vandenberg had just given him reason to suspect someone else for Rosalind's murder. The question was, why?

The summer season was in full swing in Newport. With the fear caused by the deaths on the Cliff Walk now a thing of the past, the cottagers threw themselves into the serious pursuit of pleasure. New ensembles from Paris or New York were ordered, worn, and discussed with much solemnity by the fashionable; the Casino held its annual subscription ball, while Tennis Week, at which the national championship would be decided, was in full swing; and everyone gossiped. And, on a balmy August evening, Belle Mer threw open its doors to the 400 to celebrate the engagement of Brooke Cassidy to Eliot Payson.

The night of the ball, Brooke burst into her room, frazzled and on edge. The first guest was due to arrive in forty-five minutes, and she wasn't even dressed. Having to oversee preparations for the ball, as well as being its guest of honor, was a bit much. "Annie, help me get these buttons undone. And hurry! There's no time to waste."

Annie, acting as Brooke's maid for the evening, came over and deftly worked at the buttons on Brooke's frock. "If you don't mind me saying, Mrs. Olmstead works you too hard, miss."

"I don't mind it, usually." She blew out her breath, lifting a strand of hair. "But there's just so much to see to, apart from the ball." Her eyes met Annie's in the mirror. "You know what you're to do?"

"Yes, miss. I've drawn your bath, by the way, so if you hurry you should be done in time."

"Yes, yes." Clad now only in chemise and frilly underdrawers, Brooke turned toward Annie. "You will be careful? You'll remember to stay behind the potted palm near the door—"

"Yes, miss, and listen to the voices as people come in. I'll be careful to stay hidden, that I do promise. And if I do hear him,

I'll tell you right away. Or Charl—Sergeant Sweeney. Nothing to it, miss."

"I hope not. I do wish we could have the sergeant in the Italian Hall, but too many people know his face."

"I know. I wonder, miss. How do you think he'd look dressed as a footman, in breeches and hose? I'll bet he has fine legs."

Brooke stared at her. "Annie."

"It's a thought, miss. Now quick, into your bath, or you will be late."

"Yes, Annie," Brooke said, and, throwing her another look, hurried into the bathroom adjoining her room.

A short while later Annie sat ensconced behind a huge potted palm, just inside the entrance to the Italian Hall. There, everything had got done on time, and the evening looked to be a success. Miss Brooke looked a treat, she did, in her gown of oyster white satin, with its huge puffed sleeves of Alençon lace and the gold satin roses trailing down the front of the skirt, as if scattered there. A lovely gown, it was. Annie wished she could wear something like that. Well, it wouldn't be so fine, of course—she couldn't afford it—but something, anyway. For her wedding day, if she ever married? It was something she'd been thinking of more often lately.

Two men, dressed in impeccable black tailcoats, walked by her hiding place, discussing events on Wall Street that week, and their appearance made Annie straighten. She was here to do a job, not to daydream. Miss Brooke and Charlie—Sergeant Sweeney—were depending on her. Still, a lot of the guests were here already, and she hadn't heard that voice yet. She shivered. She'd know it when she heard it again, that she would. Likely she'd never forget it. Already she'd heard it in her dreams, and she feared she always would.

Out in the hall, the orchestra, placed in the gallery above, was playing ragtime, and people were dancing the two-step, the latest dance craze. Oh, it was a fine sight, the gentlemen in white tie and black tails, the naval officers, invited so that there would be enough men present, resplendent in their white dress uniforms. In contrast, the ladies' gowns were sumptuously colored, and there were enough precious jewels to run a small country. The Mrs. Astor herself, dressed in her customary white satin, surely was wearing a fortune in diamonds, from the triple-strand necklace that was rumored to have more than two hundred stones, to the magnificent brooch on her bosom, to the tiara, glittering upon hair that was suspiciously dark for a woman of her age. Lord, what she wouldn't give for just one of those diamonds, Annie thought, wistfully.

In contrast to the guests' finery, the hall was almost plain in its decoration. Oh, there were vines of flowers festooning the galleries and tubs of roses set everywhere, as well as more potted palms, but Mrs. Olmstead had, for once, wanted the decorations kept simple. This was Miss Brooke's night. All attention was supposed to be on her. Annie's eyes sought and found Brooke dancing with Mr. Payson, making her smile. They made a lovely couple. Maybe not what she'd have chosen for Miss Brooke, but a good match, all the same. She was still watching them when someone stepped in front of the palm, blocking her view.

Biting her lips, Annie cursed under her breath. If the man didn't move, how was she supposed to do her job, let alone watch the ball? Yet she couldn't say anything, and thus give herself away. She sat back, annoyed, but resigned to wait until the man, whoever he was, decided to move.

"Annie." It was a whisper, and it sent convulsive shivers down her spine. She'd heard that voice before, oh yes, she had, with all its menace and threat, but never had she thought to hear it in quite this way, in the middle of a crowded ballroom. "Hello, Annie. Remember me?"

Annie swallowed and stayed absolutely still. Maybe if she didn't move . . . "I remember you. And I see you, you know," he said. At that she did move, her hand jerking involuntarily against the palm, causing its leaves to rustle. "Oh, yes." A hoarse chuckle. "I know you're there. Intriguing hiding place, but you'll have to come out sometime, won't you? And when you do, I'll be watching." Another hoarse chuckle. "Remember that, Annie. And remember Illumination Night."

With that, the man moved away. Paralyzed by fear, Annie gripped the sides of her chair, but some part of her mind was on her task. Leaning forward, she peered through the fronds, trying to see who it was. A gent, that much was certain, of medium height and dark hair. More than that she couldn't see, however. His back was to her as he walked away, and in a moment, he was swallowed up by the crowd, just one man among many, dressed in black. She had lost him. He was gone, but he was also still there. Of that, she had no doubt.

Well, she wasn't going to sit here like a target and let him get her! No, not her, Annie McKenna. She was smarter than that. After all, they had a plan, didn't they? Didn't matter if she came out now, he'd seen her already and she had no doubt he was telling the truth. He would be watching her.

The thought almost made her dive back behind the palm for protection, but pride kept her going. There was no safety there. Safety lay across the crowded floor. Picking up a tray, she made her way across the room. No one paid her any heed; she was just a maid, after all, and she wasn't going to look around to see if someone were watching her. She would not—would not!—imagine that at any moment a hand would descend upon her shoulder, dragging her away and locking on to her throat, and—.

"Miss Brooke." Fear made her voice breathless, as she came up to Brooke, standing in a small group that included Mr. Payson and the Olmsteads. "Mrs. Smith needs to see you in the kitchen a minute."

"Oh, bother. Now?" Brooke said, but she moved away. This was the signal they had arranged earlier if Annie heard anything.

"Yes, miss. I'm sorry, miss."

"Oh, Brooke, now?" Winifred wailed. "But your uncle is just about to make the announcement."

"I won't be a minute. Excuse me," Brooke said, smiling, and walked away, by Annie's side. "Well?"

"He's here, miss."

Brooke gripped her arm in excitement. "Is he? Did you hear his voice? Where is he?"

"I don't know, miss. But"—Annie swallowed hard—"he threatened to kill me."

14

Brooke stopped dead. "Who is he?" she demanded.

"I don't know, miss, and that's a fact. Kept his back to me the whole time, he did. But I'll never forget that voice." She shivered. "He said, 'Remember Illumination Night.'"

Brooke took Annie's arm and began moving through the crowd again. Dear heavens, that was a threat. So long as Annie was with someone, however, she should be safe. Brooke dreaded to think of what might have happened had they not planned for this.

Charlie was sitting at the long table, chatting with Mrs. Smith, when Brooke and Annie walked into the kitchen. One look at them, and the smile on his face faded. "He's here?" he said, getting to his feet.

"Yes. She didn't see him, though," Brooke said.

"He kept his back to me," Annie explained.

"And he threatened her. Tell him, Annie."

Charlie's face grew darker as, haltingly, Annie told of her experience. "I think, though, if I go back I could figure out who it is—"

"No." His voice cut across hers. "You've done enough, Annie. At least we know he's here."

"Do you think she's safe, sergeant?" Brooke asked.

"No. Not here. We'll go on with the rest of the plan."

"Well, I'm glad to hear that!" Mrs. Smith exclaimed, coming forward with Annie's hat and coat. "I was worried about this, I don't mind telling you. Here are your things, Annie. Got them ready for you, just in case."

"Good thinking, Mrs. Smith." Charlie winked at her, and to Brooke's vast amusement, the housekeeper blushed.

"Go on with you. Flirt with someone your own age, sergeant."

Charlie's grin was unrepentant. "I just might. Well, Annie? Are you ready?"

"Yes, sergeant. Oh, miss. Are you sure you'll be all right?"

"I'll be fine, Annie." Brooke accompanied them to the back door. "No one knows that I'm part of this."

"But you left the hall with me, miss—"

"And if anyone asks, I'll explain you took sick. Now, you'd best go. Can you tell me where you're taking her?"

Charlie shook his head. "It's probably better if you don't know. She'll be safe, though. I can assure you of that."

"Good. Take care of her, then."

"I plan to," Charlie said, and escorted Annie out the door.

Silence fell in the wake of their departure, a curious silence not broken by the bustle of maids and footmen in and out of the kitchen. "Well. I'm thinkin' we'll be hearing wedding bells there," Mrs. Smith said.

"What?" Brooke glanced toward the door. "Annie and Sergeant Sweeney?"

"Indeed. And a good match it would be, I'm thinkin'."

"Yes." And speaking of that, she should head back to the ball. "Thank you, Mrs. Smith. And remember, not a word to anyone."

"You think I'd do anything to hurt Annie? Not likely. Now just you get back to your ball, miss—yes, what is it?"

Brooke turned at the sharp tone of Mrs. Smith's voice to see Miles Vandenberg standing in the doorway, looking distinctly out of place. "Miles?" she said, crossing to him. "Is something wrong?"

He smiled down at her as she reached him. "Funny, that's what I was going to ask you. You left the Hall so quickly I thought you might be ill."

"No. A minor emergency here, that's all."

He nodded. "I see. Well. They're waiting for you, Brooke."

"Yes, I know. I was just going."

"I'll walk back with you," he said, holding out his arm. After a brief hesitation, Brooke laid her fingers on it. It wasn't Miles's fault she was reluctant to face what lay ahead.

"Very well, then. Let's go," she said, and walked back to the hall for the announcement of her engagement to Eliot Payson.

Matt glanced at the report one more time and then set it down. Paul Radley had been on the *Priscilla* from New York the night Rosalind was murdered, and had produced a ticket stub to prove it. The officer who had done the initial check on Radley's movements had confirmed it in his report. Still, it bothered Matt. Why had Vandenberg said what he had if Radley had been on the steamer? On impulse, he strode to the door of his office and put his head out. "Charlie."

Charlie appeared in the corridor. "Yeah, detective?"

"Come here for a minute, will you?" he said, and went back to his desk.

"What is it?" Charlie asked as he walked in.

"This report about Paul Radley. I want him checked out."

"We did it already, Cap."

"I know. Let's do it again. He was at Belle Mer last night, wasn't he?"

"Yeah."

"Okay. We'll need to find out where he was on Illumination Night. Also, let's find out how often he came down from New York, and how."

Charlie shrugged. "All right. About Nellie Farrell."

Matt looked up. "What?"

"Nothing." He shrugged again. "I've had men going up and down her street again, talking to her neighbors. I even went to the Reading Room and talked to some of the members, but they all claimed they didn't know her. Can't say I blame them, considering what that would mean." He glanced down at his notes. "The neighbors didn't like her much, but she didn't bother them. Apparently she kept to herself. About the worst anyone can say about her is that sometimes late at night they'd see her greeting a man at her door. Medium height, dark hair, a gentleman by his dress. But we knew that."

"It could be anyone," Matt said, but he didn't think so. It sounded like Paul Radley. He was, after all, the likeliest person to have met with Rosalind, particularly if he had come down from New York on a night different from what he'd said. He was also the likeliest man to have fathered her child, and he had been at Belle Mer last evening. The sketchy description came disturbingly close to that given by Annie. Not for the first time he was glad they'd arranged for her safety; at this moment she was with his parents in Middletown. Otherwise, the Cliff Walk Killer would likely have claimed another victim last night. "It was stupid of him."

"Who?"

"Our murderer. He has to know we've arrested someone. Why not just let Annie alone?"

"We don't know what he had planned for her. If it's the same man as did Nellie, he uses different methods." Charlie's face darkened. "I'd like to get my hands on him."

"So would I." Matt leaned back. "I don't think we've heard the last of him."

"You think he'll try again?"

"I don't know. Killing doesn't seem to bother him, does it?" Charlie's mouth tightened. "I'm glad Annie's safe."

"So am I."

"Matt." Charlie's voice was hesitant. "Whoever it was had to see Miss Cassidy going out with Annie last night. You think she's safe?"

Matt's head shot up. "Brooke? Dammit, she'd better be. I don't see what else we could have done last night." He rose and began to pace. "If Annie'd gone out alone, she would have been a target."

"Yeah. And now Miss Cassidy might be. He might think she knows where Annie is."

Matt looked at Charlie for a moment without seeming to see him, and then grabbed his jacket. "I'd better warn her."

"Yeah." Charlie rose. "And I'll get busy on Radley."

"Good," Matt said as he walked out, his mind already on other matters. Until Charlie had pointed it out, he hadn't considered that Brooke might be in danger. She would have to know, so she could be careful. Because if anything happened to her, he would have to do something about it. Even if she were going to marry someone else.

"Excuse me, miss," Hutton said, and Brooke, sitting in a white wicker chair on the loggia, book in hand, looked up. "Detective Devlin is here. Do you want to see him?"

"Hello, Brooke," Matt said from behind Hutton. "Do you mind?"

"No, Matt." Brooke rose, smiling a little. Ordinarily Hutton would never let visitors in without checking first to see if they were welcome, but the entire staff looked on the police a little more kindly now. They knew, if the Olmsteads didn't, what Matt and Charlie had done for Annie. "Bring us some iced tea, Hutton."

"Yes, miss. If I might venture to suggest, miss, perhaps the gentleman would like something stronger."

"I would, thank you," Matt said, before Brooke could answer. "Whiskey, please."

"Very good, sir," Hutton said, and went back inside.

"He likes you," Brooke said, and Matt turned to her.

"What? Why?"

"He called you a gentleman. Sit down, Matt." She indicated a chair near hers, and they sat for a moment in companionable silence.

"This is nice," he said, looking up first at the mosaic ceiling, and then past the lawn to Sakonnet Passage, and the blue Atlantic beyond. "I could get used to this."

"Yes, well, it's not quite so nice in the fog, but I have to admit this is my favorite part of the house."

Matt twisted his head to regard the house. "You've come a long way, Brooke."

"From the Fifth Ward? Yes, in some ways. Thank you, Hutton." This as the butler set a tray with their drinks down upon a table. "I take it you're not here on official duty?"

"Actually, yes, I am. Why?"

Brooke looked pointedly at his drink. "That."

"Oh. This." He cradled the crystal tumbler in his hands and looked out at the view again, this time with a frown creasing his brow. "Something's come up."

"Something serious?"

"Yes. Last night, when you went to the kitchen—"

"Is Annie all right?"

"Yes. Fine. It's you we're concerned about now."

"Me?" she said in surprise. "But I'm fine."

"We know the killer was here last night, Brooke." He regarded her soberly. "He saw you leave with Annie. Of that you can be certain. And he must be wondering now how much you know, and how much of a danger you are to him."

A chill went through Brooke. "You think he might come after me?"

"I don't know. It's a possibility."

"Dear heavens. But Matt, I don't know anything."

"You know the real killer hasn't been caught. You know that it's someone you know."

"Dear heavens," she said again. "What do I do?"

"I don't know, dammit. Sorry," he said, in apology for his language. "I'll talk to the guard here, but I don't even know who to warn you about. I can tell you this, though." He hunched forward. "Stay close to home. Don't go out on the estate unless someone is with you. Do not ever go out alone. And don't be alone with any man until this thing is settled."

"Not even Eliot?" she said, faintly.

"No. Not even him."

"But he didn't attack Annie. You know that. He was on the Burnhams' yacht with me that night, and last night we'd just finished dancing when Annie came up to me."

"All right," Matt said after a moment, grudgingly. "Payson's probably all right. But no one else, Brooke."

"No. I promise." She looked off across the lawn without taking in any of the view. When Rosalind's body had been found she had felt the menace coming near to her, but never had she expected it to come this close.

"I don't really think he'll come after you." Matt's tone was almost soothing. "He has to know he couldn't get away with it. I just want you to be prepared."

"Thank you, Matt." She flashed him a quick, strained smile. "I promise I'll be careful."

"Good." He set the tumbler down on the table and rose. "I don't want anything happening to you," he muttered.

"Excuse me?" Brooke said, not certain she'd heard correctly.

"I said I don't want anything happening to you." He turned and glared at her. "Even if you did leave me."

"I didn't leave you, Matt!" She rose hastily to her feet, facing him. "My parents died. What was I supposed to do?"

"You could have married me, dammit."

"You didn't ask."

"I didn't think I had to."

"Didn't think you—!" She stared at him. "Of all the nerve!"

"What was I supposed to do?" he demanded. "You were upset about your parents. Was I suddenly supposed to start courting you?"

"You could have given me some sort of sign."

"I thought I had. I thought we had an understanding. And don't say you didn't know. You knew. God, when you left . . ."

"Maybe I would have stayed," she said quietly. "Maybe if I'd thought—I needed family, Matt. I told you that before. When I left I never intended to turn my back on my old life, never! Don't you think it was hard for me, leaving all my friends and everything I ever knew? And then to be plunged into society— no one knew me, no one would accept me for myself for a long time. They still don't." She hesitated. "You never said anything, Matt."

"And I can't very well say anything now," he said, bitterly.

"Why? Because of this?" she challenged, waving her hand to indicate Belle Mer and all it represented. "You don't know me at all if you think this matters to me."

"It matters to me, dammit."

She stared at him. "Why, you snob."

"Brooke."

"You are, you know. You've always resented anyone with money, and now you're judging me because I have rich relatives, because I don't live in the Fifth Ward anymore."

"Dammit, Brooke, you're engaged."

Silence fell. "So I am," she agreed after a moment, looking down at her ring and twisting it on her finger.

He followed her gaze. "Do you love him?"

"I—we like each other. We're well suited."

"That's not what I asked. Do you love him?"

"Oh, Matt." Wearily she brushed her hair away from her face. "Love isn't always the most important thing."

"Hogwash. You know better. Your parents had it. My parents have it. What do you think has kept them together for so long?"

"Matt, it's complicated—"

"No, it isn't. You either love him, or you don't." He stared at her, hard. "Do you love him?"

Brooke looked fixedly at her ring. "No," she said, in a very small voice.

"But you're going to marry him anyway."

"Yes."

"Dammit. I see." Matt snatched up his hat and stomped toward the glass doors that led inside. There, however, he stopped. "You tell me you haven't changed, Brooke." He turned to look at her. "But you have, you know. You have," he said, and turned away.

"Matt," Brooke said, but it came out softly, almost a squeak. Calling him back would do no good. He was gone. And never, Brooke thought, dropping into her chair and sinking her face in her hands, had she felt quite so alone.

Matt threw himself onto his bicycle and pedaled off at a furious pace for the station house. He'd had enough of Bellevue Avenue and the people who lived on it. Give him ordinary people, the townies and the workers, any day. Conflicts with them were likely to be straightforward, almost easy. He was not a snob, as Brooke had accused him. There was, however, no question in his mind that the rich were a different breed of people. He'd do well to remember that.

At least he'd done his duty, warning Brooke of any possible danger, and he'd make sure she was protected. He'd do no less for anyone in such a situation. That was all there was to it. Other than that, he needn't think of Brooke at all. Swinging off the bicycle at the station house, he glanced at the clock set high in the wall. At the same time he heard the distant sound of a ship's horn, and the two events converged in his mind. Quarter of eight, time for the New York steamer to come in from Fall River. Matt jumped onto the bicycle again and headed down Thames Street. Since the Fall River Line kept no passenger records, he'd relied on testimony from a steward as to whether Paul Radley was aboard the steamer on the night he'd claimed. Maybe he was wasting his time, but he felt a sudden urge to confirm that fact. What Miles Vandenberg had said to him the other day bothered him. What if Radley had indeed been in Newport at the time of Rosalind's death?

If any one place epitomized the two different Newports, the workaday world and the social capital, it was Long Wharf. Here the fishing boats tied up and unloaded their catch, leaving a perpetual aroma that overlay everything; here, as if this were a street, were tenements and saloons and boatbuilders' shops. At the end of the wharf, however, things were very different. A crowd of well-dressed people waited to board the steamer; Matt recognized more than one cottager in the line. Showing his badge to the ticket collector, he went to the head of the line, watching as the steamer *Priscilla* rounded Goat Island, preparatory to docking. The big white boat, almost as large as a trans-Atlantic liner, made a splendid sight as she docked, all lights ablaze and the paddle wheel foaming the water. Matt had never actually been aboard a Fall River Line boat. He certainly was seeing a different side of life on this case, he thought, as he had once before.

As soon as *Priscilla* docked, Matt bounded across the gangplank, intent on his errand and very aware of the time constraints, since the boat was scheduled to leave again in half an hour. He'd ask his questions and get out, he thought, and then stopped, brought up short by the room spread before him. While passengers pushed past him, he stood and stared at the Grand Saloon. It was huge, easily as big as several tennis courts, and the ceiling soared high above, its domed chandelier twinkling with hundreds of lights behind its opalescent glass. Dazed, Matt wandered across the room, his feet sinking into plush red and gold carpeting, taking everything in, from the gilded columns to the fine velvet-upholstered furniture. Good God, this wasn't a boat, it was a floating palace. How must Nellie Farrell have felt, traveling in such splendor, he wondered, and abruptly returned to earth. He had a job to do.

The ticket collector had given him directions to the pilot house, where Matt planned to speak to the captain, but even so he got lost. There were too many staircases to climb, too many corridors to negotiate. Confused, he stopped at the entrance to the dining room, astonished again by its size; it looked as if it could hold all of the boat's 1,500 passengers. White-jacketed waiters circulated through the room, laying out china and cutlery upon white linen tablecloths. He was about to stop one to ask for directions, when someone spoke behind him. "The dining room isn't open yet, sir. If you'll come back after we leave the wharf, we'll be happy to serve you."

Matt turned to see a man wearing a black dinner jacket. "I'm not here to eat. Actually, I'm lost." He showed the man his badge. "Detective Devlin, of the Newport police."

"Devlin." A look of dismay passed swiftly over the man's face. "Are you looking into Miss Farrell's murder?"

"Yes," Matt said, startled. "Did you know her?"

"Only as a passenger. She was a lovely woman."

"Did she travel often?" he asked, curious as to how much the waiter had noticed.

"Perhaps once a month, but she wasn't someone you'd forget. Very full of life, and very happy to be aboard."

Again Matt felt a pang of sorrow for Nellie. "I don't believe I caught your name. You are—?"

"John Harris. The head waiter, sir."

"Mr. Harris." Matt nodded, rapidly calculating times in his

head. He needed to speak to Captain Simmons, to get permission to interview the crew, and yet Harris's knowledge was too valuable for him to ignore. "Are you familiar with your other passengers?"

"Oh, yes, sir. I have to be, you see, it's my job. And the people we get expect fine service." He straightened, throwing out his chest. "I don't hesitate to tell you, sir, we get the best of society on our boats. Astors, Vandenbergs, Belmonts, even presidents. President Cleveland travels with us regularly, you know. I believe we've had every president since Lincoln aboard, at one time or another."

"Really," Matt said, impressed in spite of himself. "Do you know Paul Radley?"

"Senior or Junior, sir? I ask, because Mr. Radley Senior doesn't make the trip very often."

"I'm interested in his son."

"Paul Radley, Junior." He looked thoughtful. "Yes. He was with us last Thursday, as always."

"Thursday," Matt said, sharply. "I understood he came from New York on Friday nights."

"Oh, no, no. He's usually with us on Thursdays. Except, of course, on alternate weeks, when I presume he's on the *Puritan*. *Priscilla* and *Puritan* alternate nights, you know. Now, I remember he was with us last week, because of his breakfast. Passengers may have breakfast in their rooms, so long as they ask for it the night before, but they have to come to me to collect it. Last week Mr. Radley was not at all pleased with his meal. In quite a taking, actually. The steak wasn't done to his liking." He leaned over, his voice lowered. "I believe, though, that he ordered it incorrectly. We rarely make such mistakes."

Matt's mind was whirling. If what Harris had just told him was true, it changed everything he'd thought about the case. "Mr. Radley told us he came down on a Friday night several weeks ago, in stateroom number twenty-two."

"Number twenty-two?" Harris's lips pursed. "That's odd."

"Why?"

"That stateroom is close to the boilers. Very uncomfortable, you know, with the noise and the heat, particularly in the summer. Mr. Radley usually takes an outside room." He nodded, decisively. "Yes. I distinctly remember that last week he was in number forty-five."

"Would you have a record of that, Mr. Harris?"

"Yes, I should have his order for breakfast."

"Good. I'd like to see it" He frowned. "But why—" he began, just as the boat's horn blew. Damn. There was so much he had still to learn, and so little time left. "Are there stewards for the staterooms I mentioned?"

"Yes, but they'd be busy just now. In fact, sir, I must get back to my duties—"

"I realize that." Matt spoke rapidly. "I need to speak to them, however. The stewards from the *Puritan*, too. Who could I see to arrange for them to come to the station house?"

Harris's lips pursed again, but then he nodded. "I can take care of it for you, sir. Mind you, Captain Simmons probably won't like it, but I'm sure he'll want to cooperate. As I do." He glanced away. "Miss Farrell was a lovely woman," he said again.

"I'd appreciate it. We won't keep them long."

Harris nodded again. "I'll see what I can do, sir."

"Thank you," Matt said, holding out his hand and then turning as the ship's horn blew another blast. If he didn't get off soon, he'd be heading for New York himself, and that wouldn't do. Not with this new information in hand.

Grinning, he left the *Priscilla* and swung onto his bicycle again, heading for the station house through the gathering twilight. It looked as if they'd finally gotten a break in the case. Once he learned what he needed from *Priscilla*'s stewards, he could go ask Radley some pointed questions. And, with any luck, he would find the real Cliff Walk Killer.

15

"You're quiet this afternoon, Brooke," Eliot commented as he pulled on the reins and brought his team to a stop. Midafternoon, and they had, as usual, taken part in the carriage promenade along Bellevue Avenue, along with all the other fine turnouts. No matter how often Brooke saw it she was impressed: the coaches, barouches, landaus, and victorias, all spick and span, with the horses groomed and currycombed so that they looked almost artificial. Even more striking was the solemn formality of the parade, with the drivers sitting stiff as statues and the passengers, usually ladies, nodding regally as they passed each other. She and Eliot had left that behind for the moment, however, driving out onto Ocean Avenue to Brenton Point. At this rocky promontory, the waves crashed against the rocks unceasingly. As an engaged couple, they were alone in Eliot's stylish phaeton, and no one thought anything of it. Brooke supposed she might as well get used to it.

"I'm sorry," she murmured, aware that she had said little during the drive. Her mind was occupied with other things. With the conversation she'd had with Matt yesterday. The implications of it stunned her.

"Don't be." Eliot sounded cheerful. "I like a woman who can stay quiet."

Brooke eyed him in astonishment. "Eliot! What a horrid thing to say."

"Truth." He gave her his easy, charming smile. "You're a

very restful person, not forever clacking on like so many women. We'll suit each other, I think."

Brooke's hands clenched in her lap. "Yes."

"Fine view here, isn't it?" He took a deep, deep breath. "And good, bracing air."

"Yes." Across the channel could be seen the island of Conanicut and, farther off, mainland Rhode Island; far out to sea the silhouettes of ships were visible. It was a sparkling day, with the sun shimmering upon the cobalt sea and the freshening wind kicking up waves that beat against the shoals of rocks, sending spume high into the air. It was a fine view. It was also where her parents had met their deaths five years earlier. "Could we go?"

"Why? We just got here, Brooke." He laid his hand on hers, smiling warmly. "And we rarely have the chance to be alone."

"I know." Brooke forced her fingers to relax. Eliot hadn't noticed her tension. She didn't know why that surprised her. There was a great deal he didn't see. "I don't like this place, Eliot. It's where my parents died."

"Oh? Oh. Then, by all means, we'll go." He flicked the reins, turning the horses and heading back toward town. To their left, the land side, rose the bulk of more cottages, one of granite, as if hewn from the rocks; another of Tudor design, like an English manor house. Ocean Avenue was becoming almost as fashionable as Bellevue. "I'd forgotten that. A carriage accident, wasn't it?"

"Yes." She stared straight ahead. "Something made their horse run away, and they overturned onto the rocks."

Eliot winced. "I'm sorry, sweetheart. I should have remembered that."

Indeed, he should have. Matt would have, she thought, and quickly banished the treacherous idea. "Besides, I should be home soon. We're dining at Lindhurst tonight."

"As am I."

"Oh, yes, of course. Aunt Winifred wants to discuss some things with me first."

Eliot nodded wisely. "About our wedding, I'd guess."

"Well, yes."

"Wise woman. There's a lot to plan."

"Yes." Brooke said again, and wondered that he didn't hear the reluctance in her voice. But then, as she'd just reminded herself, he wasn't the most perceptive of men.

"We'll want to have it at Grace Church," he said. "The wedding breakfast will be at your home, of course. Have you thought about bridesmaids?"

"No."

"You should. Very important in a wedding. You want someone who is attractive, but who won't outshine you."

"Thank you very much!"

He flashed her a quick smile. "Not that anyone could, of course. We'll have to think about the guest list, too. I'm afraid I have a prodigious amount of relatives."

"Eliot, must we talk about this now? We haven't even set the date yet."

"Yes, and why not?" He fixed her with a stern look. "People are asking, you know."

"I know," she murmured. "Aunt Winifred is talking about next May."

"May." He nodded, lips pursed. "A good month. Warm, but not hot. I approve."

"You don't wish to be married sooner?"

"Of course I do, darling." He flashed her a brilliant smile. "But we need to plan, don't we? This gives us the time. We are going to have a wonderful life together. Think of it, Brooke." His eyes looked almost unfocused. "We'll travel wherever we want. We'll be here in the summer, of course, New York in the fall, and I was thinking perhaps Florida in the winter. Oh, and we'll cross the ditch to Europe, as often as you wish."

"Is that really how you see our future?"

"Yes, why not? Oh." His smile was smug. "You want a home. And children, I suppose. Well, I'm not opposed to that, so long as they don't distract you too much."

"From what?"

"From your real purpose in life. We are the *crème de la crème*," he went on, his voice growing passionate. "We are the smart set, the top of society, and we can live any way we choose. Not just traveling, but at home, too. Think of how we'll entertain in our own home, Brooke. We'll go to parties, of course, but we'll have our own, and we'll set the styles. We'll—"

"I can't," Brooke burst out.

"Can't set the style? Of course you can, darling." He cast a critical eye over her outfit. "I will admit that you could be more original with your ensembles, but you'll learn. I'll teach you. You'll be the most stylish matron in New York."

"I don't want to be stylish."

"Of course you do, darling. Everyone in our set wants to be."

"I don't!" She pulled her hands free from his restraining grip, staring up at the sky. "I don't want to be stylish. I don't want to winter in Florida, or travel to Europe, or hand my children over to a fashionable nanny. I don't, Eliot! And I most especially do not want to spend my entire life socializing. I want more."

Eliot's look was blank. "What more is there?"

"What more? Oh, Eliot."

"No, tell me. I really want to know. Why aren't you happy about our plans?"

"Your plans, Eliot. Yours, not mine." Frantically, she pulled at her gloves. "I thought I could do it. I thought that when everyone told me how well suited we are, they were right. Well, they weren't, Eliot. They were wrong. Wrong. Here." She held out the diamond ring he'd given her not so long ago. "I want you to take this back."

He stared at her incredulously. "You're breaking the engagement?"

"Yes. I'm sorry, Eliot, but I can't marry you."

"Can't—oh, I understand." To Brooke's surprise, he chuckled. "You're having second thoughts. But that's normal, darling. Once you get through this, you'll see—"

"No." Brooke kept her gaze and her voice steady. "I mean it, Eliot. I can't marry you."

Slowly Eliot reached out and took the ring, never taking his eyes from Brooke's. "You're serious."

"Yes, Eliot."

"Look, is it the drinking? Because, if it is, I'll swear off, I promise—"

"It's partly the drinking. You do drink too much, Eliot." She gazed up at him, willing him to understand. "But it's more what's in me. I can't do it. I'm sorry, but—"

"Damn it to hell." Eliot threw the ring to the floor of the carriage and flicked the reins, hard, sending the horses galloping along the narrow road.

"Eliot!" Brooke cried, grabbing on to the side of the carriage as it swayed. "Slow down! We'll crash at this rate!"

"I don't give a damn. Dammit, Brooke!" He pulled on the reins, and the carriage slewed to a stop. "Why?" he asked, sounding bewildered.

She swallowed. She owed him honesty, if nothing else. "I don't love you, Eliot."

"Love? What does that have to do with it?"

"More than you realize. Here." She reached down and scooped up the diamond from the floor, pressing it into his hand. "Give this to someone who can love you, Eliot. You deserve it."

Eliot pushed the ring into his trouser pocket. "Is there someone else? Is that it?"

She hesitated. "Yes, there is." For all the good that did her.

"Dammit," he said again, and picked up the reins, driving off at a more moderate pace. "Why did you wait until after we announced it? Now we'll have to deal with all the gossip."

"Eliot, I'm sorry—"

"Don't, Brooke. Don't say it." His gaze remained straight ahead, and a muscle twitched in his jaw. "Don't say anything."

"All right." Brooke shrank into the corner of the phaeton, as far from Eliot as possible. She'd never seen him this way, so angry, so dark and dangerous-looking, not smiling, congenial Eliot. There were depths to him she'd never before suspected. The thought chilled her, reminding her of the warning Matt had given her yesterday. But Eliot was safe, she reminded herself. He'd been with her when Annie was attacked, and again when she was threatened at the ball. Surely he wouldn't do anything to hurt her, though they were, to all intents and purposes, alone, their only companions a carriage far ahead. He wouldn't, would he?

It was a relief to reach more populated areas at last, near Bailey's Beach, where other carriages passed them, their occupants waving and calling greetings. It was a relief to turn onto Bellevue Avenue, and a relief when Eliot pulled the carriage to a stop on the drive at Belle Mer. Brooke's shoulders, held tightly during the tense, silent ride, sagged as Eliot, ever the gentleman, came around to help her down. He gave her a searching look as she descended, his hands gripping hers. "You're sure, Brooke?"

"Yes, Eliot. I'm sure." She pulled her hand away, relieved when he didn't try to hold her. For now, she was safe. "I'll talk with my aunt and uncle."

"Yes." He stood, one foot scuffing against the other, like a little boy's. "Well. Take care of yourself, Brooke," he said, and climbed into the carriage.

"You, too," Brooke whispered, but he was driving away, the wheels of his carriage grating on the gravel, so that he didn't hear. Her vision briefly blurred by tears, Brooke watched him drive off, and then turned to go in. Poor Eliot, she thought. He was a decent man, and she was sorry she'd hurt him. Even now, though, the thought of living with him was something she couldn't face. She was glad she'd finally found the courage to break the engagement, and plan her life herself.

"Miss Cassidy," Hutton said as she came in. "There's a matter for you to deal with."

"Oh, no, not again!" she exclaimed. "Do you realize, Hutton, that lately every time I come in you tell me that?"

"Yes, miss." Hutton's face was wooden. "I'm sorry, miss."

"Oh, bother. I'm sorry, too, Hutton. It's not your fault. There's simply been too much happening lately."

"Yes, miss." Hutton's eyes were sympathetic. "But this shouldn't be too much of a problem."

Brooke yanked out the long hatpin that held her hat in place, and pulled the hat off. "Oh, very well. What is it?"

"There's a Monsieur Pepin to see you. He's in the morning room." Hutton's nose wrinkled. "He insisted."

"That name sounds familiar," she said, wondering at his reaction. "Do I know him?"

"He was the cook at the Point, miss, at least until today. He's

known for his temper, and his cooking. I heard"—Hutton si-
dled over to her—"that something set him off today and he up
and quit."

For the first time since giving Eliot back his ring, Brooke felt
like smiling. "Am I to assume he wants work here?"

"Yes, miss."

"God help us. Very well. I'll be in the morning room. Oh,
and Hutton." She turned back, smiling a little. "Thank you."

"You're quite welcome, miss," Hutton said, his bewildered
look only intensifying her amusement. He had, quite without
meaning to, reminded her that life went on, no matter what else
happened. In her world there would always be a house to run,
with all the problems that entailed. She was almost looking forward to meeting the mecurial Monsieur Pepin.

"Mademoiselle," he said, bounding up from his chair as she
entered the sitting room. "A thousand *mercis* for seeing me like
this. You are most kind, most generous."

Brooke's lips twitched. "Er, yes. I am Miss Cassidy. You are
Monsieur Pepin?"

"But of course. But, *pardon*, I did not introduce myself, *non?* I
am Richard Pepin, chef *extraordinaire.*"

Her lips twitched again as he bowed. He was short and dapper, with a highly waxed black mustache and snapping black
eyes. She could well believe he had a temper. "Sit down, monsieur. Now," she said, sitting herself, "why did you wish to see
me?"

"Ah, you *Americains,* always so blunt, *non?* To be honest, mademoiselle, I am here to do you a very great favor."

"Oh?"

"*Oui.* I am offering to you my services as chef."

"I thought you were employed by the Vandenbergs."

Pepin's eyes flashed. "Bah! Them. *Impossible!* And the staff—
encroyable! Always at my knives and my pans, putting things
here, putting things there, never back where they belong, no."
He mimed putting knives back in a drawer as he spoke. "Now
my paring knife is missing. And my pans, my precious copper
pans—one *cochon* of a maid used my omelet pan to sauté onions.
Onions! *Encroyable!*"

"Er, yes. But don't the Vandenbergs think well of you?"

"Them? Bah," he said again. "Madame, she will not eat what I prepare, no matter what it is. *Non.* Always she sends it back. And Monsieur Vandenberg, he is never home." His smile was sly. "Out with a lady friend, eh?"

"Really?" Brooke said, diverted.

"Mais oui." He gave an elaborate, very Gallic, shrug. "With a wife like that, who can blame him?"

Brooke smothered a smile. He was somehow more French than any Frenchman she'd ever met, making her wonder how many of his mannerisms were real, and how many staged for effect. "Well." She rose. "I can't promise you anything. We do have a cook already and I doubt she's thinking of leaving. But I will talk to my aunt about you."

"A cook. Bah. With me you would have a chef *premier,* mademoiselle." He, too, rose. "But I shall resign myself to my fate."

"Good." Brooke pressed the button that signaled Hutton. "Hutton will see you out," she said, and left the room, her spirits considerably lighter. Life did indeed go on. She would put the incident with Eliot behind her, just as he someday would. He would recover from the blow she'd dealt him, which, she suspected, had hurt his pride more than anything else. As for herself, she could now stop feeling guilty, and could plan her life her own way. She was free. For the first time in five years, she was free.

The stewards from the *Priscilla* had, as requested, come to the police station to explain the curious circumstances of Paul Radley's traveling arrangements. Like Mr. Harris, both agreed that he traveled on Thursday nights. When pressed to explain why he'd also taken a stateroom on Fridays, both looked at each other blankly. That particular stateroom was occupied by a Mr. Taylor, one of them finally said. He had no idea who that was, but Matt did. Taylor was Radley's valet. Why he'd traveled separately was another matter.

"We're on to something," Matt said with satisfaction after

the stewards had left. "Radley could have committed the murders."

"Yeah." Charlie flipped through the pages in his notebook. "He was here when they all were committed, but he kept that quiet from everyone. But the staff at the Muenchinger-King Cottage remember it. I checked that this morning."

"Did he keep it from Rosalind, I wonder?" Matt brushed a finger across his mustache. "He could have been the man she was going out to meet."

"Seems likely, doesn't it?"

"Mm. If Rosalind wanted to do something that wasn't allowed her, she'd have to do it in secret. Radley could have been in it with her."

"I'll lay even money he was."

"Mm." Matt brushed his finger across his mustache again. If nothing else, they needed an explanation of his odd travel arrangements. "We'll go talk to him," he said, and picked up the telephone, asking for Hôtel Soleil, the Radleys' home. That produced the interesting news that Paul had yet to arrive from New York. Matt rang off, and instantly asked for the Muenchinger-King Cottage, the tony boardinghouse where many of society's finest, with no fixed address in Newport, stayed. Yes, Mr. Radley was staying there, he was told, and yes, he could come to the phone. Matt's smile was grim as he spoke to Paul, and then rang off again. "I think we've got him," he said, rising and reaching for his jacket. "He's agreed to meet us at his house. Get us a buggy, Charlie. I want to get this settled."

"Sure thing, Cap."

A short time later they stepped down from the buggy in the drive at Hôtel Soleil, and went in, to the same paneled reception room where they had interviewed Radley before. Paul came in after a few moments, his face hard. "What is this all about?" he demanded, without preamble.

"Sit down, Mr. Radley," Matt said, refusing to be rattled.

Paul remained standing. "You will not be staying, gentlemen. Ask your questions and leave."

Matt looked at him for a long moment. "Very well. Why did you lie to us, Mr. Radley?"

"I didn't lie to you."

"No? Your staff here thought you were in New York. Why are you staying at the Muenchinger-King Cottage?"

Paul's look was disdainful. "I didn't expect to come down last night, and so I didn't notify the staff. Rather than put anyone out, I decided to stay at Muenchinger's."

"That's a thumper, Mr. Radley. You were also here the night Rosalind died."

"I was on the steamer from New York. I've told you that already." His smile was frosty. "Check with the Fall River Line if you doubt me."

"Oh, I have, Mr. Radley," Matt said, and had the satisfaction of seeing the other man's eyes flicker. "You neglected to tell us that your valet was in the stateroom you claimed to occupy. Don't bother denying it," he added as Paul opened his mouth to speak. "We have witnesses who will confirm it."

Paul didn't answer for a moment, but stood there considering them, his hands shoved into his trouser pockets. "I see," he said, finally.

"Is that all you have to say for yourself?"

"What would you have me say?"

Matt braced his hands on the table that separated them, leaning toward him. "You were here when Rosalind died. You came here on Thursday, not Friday, and you did it in such a way that no one would know. That looks suspicious to me."

"I don't really care how it looks, detective."

"Where were you that night?"

"I don't remember."

"Don't push me." Matt leaned forward even further, and again Paul's eyes flickered. "I can find that out, too. It'll be better for you if you tell me."

"What I did that night is none of your affair."

"Were you with Rosalind?"

"No. But I don't expect you to believe that."

"Where were you, then? Come on," he said when Paul didn't answer. "If you won't cooperate, we'll have to take you down to the station."

"A threat, detective?"

"No. A promise." Matt kept his gaze steady. When Paul still didn't answer, he abruptly straightened. "Guess that's it, then. Sergeant, take him in."

"No," Paul said, pulling away as Charlie reached for his arm. "Don't."

"You'll talk to us, Mr. Radley?"

"Yes. Dammit." Paul turned away, pulling his etched silver cigar case out from an inner pocket. "I suppose I've no choice. You're right. I was here. But I was not with Rosalind."

"Where were you, then?"

Paul paused a moment, lighting his cigar, and then waved out the match. "With a lady."

"Oh?"

"Yes. We've had a long-standing liaison. She's married, of course."

"And you were engaged."

Paul shrugged. "What does that have to do with anything?"

Not for the first time, Matt pitied Rosalind. "Did Rosalind know about this?"

"Of course not! It's not the sort of thing one talks about."

"Isn't it." Matt peered at him. "Who is she?"

"I can't tell you."

"Oh, come on, Mr. Radley," Matt said, setting down his notebook. "You're not stupid. You know why I'm asking you these questions."

"Of course I do. But if I tell you her husband will find out, and I can assure you, that won't be pleasant. Why do you think I travel as I do? So he won't find out. He comes down from New York on Fridays. I come on Thursdays to avoid him. If he asks, however, I have ticket stubs for Friday."

"Which is what you showed us. So. You were here on the night Rosalind died. That's opportunity. You believed she was seeing someone else; that's motive. And you have the strength needed to strangle a woman. Yet you tell us you were with a lady, but you won't tell us her name." Matt's gaze was hard. "This looks bad, Mr. Radley."

"To you, perhaps. You think I killed Rosalind."

"Didn't you?"

"No."

"I think you did."

"Then prove it. And you'd better have better evidence than you did against Olmstead," he snapped, and stalked out of the room.

"He's right, Cap," Charlie said into the strained silence. "We don't really have any evidence against him."

"Dammit, I know he's right. We'll have to find the evidence. We'll go back to the station, look at the reports one more time." His face was grim. "There's something in them I'm missing, but I'll find it if it kills me. One way or another, we'll get him."

"Yes, Cap."

"And don't call me Cap."

"Anything you say, Cap."

Back in his office, Matt took off his jacket and sat at his desk, eyeing the stack of reports balefully. Dammit. They were close to breaking this case, so close, but not quite there. Radley was right. They didn't yet have the evidence they needed against him. The last thing he wanted to do just now was to comb through reports, but it had to be done. He was not going to arrest another man without first building a solid case against him.

Pulling the first report toward him, he read it carefully, then pushed it aside and read another. And a third. In the early days of the investigation the police work had been thorough, exhaustive. Anyone who had any connection to the murdered girls had been questioned, once and then again. With Rosalind's death, the questioning had broadened to include the summer people. There were reports on the Olmsteads, the Belmonts, the Vanderbilts; reports on Miles Vandenberg and Eliot Payson, on Mamie Fish and Tessie Oelrichs. It was a name in one of these that suddenly leaped out at him, a name that at the beginning of the investigation had meant nothing, but which meant everything now. Matt put the report down and stared into space, putting it all together. Facts that had previously been unrelated now meant something: a tennis game, trips to New York, a red rose in an etched silver vase. Facts that fit so well that he wondered why he hadn't seen it all before.

"Holy Mother of God," Matt muttered, standing so fast that the papers scattered on his desk. He knew. He knew, beyond a shadow of a doubt, who the Cliff Walk Killer was.

The news that Brooke had broken her engagement to Eliot Payson spread quickly. The fact that their relationship was strained had been evident last evening at Lindhurst, when they studiously avoided each other, and it hadn't taken long for the reason to become known. Now, the morning after giving Eliot back his ring, Brooke sat in the morning room at Belle Mer with her aunt and several guests, and tried, as she sipped her tea, to pretend that nothing had changed.

The ritual of morning calls usually didn't proceed in such a way. Usually what it entailed was dressing in one's finest day ensemble, climbing into one's carriage, and stopping at the houses of various friends. There a footman would be dispatched to leave one's calling card. Then, social duty done to that particular acquaintance, it was on to the next house. Rarely did people actually leave their carriages to go inside, since the people they called on were making calls of their own. In such a way, friendships could be maintained without people ever actually having to talk to each other.

Things were different this morning, the news having brought the curious to Belle Mer. Aunt Winifred was furious over this latest turn of events; hadn't they had enough scandal this summer? In the face of her friends' questions, however, she presented as serene a front as Brooke did. Yes, she was sorry about the engagement, but far more concerned about her niece's happiness. She had plans, she proclaimed, and immediately began discussing ideas for a grand dinner party, to be held at Belle Mer. If her guests remained unconvinced, they were too polite to show it.

Over the rim of her teacup, Brooke's gaze met the amused one of Miles Vandenberg, sitting across the room. She rolled her eyes a bit as Winifred elaborated on her plans, and, taking that as a signal of sorts, Miles rose and came to sit next to Brooke on the pink brocade sofa. "So life goes on, it seems," he commented, in a voice meant for her ears alone.

"Apparently," Brooke muttered, curious as to why Miles was here, the only male in a group of women, but glad, as well. Of all the cottagers, he was the only one who seemed to share her views on society. "If everything goes wrong, give a party."

"Not a bad philosophy, actually. Thank you." This to the maid who handed him a fresh cup of tea. "Is that a new girl?"

Brooke looked up in surprise. "Lucy? Yes. Why do you ask?"

"No reason. You had a girl working here. Pretty thing, with red hair."

"Annie?" Brooke said before she could stop herself, and a nasty suspicion crossed her mind. But it couldn't be, she thought, banishing the idea.

"Is that her name?"

"Yes. Annie McKenna."

"Yes, I suppose that's who I meant."

"We had to let her go."

"Who are you talking about, Brooke?" Winifred said.

"Annie, Aunt Winifred."

"Annie?"

"Annie McKenna."

"Who? Oh, her." Winifred made a face and turned back to Mrs. Stanford, seated beside her. "Shocking thing. One of our maids. We had to let her go. Why, she was arrested on Illumination Night, for streetwalking, of all things."

"Well, if I'd known that . . ." Miles drawled, again in a low voice.

"Miles!" Brooke stared at him. "Is that who you're interested in these days? Maids who can't defend themselves against you because you're their employer?"

"You make me sound quite the monster, Brooke." He took a sip of tea. "I thought she was pretty. Nothing wrong with that, is there?"

Remembering what the Vandenbergs' former chef had told her, Brooke wasn't so sure. "I suppose not."

"Next thing you know, you'll be accusing me of being the Cliff Walk Killer."

The suspicion she'd had a few moments ago returned. "Are you?"

He stared at her for a moment, before putting back his head and laughing. "Good God, no! Why would I do something like that? Besides, he's been arrested."

"What is so funny, Miles?" Winifred called.

"Nothing, ma'am," he said, though the corner of his mouth twitched.

"Well, come and talk to me anyway. I could use some amusement."

"Of course. Excuse me, Brooke?"

"Certainly," she murmured, not meeting his eyes. Of all the absurd things for her to say! Of course Miles wasn't a killer. He'd certainly had little to do with Rosalind while she was alive; why would he wish her dead?

"Now," Winifred said in a carrying voice. "What were you talking about?"

"Nothing very much," Miles said, leaning back against the sofa. He should have looked incongruous, out of place, a man lounging against crimson brocade, but somehow he didn't. "Actually, we were discussing the Cliff Walk Killer."

Winifred pursed her lips in distaste. "Oh, that."

"Yes, that. I told you it wasn't interesting."

"Thank God he's been caught," Mrs. Warren, a stout matron of middle age, said. "Why, do you know I had trouble getting any of my staff to go out on errands? They refused to use the Cliff Walk. Can you imagine? They said it wasn't safe, even in broad daylight. Such insolence. I had to let several of them go."

"Yes, I'm relieved it's over," Winifred said mechanically. "Who are you inviting to dinner next week?"

"Oh, my dear, I let my secretary take care of that kind of detail. Of course it would be a relief to you, after what you had to go through."

Winifred's smile was fixed. "Yes."

"I still cannot get over what they did to you and Henry. And then to have it turn out that the real killer was a common laborer."

"Well, it certainly couldn't have been one of us," Mrs. Stanford chimed in. "Such a lower-class crime. And a gardener, of all things."

"Appropriate, considering the roses," Miles commented.

"What roses?"

"The ones that were found near the bodies."

"I never heard that. I must say, though, that I agree with Amelia. I'm glad he's been caught. Aren't you, Miss Cassidy?"

Across the room Brooke sat still as stone. "Yes," she said through stiff lips, hardly aware of what she said, her teacup arrested halfway to her mouth. The roses. No one knew about them. She well remembered Matt telling her that. No one knew roses had been found near the bodies, except for herself, the police, and—the killer. Dear heavens. Her suspicions had been correct. Miles Vandenberg was the Cliff Walk Killer.

16

Matt had spent the previous morning and most of the afternoon gathering evidence. John Harris had come into the station, along with the stewards from *Priscilla*, and Matt had received confirmation of what he had suspected. His suspect had made the trip between New York and Newport many times, though he'd claimed he hadn't. More interestingly, some of those times coincided with Nellie Farrell's trips to New York. Since he'd used Nellie as an alibi for the night of Rosalind's murder, that prompted Matt to send patrolmen with pictures of the suspect to Nellie's neighborhood. Though none of the neighbors could identify him conclusively, more than one said that it looked like the man who had called on her. Clinching that aspect of the case was the elderly gentleman at the Reading Room who had admitted testily that, yes, he'd known who Nellie's protector was, but until this moment hadn't wanted to implicate him. They had their man for one murder. Matt wanted more, though.

And this morning, he'd gotten it. Yesterday he'd made a long-distancer call to a Sergeant O'Neill in New York, and O'Neill had returned the call today, talking for a long time. After exhaustive questioning at the city's best hotels, he had finally found a clerk who admitted that, yes, the man in question had spent time there, and yes, he'd sometimes been with one particular girl. Yes, that girl, in the picture the sergeant was showing him, he insisted. Matt smiled grimly when he'd heard that. The girl in the picture, taken from the society pages of the

Herald, was none other than Rosalind Sinclair. Their suspect was implicated in Rosalind's death, and by association, the others.

Armed with this evidence, Matt had next to face a long interview with the chief, who was both pleased and disgruntled. The thought of arresting yet another cottager for the murders gave him dyspepsia, he said, but in the end he, too, had to admit that the facts were overwhelming. Within an hour, armed with an arrest warrant, as well as a warrant to search the suspect's estate, Matt and Charlie were driving in a buggy on Bellevue Avenue, the paddy wagon behind. They were at last going to solve the Cliff Walk killings.

It was disconcerting, then, to reach their destination and to be told their man was not at home. Only mildly frustrated, Matt presented the search warrant to a flustered butler, telling his officers precisely what to look for, particularly any knives that could have been used on Nellie, and for the heavy work shoes the killer had worn. They would wait for their man to come home, rather than try to take him in a public place, since he was expected to return for luncheon. And, by the way, Matt asked casually, where was he this morning? The butler, upset over the invasion of his domain and the disruption of his orderly routine, answered distractedly. His employer had gone to Belle Mer, he believed.

Alarm flashed through Matt, making him rise abruptly to his feet. Beside him Charlie was reaching for his hat, apparently as concerned as he was. They couldn't wait, not now. "He's got no reason to hurt her, Cap," Charlie said, as they hurried out to the drive and climbed into the buggy. "She doesn't know anything. She's all right."

"I know." Matt's tone was grim as he picked up the reins and sent the buggy speeding down the drive. Hard to explain this strange sense of urgency he felt, except that it was getting stronger. The presence of the suspect at Belle Mer meant only one thing. Brooke was in danger. "But we'll take him there, anyway," he said, and set the buggy at a spanking pace, heading for Belle Mer, to arrest Miles Vandenberg.

* * *

Brooke looked up and found Miles regarding her again, this time without amusement. There was, instead, a chilling calculation in his eyes, making her go cold inside. He knew. He knew he'd made a mistake, and that she'd figured it out.

The same terror she'd felt the previous afternoon, when she had realized that Eliot was angry enough to kill, returned, magnified a hundredfold. Miles had proven himself a killer several times over, and he had attacked Annie because she could identify him. He had—dear God, he had followed them to the kitchen the night of the ball. He was relentless, ruthless, and if he thought Brooke were a danger, he'd stop at nothing to eliminate her.

Around her the chatter went on as if nothing had happened. No one seemed to notice Miles's stillness, or that he continued to stare at Brooke. She was safe, she reassured herself. So long as she stayed in her own house, she was safe from him. Matt had been right in warning her not to be alone with anyone.

Matt. Dear heavens, he'd have to know. For all she knew, he could be off working on some other case, but she still had to let him know what she'd discovered. With shaky fingers she reached out to touch the silver teapot, as Winifred spoke to Miles, momentarily distracting him. The pot felt scalding to her icy hand, but still it provided her with the excuse she needed. "The tea's gone cold," she murmured. "I'll see about getting some fresh."

As casually as possible, she rose and pressed the button in the wall, signaling to the staff that service was required in the morning room. Then, as if leaving one's guests were a normal occurrence, she slipped out of the room, careful to keep her back straight and her movements slow, easy. Once out in the hall, however, she dropped the pretense of casualness, picking up her skirts in both hands and setting off at a run.

"Miss?" Hutton said, startled, as she passed him.

Brooke ignored him. The house's only telephone was mounted on a wall in the back hallway, where its ringing wouldn't disturb the family. It was her lifeline now. Out of breath, she reached for the receiver, rattling the handle to signal the operator. "Come on, come on," she muttered into the mouthpiece, dancing from one foot to the other in impatience and fear. "Come on the line—oh! Operator. Get me the police."

"I wouldn't do that," a silky voice said behind her, and something cold and sharp pressed against her throat, making her freeze.

"Who are you calling, please?" the operator's mechanical-sounding voice said through the receiver.

"Hang up the phone, Brooke," that same silky voice said. Miles's voice. "Now."

Brooke swallowed, and the receiver fell from her nerveless grasp, to bang against the wall. The operator squawked indignantly, but Brooke was beyond noticing. "I'll scream."

"If you were going to scream, you would have already done so." The knife pressed deeper into her skin, and she felt a drop of wetness trickle down her neck. "You know I'll use this if I have to."

"Y-yes."

"Good. Don't make me do it."

From somewhere Brooke found the courage to raise her eyes to his, cold, pitiless, remorseless. "You will, anyway," she challenged. "You can't let me live, with what I know."

"What do you know?" He bared his teeth in a smile.

"You're the Cliff Walk Killer."

"So you did figure it out." He sighed. "I'm afraid, then, there's nothing else I can do," he said, and gripping her arm, marched her toward the back door.

"Where are you taking me?"

"You'll see."

"You won't get away with this," she said, as they emerged onto the lawn, a brilliant emerald in the summer sun. The peacefulness of the scene only added to the surreal feeling of the moment. This couldn't be happening. "Too many people will see us."

"Will they? All they'll see is that we're taking a stroll."

"With a knife at my throat."

Surprisingly, he laughed. "I like you, Brooke. You've got spirit. Pity I have to do this."

"You don't, you know. If I figured it out, you know Matt will."

"Matt? Ah, yes, our esteemed Detective Devlin. No, he won't, my dear. He thinks Paul Radley is the killer."

"Paul? Why in the world would he think that?"

"Because I pointed him in that direction. Of course, all Radley is guilty of is being indiscreet enough to let himself be seen here when he's conducting an affair with a married lady. A useful fact for me to know. Relax, my dear," he said, as she suddenly tried to tug her arm free. They were halfway across the lawn now. Halfway to the Cliff Walk. "Very unwise of you to struggle. Try to appear as if we're enjoying a pleasant walk on a beautiful morning. Ah, look at the view of the sea. Shall we go on the Cliff Walk to see it better?"

"You're insane."

He chuckled. "Insane? Hardly. No, I'm very, very sane, my dear. I'm merely protecting myself."

"Is that why you did it?" she asked, as he pulled her through the gates of the Olmstead estate onto the Cliff Walk. She had to know, and if she could distract him, perhaps she could escape. "Were the girls you killed some kind of threat to you?"

"Not all of them, no. Only Rosalind."

"Then why kill the others?"

"To make it seem there was a maniac on the loose."

She stared at him. "You *are* insane."

He chuckled again, a low, evil sound, as he hustled her along the narrow, sandy path. "Rosalind had to be eliminated. I chose a way to do so that would keep suspicion from falling on me, and I made certain the police looked in a different direction. Thus, the roses. Very quick of you to pick up on that, by the way."

"You made it appear as if my Uncle Henry were the killer."

"Guilty." His self-deprecating smile didn't reach his eyes. "I knew about his hobby, of course; everyone does. Clever of me, wasn't it, to use the rose he's well known for growing? I like the Cliff Walk, don't you? So convenient. You don't agree?" he added, as she shuddered, involuntarily. "Yes, of course I tried to make the police think Henry did it, and when he lost his cuff link at the Reading Room, I found that quite useful, too. What good would it have done me to eliminate Rosalind if I got caught for it?"

"But why? What did she ever do to you?"

Miles stopped unexpectedly, making her stumble. "She was blackmailing me. She was pregnant, the little bitch—didn't know that, did you?—and she was going to tell, unless I agreed to divorce my wife and marry her."

They were close to the edge of the cliff, too close. Far below the waves broke upon cruel-looking, jagged rocks. In spite of his restraining hand, Brooke took a step back, and the knife pressed into her throat. "You were the man she was sneaking out to meet?"

"Yes. Our Rosalind liked to live dangerously. We started seeing each other, oh, last spring sometime. Clever of her, wasn't it, to use a maid's uniform? Of course, that's what gave me the idea. The other maids were perfect camouflage. I killed her here, you know," he said with chilling casualness, swinging her around, and she realized they were at the exact spot where Rosalind's body had been found. "It was easy enough to do. My right hand might be weak, but there's enough strength in my left to make up for it. No, it was really quite easy. I let her think I was giving in to her demands so that she wouldn't suspect anything, and then I followed her. Well, I couldn't very well let her do what she planned, could I?"

"B-but—"

"After all, if I got a divorce, I'd be penniless. My wife has all the money, you know. I've been poor before. It's not an experience I'd care to repeat. Nor will I do so, now." His lips thinned, making his face look cruel, hard; the face of a killer, not the man she had thought she knew. "I hate to do this, Brooke, but you've given me no choice. I will not let anything threaten my way of life."

"You won't get away with it," Brooke repeated. "This time you'll be caught. Too many people saw us together."

"Ah, but I'm not stupid, Brooke," he said, beginning to walk again, so fast that she nearly had to run to keep up with him. To her side the cliff fell away at a precipitous height, and far, far below, the hungry waves waited, beating on the rocks. "The cliff is high here. It should do quite well."

"You wouldn't—"

"Ah, but I would. So sad, Brooke. I shall have to run back to the house and admit my misdeeds. I shall tell them, you see, that I've always been attracted to you. I have, you know. That's why they'll believe me. And I shall say that when I told you you became so distraught—I am a married man, after all—that you ran from me. Unfortunately, you weren't looking where you were going, and you fell over the cliff."

"No."

"Yes. I can't very well use the knife, can I? So messy, and I'll be a suspect. But this." He grinned, but his eyes were empty, cold. "It will cause a scandal, I imagine, but I'll weather it. No one will suspect."

"Matt will!" she cried, digging in her heels as he pulled her toward the edge. "Matt will suspect and he'll come after you."

"But it will be too late for you, won't it?" He hooked his leg behind hers, and, arm flailing for balance, Brooke went down hard onto her knees. "It's over for you, Brooke. I'm sorry, but—"

"Let her go." The voice rang out in the warm summer air, carrying even over the crashing of the breakers below, and Miles went still. "Let her go, Vandenberg."

Miles looked up, and Brooke, scrambling for balance, managed to raise herself enough to see what was happening. Charlie was crouched a few feet away, his revolver drawn, but it was on Matt her eyes focused. Matt, who also held a revolver. "Matt, look out! He has a knife!" she cried.

"Ah, Detective Devlin," Miles said at the same time, pulling Brooke to her feet. "Such good timing. Do you know, we nearly had a nasty accident? Poor Miss Cassidy nearly went over the cliff. I caught her just in time."

"Don't believe him! He did it, Matt. He's the Cliff Walk Killer."

Miles chuckled. "Now why would you say something like that?"

"Let her go," Matt said again. "I know all about it, Vandenberg. It won't do you any good to hold her. Let her go."

Miles's eyes shifted from him to Charlie. "Do you know, I don't think so?" His grasp on Brooke tightened as he pulled her to him, one arm across her throat. The knife pressed into her skin again, making her briefly close her eyes. "You may have a revolver, Devlin, but I have her. I don't think you'll shoot."

"No?" Matt said, and fired.

The report was deafening, echoing off the cliffs and startling seagulls into flight, squawking. There was a sharp pain at Brooke's throat, and then she was falling, slowly, slowly, to the ground. Had she been hit? She didn't know. She knew only that the terrible pressure around her throat was gone, that for some reason Miles had released her. Or had he thrown her over? The thought jolted her, and she screamed, just as her face hit the dirt.

She was on the Cliff Walk, and she wasn't hurt. At least, she didn't think she was. She had little time to feel relief, however; hands were grabbing at her upper arms, pulling her up. Blindly she struggled, striking out, and someone yelped in protest. "Brooke! It's me, Brooke. It's Matt."

"Matt?" She looked up at him, kneeling before her, and her muscles went slack. "Oh, Matt!" she exclaimed, and threw herself into his arms. They closed around her with comforting solidity, easing her terrible shaking, making her feel safe and protected. "Matt."

"Hush. It's over, Brooke. You're safe." Abruptly he pushed her away, staring into her face. "Did he hurt you? Because, if he did . . ."

"I—I'm all right. But Miles—"

"Matt got him right in the knee," Charlie said, almost cheerfully. Brooke turned her head to see him standing behind her, his revolver held on Miles, who was rolling around on the path, hands clutching his leg and his face contorted. "Good shot, Cap."

"Thanks." Matt peered into her face, and his finger reached up to touch her neck. "You're bleeding."

"Am I?" she asked, foolishly.

"Yes. Are you sure you're all right?"

"Yes. Oh, Matt, he did it! He's the killer."

"I know."

"He told me all about it, why he killed Rosalind and the other girls—"

"I know," Matt repeated. "We got the evidence against him yesterday. We went to his house this morning to arrest him, and found out he was here. Then we found out you'd both gone outside. God." His arms tightened around her. "When I saw you with him, and realized what he was trying to do—"

"I figured it out, you see," she babbled. "He said something about roses, and I realized he wasn't supposed to know about it and he saw that I knew. I tried to call you, Matt, I did."

"I know. Brooke, I—"

"Matt," Charlie said. "We've got company."

"What?" Matt said, looking over his shoulder. He loosened his hold on Brooke. She didn't want to let him go, but she was aware of voices coming near. Looking up, she saw Hutton running toward her, looking like a long-legged blackbird. Behind him were several patrolmen.

"Detective Devlin?" one of them said.

"Bring that man back to the station," Matt pointed at Miles, "and book him."

"On what charge?"

"Assault, for now. I want him locked up good and tight."

"Yes, sir," the patrolman said, and pulled Miles to his feet with an ungentle grip. Brooke averted her head as they shuffled past her, though Miles, supported on either side by two patrolmen and in what must have been terrible pain, stared straight ahead, dignified even under arrest. She had liked Miles. She really had. If he could have fooled her, and everyone else, for so long, what other secrets might people be hiding? The thought made her shudder.

"Brooke?" Matt said.

"Yes?"

"I'll take you home."

"All right," she said, though at that moment she wasn't certain where home was anymore. Newport was lost to her, and yet she had never fit into the world of the 400. She didn't think she ever would.

"Come on." His voice was gentle. "You've had a shock." He reached for her hand, and went still. "Your ring is gone."

Brooke looked down at her hand. "I gave it back."

Matt drew in his breath. "You did?"

"I did," she said, and met his eyes. Their gazes held for a long moment, and peace settled over her. She was wrong. Here was where she belonged. Here was home.

"Good," Matt said, and, helping her to her feet, linked his arm through hers. Together, they walked back toward the gate.

"I told you I could help with the case."

"So you did. But God help me, Brooke, I never meant for it to be this way."

"Well, it wouldn't have been if I'd waited until Miles left to try to call you."

"You took about ten years off my life."

"I'm sorry," she said, and though she never again wanted to experience such terror as she had just felt, already it was fading. With it went the images that had haunted her since Rosalind's body had been found. "I think we make a good team, don't you?"

"Definitely." Matt grinned down at her. "Come on, partner. Let's go get this thing settled."

Epilogue

In the months that followed, many articles pertaining to the case of the Cliff Walk killings and the people who had been involved in it appeared in various newspapers.

From the *Newport Daily News,* September 2, 1895:
POLICE NOTES.

Detective Matthew Devlin resigned his position with the Newport police force today. Detective Devlin's arrest of Miles Vandenberg for the Cliff Walk killings caused upheaval among the force, though Mr. Vandenberg has confessed to the killings. Detective Devlin's resignation was expected, and was accepted by Chief of Police Read.

Mr. Devlin will be removing to New York City, where he has been offered a position as detective of the police force there.

From the *New York Times,* December 11, 1895:

Miles Vandenberg, of Newport, Rhode Island, was found guilty of the crime of murder in the first degree in Newport yesterday. Mr. Vandenberg was convicted of murdering five women in Newport last summer, Maureen Quick, Kathleen Shannon, Mary Manning, Ellen Farrell, and Rosalind Sinclair. The death of Miss Sinclair, late daughter of Mr. and Mrs. George Sinclair of New York, shocked everyone and brought a large number of spectators to the courtroom to hear the trial. When the verdict was read, Mr. Vandenberg showed no emotion, but Mrs. Vandenberg, an invalid, became hysterical and had to be carried from the courtroom. Judge Baker thanked the jury for their time and then lectured Mr. Vandenberg as to the seriousness of his crimes, and announced that sentencing for the crime will be on January fourth. Mr. Vandenberg was returned to the Marlborough Street Jail to await sentencing. He is expected to receive life imprisonment . . .

From the *Newport Daily News*, December 22, 1895:

Miss Brooke Cassidy of New York and Mr. Matthew Devlin, formerly of Newport, were married yesterday at the home of the bride's uncle, Mr. Henry Olmstead, in New York City. The bride was given in marriage by her uncle. She wore a French gown of ivory satin with a train embroidered with seed pearls and lace. Her veil of Alençon lace is a family heirloom, having been worn by her aunt, Mrs. Henry Olmstead, and her mother, the late Katherine Cassidy of Newport. The bride also carried an ivory fan and a bouquet of white roses and baby's breath, supplied by Mr. Olmstead from his greenhouse, and wore a pearl choker given her by her aunt. Her maid of honor, Miss Iris Gardner, wore a gown of blue silk and also carried a bouquet of white roses. The parlor where the wedding was held was decorated with white roses and narcissus.

Mr. Devlin, a detective with the New York police, was attended by Charles Sweeney. After the ceremony a wedding breakfast was held. Guests included Mr. and Mrs. Cornelius Vanderbilt II, Mr. and Mrs. Herman Oelrichs, and Mr. and Mrs. Octavius Low. The groom's parents, Sean and Mary Devlin of Middletown, were present, as was his sister, Mrs. Patrick Reilly of Boston. The bride is the daughter of the late Michael and Katherine Cassidy of Newport.

Mr. and Mrs. Devlin plan to take a bridal trip to

Europe aboard the American Line ship *New York*. Upon their return, they will reside in New York.

None of the articles mentioned that the new Mrs. Devlin had taken up amateur detecting. That was something New York society would learn soon enough.

Author's Note

Writing a historically based novel is difficult; when it includes well-known social history, it is harder. Students of the Gilded Age, and of Newport history, will notice that I took some liberty with facts. For example, the first Newport detective division, formed in 1893, only had one detective. For purposes of the story, I enlarged the division. Also, Mrs. William K. (Alva) Vanderbilt did return to Newport after her divorce, in an action called "the Newport declaration of war," but that was at a different time than I have portrayed. Real people whose names are mentioned in this book include Chief of Police Harwood Read, Judge Baker, Colonel Sheffield, Senator Burdick, Captain A. G. Simmons of the Fall River Line, and some of the members of the 400. Everyone else is fictional.

Belle Mer is based on an actual house, the Breakers, pictured on the dust jacket. For purposes of the story, I have made some changes to the layout of the house. The Breakers, as well as several other Newport mansions, is beautifully maintained by the Newport Preservation Society and is open to the public. Anyone visiting the area should make it a point to tour at least one of the mansions, to get a glimpse of a bygone era. And don't forget to stroll on the Cliff Walk, which is free to all and a wonderful walk on a sunny day. For anyone wishing to learn more about Newport, I recommend reading *The Last Resorts*, by Cleveland Amory, and *The Golden Summers*, by Richard O'Connor.

As for the entertainments, I haven't told the half of it. There was the White Ball, whose hostess wanted the Navy to anchor offshore for decoration (they didn't); the Dog's Dinner, a birthday party for dogs; the Mother Goose Ball, at which all the guests wore costumes from nursery rhymes; the infamous occasion at which Prince Del Drago, a monkey, was guest of honor . . .

In writing this book, I had help from a great many people. First and foremost are Meredith Bernstein and Jennifer Sawyer, who both believed enough in me to let me try writing something completely different. My mother, Madelyn Sweeney Kruger, and my writing buddy, Rona Zable, made up a great reading committee. In research, I had help from Detective Robert Eccleston, New Bedford Police Department, retired; Michael McKenna, Public Affairs Officer, Newport Police Department; Officer Joseph Subin of the Newport Police Department; John Gosson, curator of the Marine Museum at Fall River, Mass.; and the staffs of the Newport Public Library and the New Bedford Free Public Library. Any mistakes in this book are mine, not theirs.

I'd also like to thank all my relatives and friends who so kindly allowed me to use their names and, in some cases, to kill them off. I love you all.

Please turn the page
for a sneak preview of

NO HONEYMOON FOR DEATH
by Mary Kruger

the second book in the
Gilded Age series of mysteries
featuring Brooke and Matt Devlin.

NO HONEYMOON FOR DEATH
is on sale now at your local bookstore.

Prologue

New York City, 1896

This damned voyage to Europe was going to ruin everything. Everything. It had taken a lot of work, and a lot of thought, to make plans, to work everything out to the last detail. How did one get rid of someone else without becoming a suspect? There were so many problems involved, from the actual deed to disposing of the body. And then there was the acting. It would be necessary to put up a certain front before others; not just the police, but friends and acquaintances. The police should never be underestimated, either. Corrupt they were, certainly, ignoring all sorts of crimes, as the recent Lexow commission investigations had shown, but smart, too. It meant being careful in every reaction, appearing bewildered, perhaps even a little guilty, as innocent people so often did, but not grief-stricken. Never that. Too much was known about the real state of affairs for that to be plausible.

And so the plans had proceeded, until this damnable voyage had been proposed. No way to get out of it, either, without looking suspicious, not when one had mentioned so often the desire to go to Europe. The plans would have to be postponed—but wait. There was one unanticipated piece of luck, and a circumstance that would actually make things easier. It should be possible to think of a way around the problems this voyage posed for its one major advantage. How much simpler it would be to dispose of a body at sea.

It would happen aboard the ship, then. The person who had plotted so long, so carefully, sat back, smiling. Yes. The enemy would meet his fate aboard the ship.

1

New York, April 15, 1896

Matt and Brooke Devlin had the first major quarrel of their married life as they were about to embark on their honeymoon.

It began, of all things, over Matt's clothes. Not that he looked shabby. In the months since his marriage he'd acquired a wardrobe that startled him, including a suit from Brooks Brothers and an honest-to-God dinner jacket. He was most proud, however, of the dress blue uniform of a detective sergeant in the New York police department, which hung in his closet. Not bad for an Irish boy from Newport's fifth ward. When that Irish lad married a girl from the highest reaches of society, however, his life was bound to change, and that was part of the problem. Sometimes he didn't feel like himself. Sometimes the privileges of his new life made him uneasy.

Take this honeymoon, for example. Looking out the window of the hansom cab as it drove along Fifth Avenue to the North River pier where they would board the Atlantic liner *New York*, Matt frowned. On the face of it, it seemed a reasonable idea: to take time for him and Brooke to be alone, just the two of them, and what more romantic setting than a ship at sea? However, when they were traveling not just first class, but in a suite deluxe, and when the honeymoon was expected to last some three months, it was too much. He had been on the police force only a short time, and now he was taking an extended holiday. If that caused raised eyebrows at headquarters, it was nothing compared to his inner turmoil. He loved his work. He also loved his wife, and marrying her had meant making changes to his life. This change, however, made him feel guilty and uneasy.

And so, when Brooke had made a perfectly innocent remark that, since she intended to visit the Paris couturiers Matt should look in at a Savile Row tailor's, he'd exploded. He was a cop, by God, and an honest one, and that was something hard-come-by in these days, when everyone was routinely on the take. How did she think it looked for him to be away from the job for so long, and he only on the force for seven months? If he wasn't good enough for her, he concluded bitterly, maybe she shouldn't have married him.

Brooke's stunned silence at this unexpected attack lasted only a moment, and before long they had a proper row going. Now they were settled in opposite corners of the hansom cab, looking out the windows at the congestion caused by traffic at the intersection with Broadway, and fuming. It was a fine, warm day, if not so humid as the day before, and the signs of spring in New York were everywhere: nursery maids in the parks pushing prams; gaily striped awnings on shops; burgeoning flowers in window boxes. Neither noticed. The three months loomed before them like a prison sentence.

Matt recovered first, as always. His temper was quick to flare up, and just as quick to die down. "I'm sorry," he said into the strained silence, turning to look at her. "What I said—it was out of line."

Brooke stared fixedly out the window. He had learned, to his cost, that she could hold onto her anger as long as she wished. "I was a cop's daughter," she said, finally, without turning.

"I know." Of course he knew. Her father and his had been partners together on the Newport police force, and he and Brooke had grown up together.

"Have I ever put on airs with you, Matt? Have I?"

The hansom cab moved at last, making Matt nod in relief. Traffic was bad this morning, the streets crowded with cabs and carts and wagons, and if they got held up any longer they'd miss the ship. "You don't mean to," he said.

That made her turn. "What?" She leaned forward, her chin jutting out, and if she'd been standing her hands would have been on her hips. "When have I ever acted like that, Matt? When?"

"Well . . ." He let the silence spin out, interrupted only by the clamor of iron-covered wheels on pavement, clopping hooves, and the clanging of the Broadway cable cars. "Sometimes you do sound like your aunt."

It took a moment, but then the corners of her mouth twitched, as he'd hoped they would. Then she was smiling, if a trifle ruefully, for they both agreed that her Aunt Winifred, while meaning well, tended to be too concerned with society and position. Furthermore, while Brooke and Matt were honeymooning, Winifred would be decorating their new apartment at the Dakota. The thought made Matt shudder. "Heaven forbid. If I become like her, Matt, I expect you to tell me."

"Oh, I will." He smiled back at her, and then the smile faded. "It's just a hard time to be leaving. Here I am, new on the force. Came in as a detective and not a patrolman, and that's enough to make them resent me."

"For heaven's sake, Matt, you've been a policeman long enough, and you've certainly proven yourself."

"Doesn't matter." He stretched out his hand, and, after a moment, she took it. "Plus, I'm married to a rich woman—no, I'm not saying that to upset you," he said, as she opened her mouth to protest. "You know, and I know, that that doesn't matter to me. But others don't see it that way. Especially," his face darkened, "when I take a three month honeymoon."

"Aunt Winifred meant well," she said apologetically, for the honeymoon was a wedding gift from her aunt and uncle.

"I know." The truth was, Brooke wanted it, too. In the old days, before her parents' death, before she'd gone to live with her wealthy relatives, had she longed after such things? Or had she been as down to earth as he remembered? "I'm leaving behind a lot of work. There's that body that turned up yesterday. Looks like a robbery gone wrong, and God knows that's a lot of work. And the fraud case I was working on, he comes up for trial next week, and—"

"Matt." She put her finger to his lips. "Someone will handle it all."

"I know," he said, sounding not the least convinced.

"It's not as if you're going to be away forever. If you give it a chance, you might even like it."

His smile was wry. "That's what I'm afraid of."

"And you're not the only cop in New York."

"True." Hard to admit, though. Maybe he did need to get away for a time, away from the random violence and enforcing nonsensical laws, away from the crime-ridden world that sometimes felt like it was the only reality. "Maybe I'll even like a life of leisure," he said, with self-mockery that held just a hint of truth in it. Maybe he would, and that was part of the problem.

The cab came to a stop again. Washington Square, with the new white arch, and more traffic. But then they were turning, driving down Christopher Street through the heart of Greenwich Village. "We're nearly here."

Brooke leaned over to look out his window. "Oh, good." She straightened her hat, some silly affair of straw and feathers that somehow looked good on her. "Thank heaven we sent the trunks ahead. And the maid." She made a face. Like everything else, the maid was Aunt Winifred's idea, to help Brooke dress. Essential, considering the clothes she'd brought—and why women needed so much he didn't know—but something Brooke nevertheless disliked. So did he. "We're here in good time. Sailing day is always so confusing."

Matt held out his hand, a peace offering, accepting at last this part of his life. "I'm glad we're doing this."

Her smile lit her eyes. "So am I," she said, just as the hansom jolted onto rough cobblestones, sending them swaying, and then coming to an abrupt stop.

The door opened, and the driver stuck his head in. "This's as far as I can go. Crowded here, this morning."

Matt nodded. "Thank you," he said, handing the driver the fare, and then he rose, stepping out. In the act of turning to help Brooke down, he stopped, staring. "Holy—."

Brooke glanced up as she emerged from the cab. "What is it—oh, the ship."

"That's our ship?"

She cast him a glance as she stepped to the ground. "Yes, Matt."

"Holy—it's big."

"Well, what did you expect?" Brooke took his arm as they joined the throngs of people, all straining to reach the ship. Matt continued to stare. From this far back on the pier he couldn't see much; just the sharp clipper bow of the liner, and three tall black smokestacks banded in white, all in a line. The stern of the ship was lost in the distance, seemingly halfway across the Hudson to New Jersey. A huge ship, a floating city, and for a man from a small, insular town, who hadn't yet become accustomed to New York's crowding and chaos, it was both daunting and exciting.

Beside Matt, her arm tucked through his as they made their way across the pier, Brooke smiled. It wasn't often she saw him flustered, but certain things seemed to stun him: Aunt Winifred's extravagances, for example, and now this ship. Not that she blamed him. Brooke had made the Atlantic crossing twice before, but she found the prospect thrilling, too. Especially on a ship as large and luxurious as the *New York*.

The pier was chaos. Around them milled people and carriages and conveyances; cabin class passengers, like them, in their finery, the men's top hats glistening in the sun, the women sweltering in their furs on this unseasonably warm spring morning. Hansom cabs moved nimbly through the crowd, disgorging their passengers, while heavy drays filled with produce trundled across the cobblestones towards the sharply-slanted ramp where their goods would be loaded aboard. There were well-wishers and curiosity seekers and passengers, all raising a cacophony of sound that almost overwhelmed the rumble of the ship's engines and the sharp cries of the gulls wheeling overhead. Almost, but not quite. The chaos of sailing day meant one thing. She would be at sea again, and after being pent up in the city for what felt like ages, Brooke found the prospect exciting.

"Is it always like this?" Matt shouted over the babble as they pushed their way towards the gangplank, his hand holding hers tightly so that they wouldn't get separated in the crowd.

"Yes," Brooke called back, hastily reaching up to straighten her hat, which was in danger of coming loose as she was jostled by someone in the crowd. It was a new hat, too, of Leghorn straw with ostrich feathers dyed a pale peach to match her walking suit of peach and amber, and one of her favorites.

"Watch it there!" Matt glared at the man who had jostled her, though he was already several feet away. "Do you have everything?"

"What?"

"Your purse, watch, jewelry. Did he take anything?"

"What?" Brooke glanced down at her purse, held securely by her side. "No one took anything from me."

"Prime crowd for pickpockets," he muttered, drawing her arm through his, his narrowed eyes scanning the people around them.

"For heaven's sake, Matt. There are no pickpockets here."

"How do you know?"

"I just do. Come, there's the gangplank at last. Heavens, what a queue!"

"If we'd left when I wanted to, we wouldn't have to wait," Matt grumbled as they joined the end of a long, long line.

"It's just past nine, Matt, and the ship doesn't sail for another hour. Besides," she added with serene self-confidence, "it won't sail without us."

"Huh," Matt said, but he subsided, looking again at the ship. From here it rose above him, a solid expanse of black steel pierced at intervals by round portholes. The white-painted superstructure, like a long, low building dropped onto the deck, was surrounded by masts and funnels and davits for lifeboats, and surmounted by those three huge smokestacks. From them smoke already belched, as the ship's engines heated the steam that would propel them across the Atlantic. It looked solid and steady, and yet Matt didn't trust it one bit. He'd grown up near the ocean, and he'd heard of too many disasters at sea to be entirely at ease.

They inched their way up the gangplank, while Brooke conversed with the people around them, many of whom she knew. Matt's uneasiness grew, until at last they were at the top of the gangplank, aboard the ship. A blue-uniformed man took their tickets; another pointed out the general direction of their cabin. With that behind them the pressure of the crowd lessened, and Matt relaxed a little. Once he got settled, knew where he was, he might even enjoy himself.

"Let's explore a little bit," he said, as Brooke turned towards a doorway leading inside. "I'd like to know where everything is."

"We can't. At least, not now."

Matt followed her as she turned into the first of a bewildering succession of passages. "Why not?"

"We have guests coming to our suite to see us off, have you forgotten?" Up a staircase, and out onto a teak-floored deck. To one side was a railing, and beyond that a warehouse-lined wharf; to the other the deckhouse, dotted here and there by doors and windows and bisected by corridors. The deck itself was wide, and divided into two sections by an awning deck of canvas supported by steel, near the railing, above which hung lifeboats on davits. Nearer to the deckhouse some passengers were already sitting in steamer chairs, while the passageway formed by the awning deck was bustling with people preparing for departure. "I don't want Aunt Winifred to get there before we do."

"Can't have that."

"No, of course not, since she's paying for it."

Matt stopped. "I thought that was Henry." He understood Henry and Winifred Olmstead's reasons for paying for this trip. He did. But it was a sad day when a man wasn't even allowed to pay for his own honeymoon.

Brooke turned. "Oh, Matt. I didn't mean—"

"I know you didn't," he said, and though his voice was still clipped he reached for her arm. "Never mind. Is our suite around here?"

"It should be." Brooke stopped at one of the corridors. Glancing down it, Matt could see doors opening off it, and the other side of the deck. "In fact, it should be here," Brooke said, and, as if by magic, a white-jacketed steward appeared.

"Mr. and Mrs. Devlin? This way," he said, opening one of the doors.

"Thank you." Brooke sailed into the room; Matt, a bit more bemused, followed, stepping into a sitting room furnished with velvet-upholstered sofas and chairs. Beyond was the bedroom, equally luxurious with its big brass bed, and to the side was a private bathroom, with a convex wall to follow the curve of the smokestack. The windows overlooked the promenade deck. God only knew what this cost, he thought, turning from checking that the blinds fitted tightly, letting in neither light nor curious eyes, to see Brooke bouncing on the bed. " 'Alone at last,' she said dramatically," Brooke said, smiling up at him, and all his irritation, all his uneasiness, dissolved. This was their honeymoon. Nothing else mattered.

He held out his hand to her, and she rose, coming into his arms. She had just raised her face to his when there was a knock on the outside door, followed by the sound of it opening. "Brooke? Matthew? Are you here?"

"Oh, heavens." Brooke and Matt sprang apart, he straightening his tie, she smoothing her hair. "Yes, Aunt Winifred. We just got here ourselves."

"Really, Brooke, that was cutting it close, wasn't it?" Winifred Olmstead gazed about the suite with narrowed eyes. "This will do, I suppose," she said, thus dismissing the overstuffed sofa and armchairs, the porcelain fixtures in the lavatory, the thick pile carpets. "If one must travel, and I don't know why one should when there is *mal de mêr* to consider, then one should do so in comfort. The *St. Paul* is an ugly ship," she went on, running a gloved finger across the top of a mahogany dresser and frowning, even though the glove remained spotless, "and *Campania* rattles, there is no other word for it. Cunard always was more concerned with speed than with their passengers' comfort. No, I did well in choosing this ship for you. I dare say you'll enjoy yourselves."

Matt glanced at Brooke and then as quickly looked away at the laughter he saw bubbling in her eyes. "It was very good of you, ma'am," he said, in a voice that was only a bit strangled, and held out his hand. "Henry. Good to see you."

"And you, too, my boy." Henry's hands went back in his trouser pockets after he'd shaken Matt's hand, as was his habit. It was easy to ignore Henry Olmstead in the presence of his forceful wife, but in the past months he and Matt had grown to like each other. Even if Matt had once arrested him for murder, falsely, as it turned out. "Sure you'll survive all of this?" he added, his voice lowered.

Matt shrugged. "God knows. And then Europe, afterwards." He paused. "It's a generous gift, Henry."

Henry waved that off. "Brooke means a lot to us." He looked up at Matt, then, his eyes unexpectedly keen. "We want her to be happy."

"I know that." Something in Matt's tone must have been reassuring, for Henry nodded, and the intent look left his eyes. Matt knew the truth, though. Henry was a more complex man than he appeared. "I think," he began, and at that moment there was another knock on the door. Nodding at Henry, he crossed the sitting room to open the door.

"Matt, my boy," boomed the man who stood there. He sauntered in, his shoulders thrown back and chest thrust out, as if he owned the world. "Came to see you off. Done well for yourself, my boy, that you have."

"Thank you." Matt shot another glance at Brooke and saw that she was suppressing laughter again. "I don't believe you've met my wife's relatives. Mr. and Mrs. Olmstead, Thomas Nevesey."

"Delighted to meet you," Nevesey boomed, holding out his hand. He was a small man, and yet his presence filled the room. His sandy mustache bristled with vitality, and his tan herringbone suit, while of impeccable cut, seemed on him to be almost garish. "Let me guess. Republicans, are you?"

"Tom," Matt muttered.

"Indeed." Winifred's voice was glacial. "I've heard of you, Mr. Nevesey."

"Don't doubt you have. Your niece married a good man, Mr. Olmstead. I hope you know that."

"I'm aware of that." Henry's eyes held the same twinkle as Brooke's. "You are Matt's, ah, ward boss, I believe it's called?"

"That I am." Nevesey stood with his legs braced, as if the ship were already at sea, his thumbs tucked into his vest pockets. "Helped Matt get his job, I did. Can always use a man like him on the force."

"Er, yes," Matt put in, fidgeting, hating the appearance of impropriety. Nevesey hadn't really gotten Matt his job, but he might just help him keep it. Last year the dauntless Theodore Roosevelt had been named to the board of police commissioners; he had since waged a one-man campaign to clean up the corruption uncovered by the Lexow commission. Among other things, he had forced the resignation of patrolmen and detectives alike and brought in new people, Matt among them. Yet among all this reform, politics still lurked and ward bosses still held power. A wise police officer kept on their good side. There was no need to advertise that, however. "Would you like to see the cabin, Tom?"

"That I would, my boy." Nevesey's voice lowered as he followed Matt into the bedroom. "Looks like you've landed yourself in clover."

"It won't affect how I do my job."

"Never thought it would, my boy, never thought that." Nevesey glanced quickly around the bedroom, and his voice lowered still more. "Though when you came to me to tell me you wanted to go on this honeymoon—you know you'll have some trouble when you get back?"

Matt nodded. He'd already faced resentment from his fellow officers over his good fortune. "I expect it."

"Good. Just so you know. Of course, with Mrs. Devlin and all, can't say I blame you."

"No, sir."

"Not many men have a rich wife. Enjoy it, my boy."

"Yes," Matt said, his voice stiff.

"Bothers you, does it?" Nevesey's gaze was sharp, belying his genial, jovial manner. "Well, don't let it, my boy. Not many get the chance. Now, before I go, there's someone I'd like you to meet."

Matt followed him out into the sitting room. Winifred drew back as they passed, ostentatiously pulling back her skirts from

Nevesey, but Matt made himself ignore it. Soon enough all the guests would be gone, and he and Brooke would be alone. Maybe then it wouldn't matter that their backgrounds were so different. "Who?"

"Ambrose Smith, ship's detective. He's just outside. Helped him get this job, you know. He was a sergeant here in New York until all those commission hearings," Nevesey said, opening the door.

Which meant that he was less than honest, Matt thought, looking at Brooke, whose own look was curious. Nevesey was an irresistible force, however, and so, shrugging, Matt stepped out, closing the door behind him.

"A most distasteful man," Winifred declaimed into the sudden silence, ringing with the absence of Nevesey's voice. "I wonder you can tolerate him, Brooke."

Henry turned away from the window looking onto the promenade deck, where he'd stood since Nevesey's arrival. "Not a man to underestimate, I'd think," he said.

"No. Matt owes him rather a lot," Brooke said. "And I like him."

Winifred stared at her. "How can you, possibly?"

"Well, I do. Aunt, what do you think I should buy in Paris?" she asked, and the conversation immediately turned to the more pressing matters of Paris couturiers and style. Poor Matt, she thought, listening to her aunt with only half her attention. He was feeling much the same as she had when first she had come to live with her aunt and uncle, very much out of his element, with the added pressures of his job. She'd never ask him to give up his work; it meant too much to him. She only hoped that by the time they returned to New York he'd be more reconciled to the changes in his life.

The ship's horn blew two short blasts, drowning out all conversation and startling everyone. "That's the signal for going ashore, my love," Henry said, coming forward and taking Winifred's arm.

"Oh, dear." Winifred fumbled in her purse and brought out a lace-edged handkerchief, touching it to dry eyes. "I do hate goodbyes. Are you certain you'll be all right, Brooke?"

"On this ship? Of course. After all, I have Matt. And," she went on quickly to forestall whatever Winifred was about to say next, "Mr. Nevesey will not be sailing with us."

"I should hope not!" Indignation replaced Winifred's sadness. "A man like that on the *New York*—well! I know standards are sadly lowered these days, but we must fight against them when we can."

"Yes, Aunt," Brooke murmured, shepherding them out onto the promenade deck. The pier was thronged with people eager to see the big ship start her voyage, and from a few feet away Matt strode towards her. "Mr. Nevesey is gone, Matt?"

"Yes." He leaned forward to kiss Winifred on the cheek, a salute she suffered in silence, and shook Henry's hand. And then Henry was leading Winifred away, though she continued to call back admonitions and advice, until they reached the stairs and were gone. An absurd lump rose in Brooke's throat, and she swallowed it. No need for sadness, not when she was on her honeymoon.

The ship gave another blast on its horn, and there were shouts from lower decks and the pier as the thick cables that held the *New York* to the land were let go. Matt joined Brooke at the railing, both of them waving at the people below, as the *New York* edged out of her berth. The buildings of Manhattan began to recede; ahead was open water, and Europe. As if at a signal, Matt and Brooke glanced at each other, and grinned, silently agreeing in that moment to leave their conflicts back on land. Their honeymoon had begun.

At precisely seven that evening the gong rang for dinner. "This thing is choking me," Matt grumbled, tugging at his collar as he and Brooke turned in from the promenade deck to the mahogany stairs leading to the grand saloon for dinner. Sandy Hook Lightship, the official beginning of an Atlantic passage, had already been passed, and land was long behind them. The ship was alone, a majestic, lonely city, and the sea had taken over. The sway from side to side made footing on the stairs, now rising, now falling, uncertain at best.

"Don't." Brooke reached up a wifely hand to straighten his tie. "You look good in a dinner jacket, Matt."

"I feel like a monkey. Will I have to dress up every night?"

"Yes," she said firmly, biting back a smile. Of all the trials of his new life, she suspected Matt found his new wardrobe the worst. Certainly he complained about it enough, but in this company it wouldn't do for him to wear his old tweed suits that had come off the peg from Sherman's store in Newport. Snobbish, perhaps, but there it was. She was proud of Matt. She didn't want anyone disdaining him for such a foolish reason.

Her hand resting lightly on his arm, she was pulled up short when he stopped dead just inside the doorway to the grand saloon. "Holy. . . ." he began, and stopped, staring. This afternoon they had explored the ship, looking in at the oak paneled library with its hundred of volumes; the comfortable, clubby smoking room, where women were not allowed; and the ladies' drawing room, with its plushly upholstered sofas and ottomans. Nothing, however, matched the grandeur of this room. It stretched far, far away from them, twice as long as it was wide, with long tables covered by snowy white linen cloths marching away, converging in the distance like railroad tracks. Domed chandeliers shed brilliant light over the scene, while the softer glow from hundreds of candles in silver holders glanced upon arrangements of spring flowers: daffodils, jonquils, hyacinths; and glittered off the sparkling crystal, fine porcelain dishes, and polished silver. Upon the wall frolicked creatures of the sea, mermaids and dolphins and tritons, while high overhead arched a ceiling of glass, dark now with night. White-jacketed waiters, towels folded in precise creases over their arms, flitted among the tables, filling with sumptuously-garbed passengers, nearly three hundred of them. Only first cabin passengers here; second and third class had their own quarters, and were kept strictly separate. Matt wondered now if he'd feel more comfortable there.

"I don't believe this," he said, flatly, moving forward at last as someone jostled them from behind. "It's as grand as anything in Newport."

"And you dislike it just as much, don't you?" Brooke said, slanting him a look.

"I didn't say that. It just—takes getting used to."

Her hand tightened on his arm, as if in reassurance. "We'll be spending a lot of time here," she said, as they followed a waiter to their table. "There's an organ, up there," she pointed to an oriel window set high in the wall far across the saloon, "and a pulpit there, for Sunday services." Another oriel window, in the opposite wall, behind them. "Any entertainments they have planned will be here. We'll have to look in the ship's newspaper."

Matt hesitated as the waiter turned a swivel chair, bolted to the floor, toward him, and then he sat. Beside him Brooke was already seated, smoothing down the skirt of her pale green satin gown. He liked her in green, though he wasn't certain he liked the low cut of this gown, or the fact that the man across the table was winking at her. "The ship has a newspaper?"

"The ship has everything. Mr. Hoffman." She was smiling at the man who had just winked at her again. "What a pleasure to see you here."

"Miss Cassidy." The man beamed at her, and Matt's temper rose. No matter if Brooke knew him; she was *his* wife, and nobody was allowed to treat her in such a way. "Sorry, it's Devlin now, isn't it? Julius Hoffman," he said, holding out his hand to Matt. "You're Detective Sergeant Devlin."

"Yes," Matt said, slightly taken aback, and looked to Brooke for guidance. Hoffman was vaguely familiar, but Matt had met so many people in the last few months that even his trained eye couldn't recognize everyone. He was a middle-aged man, balding, and not above medium height. His dinner jacket, though well cut, sagged upon his sloping shoulders. His black mustache bristled with vitality, however, and the eyes that met Matt's were dark and bright and shrewd. Not a man to underestimate. "Have we met?"

"Mr. Hoffman is a broker," Brooke explained, lightly touching Matt's hand; only the little line that had appeared between her eyes showed that she was annoyed. "He was at Aunt Winifred's New Year's Eve party."

Now Matt remembered. That awful evening, when he and Brooke were so newly married, and the society of New York had stared at him as if he were an oddity. Hoffman, at least, had been friendly. "I remember, sir," he said.

"Call me Julius," Hoffman said, and winked again, this time at Matt, who blinked. "You remember my family. My wife, Adele." Julius indicated the woman sitting next to him, a tall, regal beauty, her fair hair pulled back into a top knot that emphasized the clean, pure lines of her face. She nodded as she sipped from her crystal water glass, barely acknowledging the introduction. "My daughter, Julia." Another fair-haired beauty, seated next to her mother, who also afforded Matt a scant nod. "And my son, Chauncey." A sullen youth, next to his father.

"You're traveling to Europe for pleasure, then," Brooke said, laying aside the menu the waiter had handed her. Matt was still studying his, frowning a little. The menu was in French, and though in the last few months Matt had attended many society dinners, he still wasn't sure what he would be eating. *Consommé printanier* to start with, some kind of soup, apparently, followed by trout done up in a fancy sauce. With the soup would be served an Amontillado sherry; to drink with the fish, a German riseling. For the entrees there were veal marengo, whatever that was, and *ris de veau suprêmes*. It took him a moment to figure out that the latter dish consisted of sweetbreads; queasily he wondered if Brooke would be embarrassed if he asked for good old American steak, or *bifsteak*, as it was likely to be called aboard the ship. With the entree there would be a rich red Bordeau; with the dessert, a chocolate souffle, Dom Perignon. By the time this voyage was over, Matt thought, at last laying the menu onto his dinner plate, he would likely be both dyspeptic and a dipsomaniac.

"Business and pleasure," Julius was saying, in answer to Brooke's question. "Hoffman, Langdon and Company is looking to expand into Europe in the future. We're thinking of opening a London office. You've met Richard Langdon, haven't you? He's at that table over there."

Beside him, Brooke turned to look at the man Julius indicated with a wave of his fork. "Who's watching the business, then?" she said, smiling.

"It's in good hands, Brooke. We've trained good people to run the firm while we're gone. Actually, Richard was going to come by himself, but we have our own reasons for traveling. My daughter's getting married. To the Earl of Lynton."

"Yes, I know." Brooke picked up her own fork as the fish course was set before her, and smiled at Julia. "My best wishes for your happiness, Miss Hoffman."

"Thank you," Julia mumbled, her head bent, and Julius beamed at her past his wife.

"Only the best for my daughter, eh, puss?"

"Father, I've asked you not to call me by that terrible name." Julia shot him a severe look. "And marrying Lynton isn't my idea."

"It is the best for you," Adele proclaimed, apparently agreeing with her husband in this instance. "And to have the wedding at the earl's estate is definitely a *coup*. You were married at your uncle's house, were you not, Mrs. Devlin?"

Brooke looked at Matt, and smiled. "Yes, we were."

"A small wedding, as I recall."

Brooke kept her smile firmly in place, even as Adele's eyes flicked over her, as if looking for some hidden secret. "Yes, very intimate and warm." She laid her hand on Matt's arm. "We're on our honeymoon now."

"Are you."

"The police don't mind letting you go, Devlin?" Julius said.

"They'll manage without me," Matt said, taking a sip of water to cover his feelings. Julius might be friendly, but he was sharp, and Adele, for some reason, was hostile. Against them, he and Brooke had banded together. He could feel it.

"Not what I hear," Julius said, chuckling slightly. "I hear you're expected to go places."

"Oh?"

"Especially after the way you handled that mess in Newport last summer."

Matt glanced at Brooke before answering. "That was a different situation."

"Your father was a policeman, was he not?" Adele put in, looking straight at Brooke.

"He was," Brooke answered quietly.

Under the table Matt squeezed her hand. "I think Brooke would have made a good cop herself," he said, earning a startled glance from her and another blank look from Adele. What, he wondered, would it take to bring any emotion into those ice-blue eyes? And what must it be like to live with her?

"If more police looked like Mrs. Devlin, maybe I wouldn't mind getting arrested," Julius said, winking.

"Father," Julia protested, leaning forward. "That's a terrible thing to say. And you're winking again."

"Am I?" Hoffman looked blank, and then smiled, sheepishly. "Sorry. A habit of mine when I'm tense."

"Oh, I'm not offended," Brooke said quickly, still looking at Matt. "Do you really think I'd be a good policeman?"

"You're stubborn enough," he said, smiling to show it was a compliment.

"It's a difficult job, Brooke, as you no doubt know," Julius said. "I have nothing but respect for the police."

"You've spoken out on corruption, haven't you?" Matt asked quietly, suddenly remembering where else he'd heard Hoffman's name.

"Yes, and I'm proud of it. A man must do his civic duty, and if that means exposing corruption among the police, then so be it." He stabbed at the air with his fork. "But just because there are a few bad apples doesn't mean the force isn't solid. The police have a difficult job, always dealing with deceivers and crooks."

"Mm-hm." Matt nodded, unconvinced, noting with only half his attention the startled look Adele gave her husband. The last thing he wanted to discuss just now was corruption among the police, or to defend the indefensible.

"A man like yourself, for example," Julius was saying, and Matt looked up, his face polite. "I followed the Newport thing from the beginning. When I read about the first maid getting killed on the Cliff Walk, and then the others, I knew there was something wrong. How many did he kill, altogether?"

"Five," Matt said, his estimation of Hoffman rising. In Newport, few in society had cared about maids getting killed, until one of the victims turned out to be one of their own.

"A distasteful subject," Adele said, her lips pursed. "Especially when someone from society was arrested. I find it hard to believe that he could do such things."

"He confessed." Brooke's voice was quiet, her face serious, and Matt touched her hand. Neither of them would ever forget the day when Brooke had so nearly become a victim of the Cliff Walk killer herself. "Tell me, Miss Hoffman. Are you really getting married on the earl's estate?" she asked, and the conversation at last went onto other channels.

Somewhat to Matt's surprise, the dinner was pleasant. The food was superb, the wine excellent, and if the ship rolled a bit too much, causing china and crystal to shift on the fine linen tablecloths, that was one of the hazards of going to sea. Even the conversation was enjoyable, about the unseasonably warm weather, Julia Hoffman's upcoming wedding, and the entertainments they could expect during the voyage, including tomorrow night's play to be put on by some of the passengers, with Julius Hoffman in a leading role. Matt was greatly relieved, though, when it was at last over. For six days he would be obliged to be polite to polite society, but not, he hoped, every moment. This was, after all, his honeymoon, and his first holiday from work for years. Smiling at their dinner companions, he and Brooke left the grand saloon, where already the tables were being cleared and the oriel window was opened for an organ recital. There'd be time enough to sample the ship's entertainments another night.

The April night was brisk. At their suite Brooke threw a shawl about her shoulders, and they went out to the promenade deck, leaning on the railing and looking at the reflected lights of the ship in the sea, far below. The ship rolled in the swells, making Matt feel just a bit queasy after consuming such a big meal, but he ignored his stomach to concentrate on other things. The moon, for example, a sliver of pale light in the sky, and the stars, so much brighter here than ever they were on land. And the woman next to him, not caring if the wind ruffled her hair or gown. It was one of the things he liked about Brooke, that such things didn't bother her. He put his arm about her shoulders, as if to keep her warm, and she smiled up at him.

The promenade deck was nearly deserted, few wishing to brave the cool night air when the delights of the grand saloon beckoned, but even so he led her across to the deck house and a sheltered alcove where they could have privacy. They were, after all, a couple on their honeymoon. They spent some pleasurable moments together, until sounds from farther along the deck intruded into their private world. A loud splash, a cry, the sound of running footsteps, and then the words that everyone at sea dreads to hear: "Man overboard!"